Secret SANTA

A CHRISTMAS MAGIC NOVEL

LICHELLE SLATER

Copyright © 2018 by Lichelle Slater
All rights reserved. No part of this book may be reproduced in any form without written permission from the author.

ISBN-10: 1724284177
ISBN-13: 978-1724284174

Printed in the United States of America
Cover Design and Interior Formatting by Bridgette O'Hare of Dark Unicorn Designs

Edited by Christina Walker of Supernatural Editing

TO MOM AND DAD

Thank you for giving us so many
wonderful Christmas memories.

CHAPTER ONE

Bell jumped out of bed well before her alarm sounded and slipped on her worn reindeer slippers before scrambling down the stairs. December first—the first day of the busiest season of the year, and Bell's absolute favorite time. She didn't even bother with making her morning cup of hot cocoa, the excitement in her eyes as bright as a child's on Christmas morning as she dashed into the living room. Her Christmas tree lights were still on—they didn't turn off until six-thirty, when she left for work—adding to the brightness of the upcoming season.

Her heart jumped with giddy excitement when she spotted a thin, leather-bound book beckoning from the coffee table. She knelt on the thick gray rug and traced her fingers over the cover, feeling the design of the pressed red border. At her touch, "Spirit List" appeared in shimmering gold letters across the cover, lighting the small living room.

Bell couldn't get the smile off her face, and her hands trembled. Despite a few years' worth of experience being one of the Secret Santa elves, she still felt the excitement as if this was her first time.

Secret Santa

Upon opening the cover, swooping font appeared on the first page as if it were being written right in front of her:

Dear Miss Bell,

I am pleased to celebrate another year of Christmas with you. You have done such wonderful work as a Secret Santa. As you are aware, you have one of the most important responsibilities any elf can have—revitalizing the light and magic that Christmas brings into the hearts of those around us.

Here is your list of those who need your special light this season. Please remember to keep your notes private, and to stay as anonymous as possible. May you have a wonderful Christmas Season and ignite your own Christmas Spirit.

Merry Christmas,
Santa Claus

"Merry Christmas to you too, sir," she whispered. She sat on the edge of her couch and settled the book on her lap. Each page crinkled softly as she turned them, and each had the name and pertinent information of an individual somewhere in Owentown.

Name: Anderson, Kristi
Age: 29
Marital Status: Single
Job: University Student
Address: 304 Park Dr.

Name: Carson, Zack
Age: 47
Marital Status: Married, 4 kids
Job: Carpenter
Address: 8347 Richmond St.

She was mildly surprised to see Mr. Carson's name on the second page. On the outside, everything in the Carson family appeared to be going well. He owned the local construction company working on the Forest Subdivision, and she thought they had just landed a big and important business deal.

Bell continued to flip through the pages, recognizing some individuals only by name—like Luke Gibbons—and others she knew personally—like Betty Johnson, who owned the diner. Fredrick Owen also vaguely surprised her. Fredrick was the great-great-great grandson of Eric Fredrick Owen—the founder of Owentown. Last time she'd seen him, he had appeared happy and the family business seemed to be thriving. Perhaps he was feeling lonely this season? His divorce had finalized the year before, and he wasn't even in the Secret Santa book last

Secret Santa

Christmas.

As she turned the pages, searching the names, there was really only one in particular she was looking for and she spotted it between Fredrick and Jeremy Pole: Drake Pine, thirty-two, owner of The Red Dragon Tavern, single, living at The Red Dragon Tavern.

Bell almost groaned out loud. This was the third Christmas in a row his name had appeared in her book. Her first Christmas here in Owentown, Drake's father had passed away, leaving the tavern to his son. It had been a difficult time to try and bring joy back to everyone in town, and impossible for Drake. He'd resisted her efforts the next Christmas as well, causing her to increase her efforts throughout the year, but each attempt failed.

She drew a breath. "Not this year, Drake. This Christmas is going to be different!" she said with a determined nod of her head. "I'll help you remember what makes Christmas special, no matter what it takes!"

Besides, she didn't have much of a choice but to succeed. If she didn't help him feel the joy of Christmas, she still wouldn't be allowed to return back home to the North Pole.

Finished with her careful examination of the book, she knew fifteen people in all needed a Secret Santa this season. Bell marched to the kitchen, set the book on the counter, and grabbed her town map—which she kept rolled up and tucked behind the broom in the pantry. She rolled the rubber band off the tube and spread the map out across her table, carefully using the reindeer figurines she had as a table decoration to hold the corners of the map. Next, she pulled out her favorite red star, and gold glitter stickers from the office drawer.

She set the book on the table and began finding the homes on the map, setting a red star on each home's location. When that individual's spirit was rekindled, and their name disappeared from the Secret Santa book, Bell would cover the red dots with the gold glitter stickers. She had used this map each year, and while she felt the longing for home in her stomach, she couldn't help but feel an immense sense of pride as she looked over all of the golden stars. Except one. Drake's red dot still remained.

But not this year! She would be covering his with a golden star for certain! Now she had the houses mapped, she stuck a pen in the gap of the spine of her book. No better day to start than today, December first!

Her days needed to be carefully planned, and she couldn't neglect her own responsibilities. Bell used the blank pages at the back of the book to jot down the order in which she could visit people—she would stop by Betty at the diner first, grab some breakfast and try to find out why she was on the list. Betty was typically the light of Christmas, so for her to be in Bell's book meant something was going on behind that joyful façade. After Betty, she would have to head to work at her bakery and use that time to plan. She could take a lunch and possibly see two people at once.

But one thing at a time.

Secret Santa

Of course, with this being Bell's third year as a Secret Santa, she hardly felt like an expert, but did know one thing for sure: things couldn't be changed overnight, despite how much she wanted it to. She knew some people would take a long time (like Drake), and some might only take one moment. She just had to figure out the right moment for each person.

Until then, to the diner for some hot cocoa and eggnog French toast! Bell nearly walked out the door when she remembered she still wore her pajamas. "Ah!" she exclaimed and ran upstairs to dress and get ready before she braved the winter air to drive to work.

Bell parked next to her bakery, just a few buildings down from the diner, and braved the cold as she quickly scampered to the diner. When she stepped through the door, the overhead bell jingled.

"Oh, Bell, I'm afraid we're closed right now."

Bell gave a quick glance around, having not realized it was completely barren. "Oh, I'm sorry. I didn't notice." She blushed and looked at Betty, but her smile fell.

Betty stood behind the counter, wringing her hands. Worry was not a common expression on Betty's gently wrinkled face, yet her brows were pinched.

"Betty, what's going on? What happened?"

Tears lingered in her pale green eyes. "I left ahead of Frank and Shane, and Shane just called me and told me her dad slipped on some ice on the way over and took her down with him. She said she was taking him right to the hospital."

Bell rushed over and took her hands. "Do you need me to drive you there?"

"I can take her!" Grant called from the kitchen, already wearing his coat.

Betty drew a shuddered breath. "I was just going to stay and run the day by myself."

"This is your husband and daughter we're talking about. Everyone will understand if you don't open the diner today! Where is your coat?" Bell dropped her hands and went behind the counter to snag it off the hook.

"I can make it," Betty said when Bell held the coat out to help her put it on.

"Are you sure? I really don't mind driving you. My car is just parked at the bakery."

"No, no, I really will be fine. Thank you, Bell," she smiled, giving Bell a tight squeeze. "Thank you."

"You let me know whatever you hear, alright?" Bell helped Betty to her car, parked on the side of the building, and waited until she knew Betty could drive on her own. She waved as Betty pulled out onto Main Street, then turned and went back to the diner.

Grant had already locked up and shook his head. "I'm glad you showed up. I tried to get her to leave, but you know how stubborn she can be."

Bell smiled. "Yes, she can be. So, do you have something to do today?"

"Eh, I can manage," he chuckled. "Might do some last-minute Christmas shopping."

"Oh? For who?" She raised both eyebrows.

Secret Santa

He laughed. "My dog. Don't worry, I haven't been dating anyone."

"Oh, stop. I figured you'd already got your shopping done for James and Klara."

"Yeah, the twins are pretty easy to shop for." He tugged his zipper to his chin. "Well, I suppose you should be off to your bakery. I might stop by after I pick the kids up from school to get them a treat." He winked.

"You know it's Christmas treat time!"

He laughed. "Don't I!"

After a polite farewell, they went their separate ways. Grant was a kind man, whose wife had passed before Bell arrived in Owentown. He was always happy, even working two jobs and raising the kids on his own.

Bell made her way back to her bakery. She had her own hot cocoa maker, and still had a couple pumpkin cinnamon muffins left over from a day or two ago she could snag for breakfast. After eating, she could begin the treats she'd been waiting for the most. Out with the pumpkin, in with the peppermint!

Bell switched on the lights to the kitchen, turned the ovens on to preheat, and got the cocoa maker going. She found the last two left over muffins and popped them in the microwave for a few seconds. Then she plugged her phone into the charger and store speakers, quickly finding her favorite music app and turning on the Christmas radio station, and *finally* put on her new Christmas apron—red with small bells along the top and *Santa's Best Baker* eloquently embroidered across the front. Jamie, her best friend, had given it to her on Thanksgiving Day.

Bell poured her cocoa into a mug, added a splash of hazelnut flavoring, and took a sip. Perfect. She'd prepped the gingerbread cookie dough the day before after closing the shop for the day, so she could easily cut them with gingerbread man, stars, reindeer, and Santa cookie cutters. She would reserve the elf and tree cookie cutters for the sugar cookies.

By the time the dough was as used as it could be—with bites of muffin and sips of cocoa in between—the ovens were ready. Bell slipped the cookie sheets in and finished the last of her cocoa. After dropping the mug in the sink, she turned up the music, "All I want for Christmas is You" blaring overhead.

She danced back to the refrigerator and grabbed the sheets of dark chocolate and white pepper mint fudge she'd made. They had turned out beautifully, with broken candy cane pieces sprinkled across the top. She delicately cut them into four-inch squares, placing some in red and white cupcake papers, then slipped them all into the display case. This would allow them a little time to soften while she started making the fresh batches of sugar cookies and Christmas cupcakes.

Bell spent the next few hours preparing her typical batches of familiar items—standard chocolate, yellow, or white cookies and cupcakes with various nuts or frosting. Finally, she got to work on what she truly wanted: cranberry and pecan muffins, peppermint cupcakes and cookies, caramel cupcakes, and a whole new flavor she'd

Secret Santa

never tried before. She was going to make a hot cocoa cupcake with melted marshmallow and fudge in the center, a marshmallow buttercream frosting, and a mini candy cane on top of the frosting to look like a sweet little mug of cocoa.

Time always passed too quickly, and the display was filled before she thought it was possible. She turned the outside lights on to Bellisima Bakery, and the dining room lights. Her little bakery glowed with happy red and green lights she'd set up on Thanksgiving Day while everyone spent the day with family but had refrained from turning them on until now.

She went into the back to continue piping the frosting on the last of the peppermint cupcakes until she heard the door open. Setting the piping bag on the counter, Bell walked out to greet another friend. "Hey Amy! How are you?"

"I'm doing okay. I couldn't wait, though. I knew you would have the peppermint treats out today, and my kids have been dying to get their hands on your gingerbread cookies!"

Bell laughed. "Well you came at the perfect time! I just happen to have them all. How much of each would you like?"

"Give me a dozen gingerbread cookies, four chocolate peppermint cupcakes. Ooh, are those hot cocoa cupcakes new? I better get four of those too!" Amy laughed.

"I hope you like them. I've been experimenting for a little while."

"I'm positive we will love them," Amy insisted. "Oh, one more thing. You tend to know a lot of people who need help with things around town. Mark and I like to involve the kids in helping someone every year, so if you know someone, would you send us their way?"

"Sure," she said, placing the box on top of the counter. "I'll keep my ears and eyes open."

After Amy left, Karla walked in, followed by Chase, and before Bell knew it she was in a rush. A couple of hours passed, and the treats quickly became scarce. She would need to grab a quick lunch and bake some more. Somehow, she managed to whip up a batch of gingerbread and sugar cookie dough, roll it out and get it in the fridge before she finally left for lunch.

Bell tugged her coat tighter. How was it possible for the air to get even colder with the sun up? She stopped at the corner of the street and pursed her lips. The diner was still closed, of course, but thinking about the diner reminded her to call Betty and check up on Frank and Shane. Where could she go for lunch? Maybe she could get some lunch at Drake's tavern. They were open for lunch, and she sometimes stopped in. It would be the perfect opportunity to see Drake and get food simultaneously.

Changing direction, she walked around the block only to find the tavern's lights out with a CLOSED sign too. "Grocery store food it is," she mumbled. Again, adjusting her plans, she turned back to her bakery. Getting in her car, so she could drive the couple of blocks down to the

Secret Santa

grocery store without freezing, she buckled up and found herself in the parking lot a couple minutes later.

Luckily, the place wasn't too busy. Some people were Christmas shopping, but it was a school day, so kids and parents were at work. Bell knew she'd just grab something from the Deli, but when she stepped through the main doors, she noticed the dozens of wreaths hanging to her right. She had completely forgotten to get one for Drake this year!

Unfortunately, they'd been picked through—of course—and she didn't have much of a variety to choose from. There were cheesy reindeer wreaths, wreaths with fake snow and plastic snowmen figurines, and one that was apparently supposed to be a sleigh, at least according to the tag. But at the very back, Bell noticed a very plain-looking and disheveled holly wreath. She smiled. That would be Drake's. She grabbed it and hurried to the deli for a sandwich and some yummy tapioca pudding.

When she got back out to her car, she set the wreath on her front seat and grinned. "Alright. A little bit of elf magic will spruce this right up."

She rubbed her hands and winked. The silvery light of magic swirled around the wreath. The green leaves unfolded and filled out, the scuffed holly berries repaired and became a brighter red, and little pinecones appeared all over, making it a very handsome wreath.

Bell grinned, satisfied with her work, and grabbed her phone to call Betty while she drove back to her bakery.

"Hello?" Betty's tired voice said.

"Hey Betty, it's me. Bell."

"Oh, Bell!" Her voice perked right up.

"I just wanted to call and see how Frank and Shane are doing. Have they had x-rays and stuff?"

"Yes. Shane is really sore, but no broken bones. Frank has a broken arm, and a very bruised hip, but they're both about to be released. Then we can get home and have some fresh chicken noodle soup before I open the diner up for dinner at least."

"I'm glad to hear they're doing okay." She turned into her shop parking lot. Mallory was already there, bundled up and waiting for some treats. "You really shouldn't worry about opening the diner tonight. Just be home with them."

"Even opening up tomorrow, I just…don't know how I can run it without them," Betty sighed.

"Well, Grant can finally take over in the kitchen, and I'm sure someone would be willing to come help so Shane can get some rest." Bell grabbed her bag of lunch, and Drake's wreath, pinching her phone between her shoulder and cheek.

"I guess you have a point. I mean, Frank has been training Grant for a situation just like this." She chuckled. "You always know just what to say."

Bell laughed. "I just try to be sensitive. Is there anything I can do for you right now?"

"No, we'll be fine. Thank you, Bell."

"You have a good day. And you go home and rest too," Bell insisted. She hung up and climbed out of her car.

Secret Santa

"Hey Mallory! I just ran to the store to grab some lunch. I'll open the door and you can go in, sit down, and warm up. I've got one quick errand to run," she explained, hurrying carefully to the door.

"I'm so sorry! I can come back later."

"It's really not a problem," Bell smiled. She unlocked the front door and pulled it open. "You go sit and I'll be right back."

Mallory gave her a grateful smile. "Thank you."

"You're welcome." Bell let the door close and she carefully jogged down the street to Drake's tavern. She had no idea why he had a wreath hanger on the door without a wreath. She settled the beautiful wreath on the hook and stepped back to straighten it. "There we go. Perfect. Back to the bakery, and then I can swing by Kristi's on the way home."

❄ ❄ ❄

Drake had tried to stay in bed all day. The nice thing about running the only tavern in town was the sleep schedule—he could sleep until whenever he wanted, really, and still have time to prep before opening for lunch. Sometimes he would skip lunch altogether. After all, there were only one or two customers he managed to get at lunch.

Not today, though. The heater had shut off at some point during the night, resulting in a very frozen face.

Again.

A part of him had still debated getting out of the warmth to fix it, but he knew what his father would say. *"An early morning means a productive day!"* Drake could practically hear his voice, and immediately got out of bed to investigate the cause of the furnace shutting off. He knew it wasn't a breaker. It was never that easy.

With a grunt, Drake managed to pull himself out of bed, his feet landing on the cold rug beside his bed. He shuffled through the dark toward the light switch, rubbing his hand over his beard and yawning. In his begrudgingly awake state, he managed to slam his shin against the coffee table and hopped to the wall to blindly sweep his hand to turn on the light.

He switched the light on and blinked against the brightness to check his exposed shin for damage. "I swear I need to move that stupid coffee table," he grumbled. He threw a glare at the offending chunk of wood in the middle of his studio apartment above the Red Dragon Tavern.

Drake sighed. The damage would leave a welt, but it wasn't bleeding, and was already nicely forming above the bruise from last Saturday.

He went about his morning routine: a long, hot shower to warm him up—which he immediately regretted when he stepped back out into the cold to dress—a little trim on his neck to keep his beard looking clean, conditioned it, then ruffled some hair gel through his dark hair before finally getting dressed.

Secret Santa

The stairs creaked under Drake's worn sneakers as he trotted down to the main level of the tavern, the stairs spitting him out into the kitchen. He'd gotten used to the feeling of being alone, the sound of it, but music helped break things up. So, he pulled his phone from his pocket, connected it to the Bluetooth speaker in the kitchen, and opened a random music app to listen to some good ol' rock and roll.

While Bon Jovi started livin' on a prayer, Drake Pine grabbed the tools and started checking the furnace, hoping it was a simple fix. But nothing was simple.

After only a few minutes, the back door screamed open and he heard someone stomping their feet. It must have snowed last night. "Drake, you up?" Chris called.

"In here!" Drake called back, leaning to try and get a better view.

"Man, the furnace is out again?" Chris announced as he appeared.

"Yeah, I don't get it." Drake shook his head.

"Well, looks like it's time to update the thing." He clapped Drake on the shoulder.

Drake raised his eyebrow. "You payin' for it? 'Cause if you are, by all means, go for it."

"Maybe we can take advantage of the Christmas spirit and put a donation jar on the bar. We could call it…" Chris scratched his chin. "Ah! We could call it: 'Warm Drake's only Christmas heart.' Huh?"

"That's terrible," he said flatly.

Chris shrugged, and Drake finally smiled.

He chuckled and shook his head. "Well, it looks like I'm calling Henry on this." He rubbed the back of his head.

"Good luck. While he's here fixing it, you should join Heather and me to—"

"Oh no you don't," Drake intervened. "I am not doing anything Christmas related." He set the flashlight back on the furnace where it belonged and tugged the string of the overhead light off.

"That's not what I was going to say," Chris said, following him to the back door.

Drake rolled his eyes. "Why would I waste my money giving other people stuff? Everyone in town looks at me like I'm some wounded puppy."

"It's the eyes, Drake."

He stopped and eyed his best friend—the only friend who had stuck with him through all the drama of losing his dad. "My eyes?" he asked.

"You do this look and it looks just like a wounded puppy. People can't help but feel a little sorry." Chris grinned innocently. "Look, we were just wondering if maybe you want to eat dinner with us. And possibly Kristi."

Drake stared at him blankly. He'd dated Kristi back when they were in high school, why on earth would he pursue her now? "I'm going to guess you already set up the date."

Chris's smile stiffened, like a child caught in a lie.

"Chris." He rolled his eyes and walked into the dining

room to light the wooden fireplace. "Why are you trying to set me up?"

"She's a fun girl! She's a teacher at—"

"I know. This town isn't exactly huge, and it hasn't exactly changed." He tossed the logs in the fire and looked over his shoulder. "No offense, Chris. I just don't feel like I need to have a girl. Especially just because it's Christmas. She'll get all flirty and attached and think it's some sort of romance movie and that we're going to fall in love because there's some sort of Christmas magic at play. I'm not ready for any sort of a relationship, but especially not one starting around this stupid holiday."

"I will make sure she knows it's just a friends thing, then. Just us going to dinner."

Drake scowled. "You do know I run the tavern, right? What if customers come in?"

"The whole five you're going to get all night?"

"Hey, five people is still five people."

Chris shrugged. "So we will multitask."

"Because that's not rude." Drake put his hands on his hips and finally rolled his eyes. "Only if my furnace gets fixed."

Chris nodded once. "Deal. Oh, hey. Did your secret Santa leave a Christmas wreath again?" He nudged Drake.

"Not yet. Oh, speaking of which." He grabbed the wreath hanger he kept stored on the bottom shelf behind the bar. He opened the door and centered it before closing and re-locking it. He turned to find Chris leaning against the kitchen doorway with a satisfied grin. "What are you smiling at?"

"Nothing. Let's go get Henry." He headed out the back door.

Henry ran the furnace and plumbing store and company and had for as long as Drake could remember. Drake's father had worked with Henry when they built the tavern and barn out back. Drake had stayed in contact, with frequent visits in the past year due to the beloved furnace.

Henry made eye contact with Drake as soon as he entered the building, and immediately called out, "I'm heading over to the Red Dragon! Call me if you need anything!"

Drake gave him an apologetic smile. "Thanks, Henry. I don't know what else to do."

"Well, let's look 'er over and see what's up."

"You want to just ride with us?"

"Nah, all my tools are out in the truck. Thanks, though." He finished putting on his coat and pulled his keys from his pocket.

Drake held the door open so Henry could follow, then drove back to the Red Dragon Tavern. Henry arrived shortly after and they congregated in the kitchen.

Drake leaned against the counter next to Chris, both watching Henry take apart the furnace one piece at a time. "So, what do you want to eat for dinner? I was thinking something with pasta. Heather has been eating a lot of pasta lately. It's all she craves right now."

"That's weird," Drake said offhandedly.

Secret Santa

"I know. So, what do you want? Spaghetti?"

Drake saw Henry look over his shoulder at them, the kind of look old people give to young people when they know something from their vast experience. It was a sort of chuckle, shake of his head before Henry looked back at his work.

"Alfredo? Pizza?" Chris continued.

"Pizza isn't pasta," Drake snorted, finally looking at Chris.

"Duh. You weren't paying attention. Should I get prepping for lunch, Henry?" he asked.

"I don't think so. This thang's all rusted," he said in his heavy southern drawl. Even living in the Midwest for thirty plus years hadn't changed that accent. "Now, Drake, I can keep patchin' 'er up, but she's really at the end of her days." He tugged up his pants as he stood. "I think Chris is right this time. It's time to git a new one."

Drake ran a hand over his face with a groan. "You sure you can't patch it?"

"It's just puttin' Band-Aids on."

He sighed heavily and scratched his beard. "Well, there goes the motorcycle I've been saving for. Alright. Let's take a look at what you've got and find out the damage. Any possible way you could get it installed today so I don't freeze tonight?" he asked hopefully.

Henry pulled off his hat and scratched his balding scalp. "I might be able to git it t'ya by tonight, dependin' on if I have what you need. Otherwise, I gotta go inta town and git it."

"I don't need anything fancy, just functional. I'm positive whatever you've got in stock will work."

"What, you don't want to have a slumber party?" Chris laughed.

Drake rolled his eyes, "What are you, twelve? You might have to let me stay the night if Henry can't get one in. Oh man. You know what else this means?"

"No? What?" Chris eyed him.

He clicked his tongue and softened his brow. "No date. Man, that's too bad."

Chris laughed, "He paying you, Henry? You in on this?"

Henry's white brows furrowed over his dark brown eyes. "Huh?"

Drake laughed. "If I wanted out of a date, I would have just told you no. I wouldn't have paid Henry to ruin my furnace." He snagged his coat. Drake could use that for an advertising opportunity—"Eat at the North Pole!"

"If Henry can't get the furnace fixed, you can't open the tavern anyway. No one will want to eat where they freeze at the same time. If that's the case, we can still have dinner at my place," Chris suggested.

He sighed. "You're really wanting this dinner, aren't you?"

"You and Kristi were cute."

"In high school. Things change. Besides, we were, what? Sophomores? Juniors? That was a long time ago."

"Well, maybe you'll like her more now."

Drake groaned. "Look, I already agreed to this, can we

Secret Santa

just get it over with? I'll go light the fireplace. You call Heather and Kristi." He ran his fingers through his hair and looked at Henry. "Thanks."

He chuckled and nodded. "I'll call you and let you know what I can git in. Ah, and Chris, has Heather been sick in the mornings at all?"

"Come to think of it…she gets a little nauseous. I just figured it's a bug she picked up from one of the kids at work."

He smiled and patted Chris on the shoulder. "Think about that. See you later, Drake!" he called as he hoisted his tools and left the tavern.

Drake and Chris exchanged a quick look. "I'll help Henry out and then I can help you with lunch."

He stood in the dining room, hands in his pockets, and looked around at the tavern. He had a lot of great memories in this place. Where would he be without it? This would be the third Christmas without Dad, and he still felt guilty. His dad had loved Christmas, everything about it. Drake could easily picture the way his dad used to hang up lights, garland, ornaments, the tree, all of that set up around the tavern. He would even paint the window!

Drake glanced up when a shadow passed, and he saw Bell Winter slip on a patch of ice, successfully recover, and stop at his door. She hung a full green wreath with pops of red holly berries. For the first time, he knew who had been putting a wreath on his door since his father had passed.

"Did you see that?" Chris grabbed Drake, shaking him.

"Get off. I'm standing right here." Drake shrugged away, glancing back at the window to catch a glimpse of her again, but Bell was gone.

"Bell, huh? You know her?" Chris asked, grinning with his hands on his hips.

Drake shook his head. "Not really. I mean, she bumped into me at the Christmas party last year and got red punch all over my sweater." He looked at Chris with an expressionless face. "Ruined it."

"Not like you cared."

Drake shrugged and set the last chair down. "She can celebrate Christmas however she wants. I can however I want."

"Speaking of which—"

"No."

"You don't even know what I was going to ask."

"I know I was going to answer no." He walked to the back.

"Look, Drake, I get that Christmas is a little tough for you emotionally. I can sympathize. But you need to not spend Christmas alone. Come spend it with me—"

"No," he answered solidly, heading to check everything and make sure it was ready for customers. "And if you ask me again, it will still be no."

"You know what you are? A scrooge."

Drake narrowed his eyes and turned sharply. "You could just go home for the day."

Chris shook his head. "Christmas used to be your

Secret Santa

favorite! You'd always wake me up to go with you guys to get the Christmas tree. Remember? It used to sit in that corner." He pointed.

"Yes, I remember. Yes, I know that I'm a scrooge. Do you know what it's like to be reminded about someone you cared about every day, someone who is gone now and can't come back?"

"You know he'd be mad at you for holding on like this."

"Yeah, sorry I can't just get over it." He stormed into the back. "He'd be mad I broke the furnace, he'd be mad I don't let the town use the barn out back for the parties, he'd be mad I live upstairs instead of in a cute little place of my own."

"Drake, dude."

"I'm going outside to cool down." He slammed the door shut behind him. Who was Chris to lecture him? Chris had the perfect life—both parents happily living just two hours away, a wife, two jobs he could really work whenever he wanted. Drake only had the tavern to lean on, and not only did he struggle to gain new patrons, less and less of the regulars returned. He still couldn't figure out why. But if he didn't figure it out soon, he'd lose the tavern and end up homeless. But even worse, he would have nothing to remind him of his father.

Drake opened the doors to the barn and stepped into the vast emptiness. His dad had converted it to a celebration hall when Drake was in high school. He remembered working hours with his dad, listening to old music, laughing, telling stories. His dad had been his best friend. The city had used the barn for the yearly Christmas celebrations since, and the year after his dad died, someone had the guts to ask him to use it for the city's annual celebration.

He exhaled and looked up at the dusty chandeliers, hands shoved in his pockets. "I miss you, Dad," he whispered. "I know I need to figure out a lot, but...how can I just let go of you? How can I just accept you're in a better place?" He put his hand against one of the standing pillars. He couldn't tell if the ache in his chest had deepened or if it was trying to heal. Maybe he was the Grinch and his heart was just shrinking a little more.

He left the barn, locking the door again, and grabbed some snow-covered logs to set inside and warm up so they could add it to the fire and hopefully keep the dining room warm.

"Hey, I'm sorry."

Drake looked up at Chris and straightened. "No, you're right. I gotta figure out how to let go."

"It's not easy. I know that, and it was rude of me to call you a scrooge."

He shook his head. "Yeah. I'm more like the Grinch. How can I stop Christmas from coming?" He tried a smile.

Chris returned by giving him a crooked grin. "You can't. But I can't force you to embrace it, either."

The phone rang, and Drake glanced at Chris. "Hold on a second. Hello?"

Secret Santa

"It's Henry. Just lettin' you know I found a furnace that'll fit perfectly for the tavern. I might even be able to git her done before dinner."

He sighed. "Whatever you can do will be perfect, Henry. Thanks."

"I'll be over when I can."

"Sounds good." Drake hung up and looked at Chris. "Well, Henry found a furnace, and we might have it up and running before dinner."

"Well, with that fireplace going we will at least have one warm spot for dinner." He headed inside, holding the door open for Drake to follow.

❄ ❄ ❄

Bell finished up the day, turned off the lights, locked the front door, and wiped everything down. She was exhausted, but relieved the day was over. She set her book out on the counter while prepping another batch of gingerbread dough to cool overnight. Scanning the names, Bell hoped one would jump out at her. Kristi seemed like maybe she could use some Christmas spirit.

She wrote Kristi's name on a Christmas card, wrapped up a bundle of Christmas cookies, and tied a ribbon on the top. When that was done, she put the dough in the fridge, and put on her coat. Finally, she headed home, grateful she could stop by Kristi's apartment along the way. It stood on the southern side of Parker's Park, and Bell's house stood on the opposite end.

She rang the doorbell and stood there waiting.

Kristi answered and smiled tentatively. "Hello."

"Hi! I'm Bell. We sort of know each other, a little."

"Yeah, I've seen you around."

"I just wanted to bring you some cookies I made today." Bell held up the plate.

She smiled. "That was nice of you." She accepted the cookies. "Did you want to come in?" She gestured behind her.

"I don't want to make you feel obligated. I just wanted you to know I was thinking about you." She offered Kristi a friendly smile. "If there's anything you need, even if it's just a friend this time of year, just let me know. My phone number is on the card."

Kristi smiled almost sadly. "Thanks. For some reason this year just feels so…I don't know, lonely."

Bell's mind was already plotting ways to get Kristi involved with friends and neighbors. "I would love to go to a movie. Just call me when your schedule is free. I'm done at the bakery around five most days, except during Christmas," she ended with a laugh.

"How do you do it? How do you tolerate being alone?"

Bell's smile slid. She hadn't thought about that before. "Well…I'm sort of alone, but not really. I talk to a lot of people who come into the bakery, I try and get out during lunch to talk to people at the diner, and then I try really hard to get involved with activities in the community."

"Even when you're tired?"

Secret Santa

She shrugged. "Some nights I don't, my feet hurt too much. But I definitely get out on the weekends. And I spend a lot of time with Jamie too. I don't know if you know her, she runs Book Nook, that bookstore on Main Street. We spend a lot of time together right now, because she's alone until her husband comes home from deployment. I'm sure you could join us on our boring adventures."

Kristi smiled. "Well, Heather and I are pretty close. Do you know Chris's wife?"

"Chris…" Bell pursed her lips in thought. "He is…?"

"Drake's cook, at the Red Dragon."

"Oh, right!"

"I just haven't been very good at reaching out to her the last few months. We were supposed to have dinner today, but they had to cancel. It's no big deal though, really." She shrugged.

"I hope you two can reschedule."

"Oh, it was actually supposed to be four of us. I'm sort of doubling with her and Chris, and Drake…" She blushed.

Bell's eyebrows lifted. "Drake? As in Drake at the Red Dragon Tavern, Drake?"

She nodded. "One and only in town."

"That's great." She grinned. Bell tapped her chin, pondering a moment before looking to the side to hide her quick wink—summoning the magic within her. She wasn't sure what needed to happen to ensure Kristi and Drake ended up on this date, but if she could use a little bit of Christmas magic to help, she would do it. Of course, performing magic without knowing the ramifications was risky, but what harm could there be in setting up a dinner date?

Kristi pulled her phone from her pocket, having just heard a notification tone, and looked at it. "Oh! It's Heather. Apparently, they were able to find a furnace for the tavern and get it repaired today. I guess we're going to dinner after all."

"Good luck! Like I said, call me. Give me your number and I'll call you to make sure you get invited to our outings. Then I'll get out of your hair, so you can meet up with them." She handed Kristi her phone.

Once the phone number was in, Bell waved a goodbye and trotted back down the cement stairs, salt crunching under her shoes. A date with Drake! Maybe she could get both of them off her list today!

Pulling into her driveway, Bell suddenly remembered Amy had been by earlier that day and wanted to help someone that Christmas. Of course, she could help Betty!

Bell called Amy immediately.

"Hey, Bell!"

"Hey, I just remembered Betty could use a meal brought tonight to their house."

"Really? What's going on?"

"Her daughter and husband slipped this morning, and he's got a broken arm. They've been at the hospital all day."

"I would love to help! This will be a great opportunity

Secret Santa

to get the kids involved too. I bet they have hospital bills, so we can just put some cash in a Christmas card for them. Thank you so much, Bell!"

"You're welcome. Have a great rest of the day."

"You too!"

Bell drew a deep breath, excitement and relief filling her. Betty would be taken care of, and Amy would have someone to help this Christmas. Bell smiled to herself.

❋ ❋ ❋

"Drake! Come help me with your furnace!" Henry called through the back door.

"Coming!" Drake called back, quickly getting to his feet. "Chris, can you handle the incredibly busy customers while I help Henry?"

"I don't know. They all want drinks and appetizers. I don't know how I can manage to be in the front and the back at the same time!" he laughed.

"Just clone yourself!" Drake grinned and shook his head with a light chuckle.

"You know, I'm glad you've got him, even if Chris is a troublemaker sometimes," Henry observed, limping lightly to the back of his truck, where the furnace was strapped down.

"Me too," Drake agreed.

Drake helped Henry load it up on the dolly, wheeling it into the tavern. They began to unhook all of the old wiring and tubing from the old furnace before pulling it out of the closet and pushing the new one in.

Henry got started reattaching everything while Drake loaded the old furnace onto the back of Henry's truck. Stopping to look up at the darkening sky, he realized one thing that was true with winter—the sunsets were often beautiful, and tonight was no exception. His mom used to say they were paintings to remind us how much God loves us.

Drake strapped the furnace down and headed back inside. "How's it going?" he asked.

"Which one?" Chris asked. "Me or Henry?"

"Both."

Chris smiled. "We have seven customers. I've got them started, but you should probably check their drink situation. Oh, and Heather and Kristi should be on their way."

"What, it's already dinner time?" He looked at his watch. How had time flown so quickly?

"I'm good here," Henry called. "Just a couple more things to get situated before I can turn her on."

Drake nodded and grabbed a notepad on the way past the front counter. He went to the first table, a family with two kids. "Good evening. How are you tonight? Chris mentioned he got you started, can I get you some more drinks? And possibly some appetizers?"

The father looked at him. Drake couldn't recall seeing him in the tavern before, and couldn't remember seeing him around town either. "We'd love more drinks, and can

Secret Santa

we just order our meals? Also, any way you can turn up the heat?"

"Sorry about that, our furnace went out last night. We've been working on getting it all fixed today. I'll add some more wood to the fire for you. What would you like to eat?"

The other two tables were both couples. Drake quickly got their orders before heading into the back and telling everything to Chris. The rest of the night a couple more patrons came, which was a huge relief. One advantage of Christmas was tourists, so Drake couldn't complain about that.

After Henry finished getting the furnace running, Drake thanked him. "I've got some in cash. Let me grab the money pouch." He headed to his office.

"Drake, you don't need to give me all your cash right now."

"I've got some." He grabbed the pouch from his drawer and opened it. "How much do I owe you?"

"Well…"

"Henry." Drake gave him a firm look. "Tell me."

"I can do it fer a thousand."

Drake's brows pinched. "You sure that's it?"

Henry stepped into the small office. "I know yer tight on money, Drake. No shame in that."

He sighed heavily and pulled out all the cash he had. "That's five hundred. I'll get the rest—"

"Some other time." Henry gave him a big smile, patted him on the shoulder, and walked out the back door.

Drake gave a relieved sigh. Maybe next month he could pay Henry back.

Chris knocked on the door and stepped in. "I got Heather and Kristi situated. Want to help me with the food?"

"Any more customers?"

"Not right now."

"How convenient," Drake sighed.

He carried out a tray with salad and dressings and set it on the table in front of Heather and Kristi. Kristi hadn't changed much since high school—still had the incredibly curly red hair, striking green eyes, and lightly freckled nose and cheeks. She smiled at him, and it was the same smile he'd seen growing up, if not more hesitant.

"Hey, Drake. It's good to see you."

"Yeah." He tucked the tray under his arm. "I'm glad you two came." He nodded to Heather too. "And just so you know, your husband is conniving."

She groaned. "What did he do now?"

"Nothing," Chris said, walking out with the spaghetti already mixed with sauce and cheese on top. In his other hand he carried the toasted bread. "I have no idea what Drake is talking about. I've been here helping him with the furnace all day. And trying to come up with new slogans for his tavern. Oh, hey! What about, 'Pretend you're in an igloo! Our dragon is on Christmas vacation.' Yeah?"

Drake rolled his eyes, but still chuckled. "Yeah, that would be a great way to attract business." He took the

Secret Santa

basket of toast from Chris and set it on the table.

"But really, we've got to come up with something to—ouch!" Chris pouted at Drake, who had just stepped on his toe before taking the seat beside Kristi.

"I think maybe we shouldn't discuss business over lunch," Drake said. He looked over at Kristi. "So, still teaching?"

"Yes. I got moved to third grade this year."

"How old are those kids? Ten?"

"Eight and nine," she corrected. "They're a pretty good bunch, for the most part. Every class always has the one or two that make things difficult."

"That's too bad." Drake pushed the bowl of spaghetti her way when Heather was done serving herself. "How are you doing, Heather?" he asked. "Chris mentioned you haven't been feeling very well lately?"

"I'm fine." She smiled at Chris. "He's just a worrywart. I'm sure it's just a bug from one of the kids at daycare."

"Gotta watch out for those things. They can kill you." Drake raised his brows.

"Nah, the bugs aren't that bad."

"I was talking about the kids."

Everyone laughed, Kristi waiting a moment before joining.

Drake grinned. The Christmas season always pulled him down, and it felt good to laugh whenever he could. The rest of the dinner, however, was awkward. Kristi and Heather talked about kids they were having issues with at their work places, and he and Chris ended up talking about why neither of them were watching sports. He tried to talk to Kristi about what she studied in school, but it was elementary education, and she had no minor and nothing else she wanted to add about college. So, he tried asking her about her roommate, but apparently Rachel had just moved out to go to school and get a master's degree, so she'd been living alone. Trying to talk to Kristi was like pulling teeth, at least it felt like that to Drake.

When Heather left with Kristi, Chris sighed and folded his arms across his chest. "Well, you two just aren't meant to be, are you? I'll clean up."

"You felt how awkward it was?"

"Yeah. I mean, you were asking all the right questions." Chris stacked the dishes. "I'm sorry, I just thought you two might have some chemistry left after high school."

"Well, maybe not chemistry, but something." He loaded his hands up with dishes as well and followed Chris into the kitchen to start washing them. "Oh well. You tried."

"No Christmas magic romance for you."

"Not this year," Drake chuckled.

Secret Santa

CHAPTER TWO

A new day, and new people to visit. On the way home from the bakery the night before, Bell had run into Brian Eilen from her list. More like, overheard in passing. She'd stopped by the grocery store again to get some food and overheard him on the phone with someone, mentioning how lonely it was to live in a small town around Christmas without family close. Of course, she'd taken note of that. This morning, she couldn't figure out quite how to help him without making it obvious, since she didn't know him.

Bell flipped through the book. So far, she had new notes on Drake, Kristi, Betty, Brian, and Logan—for whom she'd jotted down "car problems," next to his name. She closed the book, gave a wink and watched it shrink to a comfortable pocket size, and headed out the door. With the diner closed, this could be the perfect opportunity to stop by the tavern for some breakfast. If they even did breakfast.

Bell pulled up out front of the tavern and glanced through the window, watching as Drake removed the chairs from the tables and set them on the floor.

Secret Santa

Apparently, it was open. Parking her car, she climbed out and stepped through the front door. No one else was in the Red Dragon Tavern at six in the morning.

The tavern was longer than wide, with a rounded ceiling carved around the edge with a beautiful swirled design and roses every few feet. Directly across from the door and front window was the bar. That entire wall was painted a deep green, and directly behind the bar was mirrored shelving with alcoholic beverages stacked neatly. Above that was a blank space of discoloration in the paint where it looked like a large painting of some kind had once hung.

To her left was a large, beautiful stone fireplace with a thick wooden mantle made from the same dark wood as the trim and edging in the tavern. All of the other wood in the tavern was much lighter, including the ceiling, windows, door, and other walls. The tables and chairs were an off-color wood, sort of red-brown. The front of the bar had large carvings of Irish knots. On the floor where the bar stools sat, there was beautiful tile work with small squares of green, white, black, and orange.

Everything appeared to have been well taken care of for years, and Bell loved the ambiance of the place. She looked at Drake and realized only then that she'd walked in and stared at the place a good minute or two. Drake had most likely been staring back at her the entire time wondering if she was going to say something.

"Uh, morning?" he greeted.

"Hey, are you open? I mean, I saw your lights on and

saw you getting ready, and the door was unlocked." She gestured absently behind herself.

His dark brows furrowed, and he leaned to look past her. "If you go out the door and turn left, there's a little diner across the street about three blocks down. And there's a coffee place somewhere in town."

"Yeah, Betty had to close the diner for a family emergency yesterday, and they likely won't open back up until tomorrow. Not only that, but the coffee shop has terrible cocoa." Bell smiled, but Drake stared, his brows still drawn together. "Would you rather I go?"

"No, no. Stay. I just don't know if I've ever had someone come into my bar and ask for a cup of cocoa. My cook isn't here, but I can manage to whip up hash browns, bacon, eggs, and some coffee if you'd like." He pulled the rag off of his shoulder and wiped the tables down. "You can sit anywhere."

"You sure? Are you even open for breakfast?"

"Not typically, no."

"I'm sorry. I just...assumed when I saw the lights." She gave an embarrassed smile.

He raised a dark brow. "Are you staying or not?"

"Yes, please." She moved over to the bar and quickly sat.

As he turned away to head back into the kitchen, Bell stole the opportunity to look him over. His black hair and beard were neatly trimmed and glossy, and he sported a red dragon tattoo down his left shoulder to his elbow—a new addition he'd gotten on his birthday back in June. Not

Secret Santa

that Bell had taken note, or anything. He was fit and clean, so the depression that had clouded him after his father's death must have been under control, although a hint of anger still lingered in the corners of his green eyes.

"My name is Bell, by the way."

"Yeah, I know," he said from the back. "Part of my job is to not forget people."

"I just wasn't sure if you would remember."

"Not exactly a big enough town to forget people in."

Her cheeks grew warm at the memory of their last interaction at the town's Fourth of July picnic. She'd turned to look at the parade while walking and ran right into him, smearing her green mint ice cream all over his blue and white plaid shirt. It was the first time they had *officially* met, though they had said polite "hellos" during a couple of community events. And she'd spilled on him the Christmas before, though that one had been planned. It just hadn't been planned that she would stain his shirt...

Drake walked back out with a tin of hot cocoa in one hand and a coffee pot full of water in the other. "So, what do you do around here, Bell?" In the background she heard something sizzling on the skillet.

She grinned with excitement. "I run that cute little bakery, Bellisima Bakery, surely you've heard of it? Even had some treats?" She took a breath. Something about his presence made her tongue feel scrambled, and she needed a breath before she rambled off about something completely irrelevant.

Drake turned on the coffee pot, then leaned against the

counter with his arms crossed. "Can't say I have."

"Well, you should definitely come by. Or I could just bring something to you. I've got some fantastic treats, and the Christmas flavors just started yesterday! Mint, gingerbread, eggnog, cocoa..." She bit her lip. Smalltalk was something Bell excelled at.

Usually.

"How long have you run that bakery now? A year?"

"It's actually been two now," she replied. "Third Christmas."

"Wow. Time flies, I guess." He studied her with hard eyes. "You sure you're really here just to drink cocoa?"

"Why else would I be here?"

"I figured the community council sent you to butter me up and ask to use my barn again this year."

Bell tilted her head. "You have a barn?"

He chuckled. "It's not a real barn, it just looks like one. That building on the lot behind this?" He pointed his thumb over his shoulder.

"Oh! I didn't know that was yours. I always wondered about that..." she lied. "No, they didn't send me. Why would they?"

"Because they want to hold the Christmas party there every year." He straightened. The coffee pot alarm beeped, and he turned and poured the hot water into a mug. He set the tin of cocoa in front of her and whipped out a spoon, holding it out to her.

Bell hesitated.

"I don't know how much chocolate you like in your

cocoa," Drake said flatly.

"Of course." She accepted the spoon. "I guess everyone is a little different, aren't they? I like three scoops." She scooped the chocolate in and stirred it. "Tell me a little bit about yourself, Drake."

He raised his brow. "You seem to be taking my job," he said with a half grin. "Usually I'm the one asking people to talk, and they pour out their lives like I've been their best friend since birth."

"Usually they have something a little stronger to drink, though?" she smiled, tapping the spoon on the edge of the cup.

He shrugged. "True."

"You are an unpaid therapist, it seems."

Drake laughed. "I guess you could say that. Some people just need a listening ear."

"And now it's your turn! So, tell me your deepest, darkest secrets," she whispered dramatically, with a wink for good measure.

That got her a full grin as Drake chuckled and leaned on the bar. "Here's a secret—this is the first time in my life I'm alone in my bar with a woman…who ordered cocoa."

"Still can't get over that, huh?" She grinned and took a sip. "This is perfect too! Only thing that would make it better would be a candy cane."

"Fresh out of those. Come back in March."

She frowned. "Won't they be a little stale by then?"

"I imagine they will be gone by then," he said.

"Intentionally?"

"Maybe." He remained leaning with one arm resting on the counter, close enough she caught his scent. He smelled woodsy, brisk and subtle, with almost a touch of pine, except the tavern had no Christmas tree.

"I couldn't help but notice you don't have the place decorated for Christmas," she said carefully, taking another sip and watching his reaction over the rim of the mug.

Drake straightened, his face suddenly a mask. "Not really a fan of Christmas. Let me go finish your breakfast." He left, clearly abruptly ending their conversation.

Bell pursed her lips, cringing inwardly. She shouldn't have asked that question. She sipped her cocoa, exhaling a breath into the mug and causing the steam to flutter up to her eyes. She'd hoped that he would be easier to reach this holiday season. Apparently not.

Last year, Drake and his mother had been fighting. Bell hadn't heard anything personally, but she had overheard rumors. Drake had spent last Christmas alone, and from what she knew last Thanksgiving and this one, too.

Last year was a disaster for Bell. She had tried to get Drake to talk to his mom by leaving his phone around on the bar with her number pulled up, but he never called. She had even tried leaving a kitten for him, which he promptly gave away. She left chocolates, sent some of Drake's friends to visit, and everything else she could think of.

Secret Santa

Drake returned several minutes later with two plates of breakfast food. "Mind if I join you?"

She smiled brightly. "Absolutely! Though, it would be a tad awkward if you sat away from me." She patted the seat beside her.

He paused, studying her again with that same hint of confusion, but he walked around the bar and took the seat beside her. "I gotta ask, how are you this chipper so early in the morning?"

"Well, I have to be at the bakery early to get everything baked fresh, that's part of what I think helps me sell so well. Day old stuff gets marked down to fifty percent off—"

"No, not why are you awake, I mean how are you so happy? I mean…normal people aren't happy like this when they're awake so early." He took a sip of his coffee.

Bell inhaled deeply, catching a whiff of the coffee's aroma. She loved the smell of coffee. Maybe she should make a coffee cake today! Remembering his question, she shrugged. "I learned a long time ago that happiness is a choice. I can wake up and be grumpy, or I can choose to be happy. More people like happy people."

He arched his brow again. "Not this early in the morning."

She laughed and picked up a piece of bacon. "Well, I find it easier to be happy. Hey, can I ask you something?"

"Depends. We're super busy right now, so I don't know if I can spend a lot of time talking." He took a bite of hash browns.

Bell glanced around and looked back at him. They were the only ones in the tavern. She was about to make that observation, but found Drake smiling at her over his coffee cup when she made eye-contact with him again.

"That was a joke," he unnecessarily explained. "What do you want to ask?"

Bell had no idea what she wanted to ask. The question had spewed from her mouth before she could stop it—one of her weaknesses. She often spoke before her brain had time to catch up or warn her to stop, and now she was in the very type of situation she dreaded. She had to make up a conversation now, and the silence between them was growing more awkward. He wouldn't talk about anything Christmas related, maybe sports? It was still football season.

"Do you watch football?"

He raised both eyebrows this time and laughed. "That's what you wanted to ask? I thought you were building up to some dreadful question." He shook his head. "Yeah, I can turn that on, if you want."

"No, I just…" She put her hand on his arm, and he sat back down. "I'm sorry. I just get all jumbled sometimes." She laughed nervously, an embarrassing little squeak. She cleared her throat. "Well, I'm kind of trying to get people's opinions on their favorite Christmas treats, so I can make them or incorporate them somehow into what I'm baking. It can be an ingredient, flavor, whatever. In fact, just smelling your coffee made me want to go to the bakery and make coffee cake, but I could totally make

Secret Santa

coffee caramel brownies. Oh that sounds wonderful!" She quickly pulled out her phone and typed it into her "notes" section, where she kept her crazy ideas for treats.

She looked back up and blushed immediately.

Drake watched her with a half-amused, half-frightened expression: his brows lightly pinched, but a small grin playing at the corner of his mouth.

"I'm...so sorry. See? I just talk. You talk." She shoved a bite of eggs into her mouth.

He shook his head. "Yeah, I mean, that sounds cool. I guess I'm trying to decide if this is a joke or something. Since, you know, I don't like Christmas."

"You can still like treats," she said before swallowing.

"I don't know." He shrugged. "Caramel? My mom used to make the most amazing homemade caramel."

"I could make some. I do use it on top of the marshmallow frosting for the s'mores cupcake, but not an actual caramel dessert." She tapped her chin. "Something flavored with it?"

"I don't know. I'm not a baker."

"But if you came in, would you be more likely to get a cupcake, pie, cookie, something else? Caramel fudge? Brownie?"

He made a face. "Caramel pie? No. Brownies, yes, cookie, yes, fudge, definitely yes."

She smiled and put it all in her phone. "Done."

He nodded and stood. "Good luck with that. You done?"

She handed him her empty plate. "Thank you so much,

that was delicious. Also, I'm going to bring you some treats when it's done."

"You really don't have to do that…" His brows dipped.

"Sure, I do! You came up with the ideas."

"The flavor."

"Well, if caramel is your favorite, you have to be the taste-tester for me. It's an unwritten rule. And on top of that, it's Christmas time! I love sharing treats at Christmas! It's one of the best parts!"

"Right." He headed into the back.

"How much do I owe you?" Bell asked, pulling out her wallet.

"We don't actually do breakfast." He reappeared a moment later and walked back to her side. "You bring me treats, I'll call it an even exchange of services."

She stood up and smiled. "Thank you. I'll be back at lunch with some treats just for you." She walked out of the tavern feeling so excited she'd been able to have a normal conversation with Drake, she completely forgot she drove to the tavern and parked her car out front. She'd made it all the way to the bakery and unlocked the back door before she stopped and looked behind her and realized her car wasn't there. She'd left it at the tavern.

Bell rolled her eyes and stepped inside.

All she had to do was come up with a delicious caramel dessert. The one thing that kept coming to her mind was salted caramel brownies. She could make a light chocolate brownie, drizzle caramel through it to bake, and cover it completely in caramel with salt sprinkled on top.

Secret Santa

Her mouth practically drooled as she wrote it all down.

By the time lunch rolled around, she had the brownies, caramel cookies, and even some salted caramel fudge. With her treats in hand, she walked back to the Red Dragon and walked in. Drake had a cluster of young women squished into a booth, an elderly couple, three men at the bar, and one man by the fireplace.

Drake had just finished setting a glass down in front of the elderly couple when he spotted Bell. He gave a courteous smile. "Hey, find somewhere to sit and I'll get you some cocoa."

Bell smiled. "Thanks. I brought you treats too." She held up the plate for emphasis.

"Oh, thanks." He walked over to her. "Wow…those actually look really good."

"Did you think I would cover them in bugs?"

They both made a face and Drake tilted his head. "Gross. How do I know you don't have some in there?"

Bell shuddered. "I promise there aren't any bugs in any of the desserts, not that you trust me about it now."

He chuckled. "Can you give me just a second? I'm going to get the drinks from this table and then I'll grab it from you."

She nodded and took a seat at one of the two-person tables in the middle of the floor. She took the opportunity to casually glance around as she set her book in front of her and thumbed through the pages. Tina was on her list, Tina Michaels, but Bell didn't know who that could possibly be. Maybe it was a teenager? Elderly person? It really could be anyone. Maybe one of the girls sitting in the booth?

She looked over at the table and saw the girls gawking at Drake from afar, whispering behind their hands, giggling, and flipping their hair whenever he glanced their way. Bell twitched her brow and looked back at her book. She really hoped she didn't come across that way.

Drake appeared back at her table and sat. "So, these are the treats you made, huh?"

"Yeah." She pushed the plate to him. "Salted caramel brownies, cookies, and fudge."

"No real caramel?" he glanced at her.

"Well, I thought about just making the caramel, then remembered you said something about your mom making the best, and I didn't want to try and beat her." She smiled.

Drake looked back at the plate of delicious-looking goodies. "Well, I can tell you one thing. That brownie looks like I may just have to eat it."

"Well, I hope you like it!"

"Wait, you're leaving?" he asked. "You're not going to sit and watch my reaction?"

Bell smiled softly. "Well, I figured you were busy, and I've got to go...run some errands, and eat lunch. Oh! That's right! I was going to eat and pay you for breakfast too!" She sat back down and started rummaging through her wallet.

Drake shook his head. "Just hold on and eat first. What do you like?"

Secret Santa

She leaned back. "Well, this is an Irish tavern. Hm. Do you have a good beef stew?"

"Yeah, and it comes with a big chunk of bread." Drake pulled a fork out of one of the rolled-up napkins on the table and took a bite of the brownie.

Bell felt her heart stop when he just sat there.

Slowly, he made eye contact with her and finally said, "This should be illegal."

"You like it?"

He leaned back. "Nah. For a Christmas treat, it's alright." He took another bite and shook his head. "I think this is the most amazing thing I've ever eaten. Don't tell Chris." He licked some caramel from his thumb.

Bell felt her ears grow warm. "Yeah? Well, I'm glad you like it."

"You better keep these here. I don't want Chris getting his hands on them, he'll eat them all." Drake stood while he finished chewing his third bite.

He put in the order and returned to his duties, taking a moment now and then to snag a bite of a dessert Bell had brought, until she was done with her lunch, and pulled her cash from her wallet to pay.

"Thanks for the treats," he said, wandering his way back to Bell's table.

"You're welcome! If you have time, you should come by and get some more."

He shrugged. "Kind of trying to stay busy." He glanced around the nearly empty tavern.

"Then I can bring some more to you." She smiled and

walked out the door. At least now he had a reason to go back, even if it was only to bring him treats.

She climbed into her car and looked around to see what streets she was close to. After starting her car again, she drove down to Richmond Street, and turned onto Charter Street. As she drove, she tapped her chin with the end of her pen, searching for Aretha's house.

"293…293…" She glanced at the paper and at the house numbers, finally stopping in front of a small blue house with dead, overgrown flowerbeds, a slightly broken and askew eave, and shingles missing from the rooftop.

Bell leaned back against her chair. Aretha definitely needed someone to provide service for her, but not just any sort of service. From what Bell could only see on the outside of the house, she needed some major repairs. With the shingles missing, there was a chance Aretha was losing a lot of heat, and the front eave of the house was a safety concern if it broke away from the house. The flowerbeds would have to wait for spring.

She might need an entire crew for this.

✵ ✵ ✵

Drake rummaged through the drawers of the desk until he found the pocket watch that once belonged to his grandfather. He ran his thumb over the crest etched into the bronze surface. His dad used to tell him it was the family crest. As a kid, he completely believed they were

Secret Santa

descendants of a royal family and maybe one day they would travel over to Ireland and meet his great-great-great (several times great) grandpa, the king.

He smiled fondly at the memory and stuck the pocket watch in his pocket. He grabbed the shoebox from the desk and carried it out the back door. He walked down the sidewalk, a bitter taste in his mouth as he passed a couple walking arm-in-arm. A woman shimmied out a store door, arms were overloaded with gift bags. She fumbled to try and reach in her coat pocket for her keys, and Drake continued walking past her. He didn't have time or desire to stop and help her. It was her own fault for trying to take care of Christmas shopping in one trip, and this late in the year.

Drake didn't fail to notice all of the "Merry Christmas" banner hanging from the street lights. "Waste of money," he grumbled under his breath. And it only got worse from there. The city had wrapped the trees in Christmas lights, they dangled across Main Street, and he knew there was also a Nativity set up with bright spotlights in front of City Hall. He would have to call them and let them know his tax dollars should be put to better use.

He finally made it to his destination: Toby's Pawn Shop. He ran his fingers through his hair before stepping into the musty air.

Toby climbed to his feet, adjusting his pants. "Heya, Drake! Been a long time."

"Yeah, it has been." He walked to the counter and set the box down. "I just…wanted to see what I can get for these."

Toby scratched his prickled white and gray cheek with one hand, the other opening the lid to look at the various trinkets Drake had managed to pull together. Toby looked at Drake over his dirty glasses. "You want to sell these things?"

"I'm really tight on money," he answered, aware how low his voice had fallen. He would be a liar if he didn't admit he was ashamed. He had to pay Chris somehow, and the electricity bill was due in a week. He cleared his tight throat. "Besides, they're just things."

Toby rubbed his nose and started holding things up to the light—the first item being his dad's cuff links given from his mom the Christmas he passed. There was a churning in Drake's heart as Toby assessed their value silently. "Well, I can give you twenty for these." He set the box on the counter and picked up a couple of golden necklaces Drake's mother had left behind when she moved out. "Fifty for all three."

Drake rubbed the back of his neck.

When Toby finished assessing the value of everything Drake brought in, and he would receive $340. He was almost $400 short. Feeling his heart sink, he nodded to Toby, who carried all of the trinkets to the counter behind him and started the process of writing up a receipt and giving Drake the cash. Drake felt numb. Now all he would have of his dad's was the tavern and barn out back. Maybe he could sell that?

"Alright, Drake. Here you go." Toby counted out the

Secret Santa

money and tucked it into an envelope. When Drake reached out to take it, Toby held on. "Are you sure you want to get rid of tall of that?"

Drake shook his head. "I don't have a choice, Toby. I've got to pay bills. I can't hold onto things." He pulled the envelope from Toby's hand and tucked it into his coat pocket. "Thanks."

"Drake, you can always ask for help, you know," Toby said.

Drake lifted his hand in a brief movement of acknowledgement and let the door fall shut behind him. At least he didn't have to buy Christmas gifts for anyone.

He intentionally ignored the woman struggling with her crying child, slipped past an old man reaching a trembling hand out holding a metal cup, and didn't bother helping the old woman step off the icy curb into the street. Everyone had their problems, and they could handle them on their own. Just like he could handle his own problems.

But when he stepped through the back door of the tavern and looked at everything, a heavy weight on his shoulders sunk a little deeper. If he lost the tavern…what would he have to live for?

CHAPTER THREE

Bell walked through the diner door, the familiar ambiance of noise, smells, and Betty's happy greeting after having been closed for a few days. She waved to Betty, who waved back even though she was busy speaking with a customer Bell couldn't identify from behind. She was about to slip into a seat at the bar when she heard Jamie call for her.

"Bell, get yourself over here and sit with me!" Jamie grinned.

Bell hurried right over to the booth and slid into the seat across from her best friend. "I haven't seen you in days! How are you?"

"Same old." Her bright smile slipped just a little, and Bell knew why. Her husband had been deployed for over a year, and the deployment this time made it his second Christmas away from home. "I noticed you skulking about Drake's place."

Bell rolled her eyes. "I wasn't skulking. Who uses that word anyway?"

"People who read books," she winked, taking a bite of

Secret Santa

a thick, homemade french-fry.

"Or own them," Bell laughed. "Speaking of which, how is the book store doing?"

"It fluctuates," Jamie shrugged. "This month is actually going pretty well, with people wanting the romance books around this season, and gifts for Christmas. I could always use some new customers, though."

"I'm afraid I'm the wrong person to ask when it comes to that."

"Your business is booming! What are you complaining about?" Jamie laughed.

Bell shook her head. "I'm the only real bakery in town, so there's not even competition. You have a lot of competition because people can buy books anywhere. I would suggest adding a little bakery section to your store, but then people would be touching your precious books with sticky fingers, and we can't have that." She finished in a mockingly stern voice.

Jamie paused. "That's actually not a half-bad idea. I mean, there are coffee places in book stores all the time."

Shane walked up to the table with a big smile and a little bit of a limp. "What do you want to eat today, Bell?"

"I thought you were supposed to be resting!" Bell exclaimed.

"I'm fine. I've been lying around for the past two days, and just wanted to get out of the house. But I promised Mom I would sit if I felt the need." She smiled.

Bell shook her head a little. "The apple doesn't fall far from the tree, huh? I'll go ahead and get…let's do your

French dip sandwich with the fries. And speaking of apples, can I have a slice of apple pie?"

"Got it." Shane jotted it down and returned to the kitchen window to call in the order.

"You're a baker. You could just make your own apple pie," Jamie said, taking a sip of her drink.

"Betty actually has amazing apple pie, and my displays are all full of other treats."

"I'm going to use the restroom. I'll be right back." Jamie scooted out.

While she was gone, Bell snuck her notebook from her pocket, looking up Mr. Carson's address. She needed to stop by his house before heading back to work. They needed his help for tomorrow to succeed.

"Who are you stalking now?" Jamie interrupted.

Bell shoved the book back into her pocket. "I'm not stalking," she said firmly. "Do you know Aretha Gilbert?"

"The grumpy old lady at the end of—"

"Yeah that one. I went by the other day and—"

"Just happened to be passing by?" Jamie raised both eyebrows in an accusatory look.

Bell frowned. "You're a sourpuss. I noticed her roof is falling apart. She's probably getting leaks and having issues regulating the warmth in her house. And one of the eaves on the front porch looks like it could fall at any moment. Grumpy or not, someone needs to take care of her."

"So, what are you trying to arrange?"

"Mr. Carson is the construction guy in town, right? I'm

Secret Santa

going to stop by his house to see if he has any ideas on how we can help get it fixed."

"Can I come?" she grinned.

Bell smiled. This might be just the thing to help Jamie too. For the first year ever, Jamie was in her Christmas spirit book. "Absolutely! Maybe we can get you to take Mrs. Gilbert to get some groceries or something while we work on her house. It would be delightful to make this a surprise."

"You can't just fix people's houses without their permission…"

"Watch me." Bell stole a fry from Jamie's plate and shoved it in her mouth.

After a rather enjoyable lunch, Jamie drove them over to Mr. Carson's house. The plan was simply to ask. Hopefully, with two of them there, he would be less likely to say no. Bell wished she knew how long it would take to fix everything, because Mr. Carson would need supplies and compensation. The thought made Bell bite her lip. She hadn't thought of that before. Hopefully, she'd be able to pay for it, whatever the cost.

They walked up to the Carson's house and Bell knocked. There was a thump and a yell, both quickly followed by the door bursting open.

Paul, the youngest Carson child, stood there with a triumphant grin. "Hi, Bell!" he yelled.

"What are you doing home?" Bell laughed. "You're supposed to be in school."

"I'm sick," he winked emphatically. "DAD!" he

shouted as he turned and ran through the house. "Dad, Bell is here! Dad!"

"I heard you, Paul."

"Dad, it's Bell!"

"I heard you! Go upstairs and get back in bed."

"But Daaad!" Paul whined.

"You stayed home from school, so you'll stay in bed."

"Fine," Paul grumbled and stomped up the stairs.

Mr. Carson finally emerged from the hallway. "Please come in and get out of the cold. Can I help you with something?"

Bell stepped in, and Jamie followed, closing the door. "I don't know if you've ever met Jamie officially, she runs the bookstore."

Jamie shook his hand with a big smile.

"Oh, right. I've seen you around before. What can I help you two with?"

"Do you know the widow Aretha Gilbert?" Bell asked.

He shook his head, frowning as he did so. "No. Why?"

"I passed by her home yesterday—it's the little blue one on Richmond Street—and I noticed the eaves are sloping at the front and looks really dangerous. I also noticed she has shingles missing. I know you're the construction man and do really good work. Would you be willing to help her out? Or know anyone who does just as good as you who would be willing?"

Mr. Carson took a breath and ran his fingers through his hair. "I don't know. I mean…I don't want to be rude, but I'm behind on my current project, and I just don't

Secret Santa

know if I can fit this in on top of everything else."

"Dad, can I help too?"

"Yeah, and me!"

Paul and his brother, Alaska, came running into the room. Alaska was ten, and loved joining his dad on the construction sites, while Paul was seven and always wanted to do anything with his dad.

Bell smiled. "I'd be willing to help too." She elbowed Jamie.

"Ow. So will I," Jamie said, rubbing her side.

"I'm sure we could get some other men to volunteer their Saturday," Bell added. "Maybe we could even get it all done in one day? With all of us helping, we might be able to get a lot done relatively quickly."

"Alright," he sighed. "I suppose taking one day off wouldn't be so bad. Maybe I can stop by tomorrow morning and see how bad the damage is."

"I haven't told her I asked anyone to help," Bell said. "I didn't want her to have the option to say no because I think she really needs it. How would you feel if we all just show up tomorrow to work?"

Mr. Carson nodded. "Yeah, alright. It will be good for all of us to help out Ms. Gilbert. What better time to help others than around Christmas?" He smiled.

"Awesome! Thank you." Bell looked at the boys. "And thank you, too. I'm excited to see you both tomorrow!" She waved and walked out of the house.

When they got back outside, Jamie leaned against Bell's shoulder. "So now we go ask people to volunteer to help tomorrow?" Jamie said.

"You find some people, and I find some people."

Jamie grinned and nudged her playfully. "Like Drake? You're going to ask Drake, aren't you? Yeah? Drake?"

"Stop it," she blushed.

"You are!"

For some reason, whenever Jamie mentioned Drake, Bell just couldn't keep her cheeks from turning red. Jamie was the only one who could see her for her true self. It was a blessing and a curse.

They'd just made it back to Jamie's bookstore, when Mrs. Flowers came running up to them. "Bell! Oh, Bell! Oh no! Christmas is ruined!" Mrs. Flowers said dramatically as she grabbed Bell by both hands. "Oh Jamie!" She turned her attention to Jamie and grabbed her hands.

"Why is Christmas ruined, Mrs. Flowers?" Jamie asked.

"I just heard the most horrible news," she continued. "The pipes froze at the school and burst! The school is flooded, and the gym's floor is destroyed! Estimates say they won't have the gym useable until after Christmas. We have nowhere to host our Christmas Extravaganza!"

Bell and Jamie exchanged a stunned look.

"There's nowhere else in town big enough to host the party," Jamie said softly.

"Exactly!" Mrs. Flowers exclaimed.

"We're going to have to cancel for the first time in the town's history?"

Secret Santa

"No, we won't," Bell interjected. "We have another place big enough." All eyes shifted to her. "Drake's barn." She knew she was crazy for even thinking it, let alone suggesting it. She hadn't been able to help soften Drake the past two years and had just barely started this year. Already, he'd re-emphasized his distaste for Christmas, *and* had even asked if she was with the community council ready to ask to use the barn.

"Are you insane?" Mrs. Flowers gasped. "I've asked for the past two years, and he not only says no, last year he told me if I came back and asked, he would burn it down!"

Bell pressed her finger against her chin. "Maybe for the past few years we've all been approaching the situation completely wrong. You've been asking him for the sake of the community, yes?"

"Of course."

"Well, what if we approached him with the suggestion this could be more of a way for us to honor and remember his father? He might be more likely to let us use it that way."

"Good thinking, Bell." Mrs. Flowers grabbed her by the shoulders. "Why don't you take that initiative?"

"Oh, no. No, no, no," Bell said, motioning with her hands. "I don't want that responsibility."

"Like you said, all you have to do is go talk to him! How hard can it be?"

"I…" She looked to Jamie for help.

"Good luck," Jamie grinned. She patted Bell on the

shoulder, stepped back, and turned to go into the bookstore, an amused smile on her face.

Bell tried to smile back, but in the back of her mind knew she was already in over her head.

Mrs. Flowers encouraged her once more before she too turned away, leaving Bell to stand alone in the cold, staring dumbfounded across the street.

Well, this day had suddenly changed.

Maybe the treats she'd given him had softened him just enough? One could hope.

She tried rehearsing what to say as she walked down the street to the Red Dragon. "Hey, Drake. Let's use your barn for the town's Christmas party in the memory of your dead father." It didn't quite seem like the best thing to say. She already got flustered around him, and now she was about to do the very thing she hoped she would never have to—talk to him about his dad. By the time she got to the Red Dragon Tavern, she still hadn't come up with a good game plan.

She drew a deep breath and stepped into the tavern. She couldn't come up with an excuse to leave. She had to walk right up to Drake, and just do it. She straightened and walked over to the bar.

The corner of his lip was lifted in a half-smile, his brows pinched. "What are you doing in here? It's not breakfast, and the lunch rush just ended…"

"I actually just came to talk to you." She rested her hands against the bar top.

"Ah. Well, Chris did manage to sneak one of your

cookies, and I had to fight him off with a sword to get them back." Drake set another stack of cups on a shelf. "What's up?"

"I'm actually here because...well, the school flooded."

"And?"

She shifted uncomfortably. "And Mrs. Flowers sent me to talk to you..."

He straightened, his lips tightening in a sour look, and his eyes narrowing. He knew what she was going to ask, and he cut her off. "So, you are with the community council."

"No! No, I just ran into Mrs. Flowers on the way to Jamie's bookstore, and she wanted me to ask you because you got mad at her last year."

"And that didn't scare you off?"

She laughed nervously. "It would take a lot more than that to scare me away."

"Yeah?" He folded his arms. "Then what would it take?"

Bell bit her lip. "The Christmas party will be canceled if we don't have somewhere to host it," she hurried. "And right now, the only place in town big enough is—"

"My barn. You want me to open the barn, so you can host your Christmas thing."

"It's not being used," she pressed.

Drake rolled his eyes. "You really are a piece of work, you know that?"

Bell frowned. "What's that supposed to mean?"

"You have no respect for people who don't love

Christmas like you do. You try and butter me up with treats before shoving Christmas down my throat? So, you can come back later and ask to use my property for your Christmas party? No, you can't use my barn. Tell the city council they can figure something else out or get over the party." He tossed his cloth onto his shoulder and started away.

"What if the city bought it from you? The barn?"

"No!" he called.

"Wouldn't your dad want you to use it? We could host the party and do it as a remembrance thing, a way to honor him and his life!" she said desperately.

He stopped in his tracks, and she saw his shoulders rise.

Okay, bringing up his dad was a terrible idea. She immediately regretted asking and wished she could take it back.

Drake walked over to her, and she took a quick breath to brace herself. "You know my father, do you? Tell me what you know about him," he said with a dangerous edge in his voice. "You don't know anything about my father. You don't know what he would or wouldn't want. You didn't even show up until after he'd died, so tell me perfect little Bell, how you know he would want me to let you all use it to your heart's delight?"

Before she could stop herself, she blurted, "I don't know, Drake. I just think if I had a dad that spent hours pouring his heart and soul into something like that he would want me to use it."

Secret Santa

His eyes narrowed. "Get out," he said, voice low.

Bell bit the inside of her lip. "I...I'm really sorry. I didn't mean to offend you. I just thought—"

"Thought you knew everything? Thought you could just come in here and bat your eyes and hang your wreath on my door and I would do whatever you want? You know, go ahead and take the wreath with you when you leave."

Bell felt her stomach churn with guilt. She stepped back, once again trying to offer an apology, but she fumbled up the words, "I'm your dad—I'm sorry about everything. Just...um." She turned away quickly, hot tears stinging her eyes. She had ruined their one chance to get the barn for the party, but worse yet, she had ruined all hope he would ever feel the spirit of Christmas ever again. How could she mess it all up with one conversation?

She grabbed the wreath with trembling hands and tried to pull it off the door, but it wouldn't budge. How on Earth could it be so stuck? She tugged and yanked, but for some reason she couldn't get it off. She yanked one last time, frustration bubbling over, and she wiped away a tear as she gave up and turned to leave.

❋ ❋ ❋

"Don't you think that was a little harsh?" Chris said from behind Drake.

Drake turned and glared at him. "What do you mean?

She came in looking for handouts, and I'm the bad guy?"

"Yeah." Drake started to retort, but Chris interrupted. "Before you talk, think. You've known her the past two years. In spite of you being you, she still persists in making sure you're invited to the Christmas party, even though she knows you won't go. She puts a wreath on your door every Christmas, despite how much she knows you're a Grinch. *And* she still had the guts to come in and ask to use the barn for the sake of everyone in town. Oh, and don't forget the treats she brought in that she made just for you." Chris paused and shook his head. "She's not looking for a handout, Drake. She was hoping maybe your heart had grown a size."

Drake's glare softened, but he kept his jaw tight as he looked through the glass on the doorway and saw her still struggling to take the wreath off. "You think I should apologize?" he mumbled.

"You think?" Chris responded with a little smirk. He went back into the kitchen.

"You're intolerable." Drake sighed and snagged his jacket off the peg and walked around the bar. He carefully pushed the door open and peeked around in time to see Bell quickly wipe a tear on her glove. He suddenly felt his stomach drop. "Uh, can I help with the wreath?" he said awkwardly.

"Oh, I can get it," she said quickly. "I just…was stupid and didn't think about the door being closed on the wreath hanger thing." She gave a quick smile and lifted up, this time sliding the wreath and its hanger from the door.

Secret Santa

"See? Not hard at all." She didn't make eye contact with him. "You have a good night." She turned to go.

"I'm sorry," Drake found himself blurting.

Bell paused for a moment before turning to finally face him, eyes still glistening. "You don't need to be. I underst—"

"Yes, I need to be. I..." He sighed. "I haven't been nice to you. I don't think I've ever been nice. It's not your fault. I guess..." He shrugged and glanced around. "I just guess I hate that you love Christmas so much." He saw her bite her bottom lip.

For a moment, she was quiet. Then she said, "Thank you for apologizing. I know how hard that is." She cleared her throat softly. "Have a good night."

"Yeah. Get home safe." He watched her start to go and felt his stomach churn again. "You know, the wreath doesn't bother me," he admitted. He hadn't meant to make her feel so bad. He often spoke without thinking; it was something his mom always scolded him for.

"Really?" she asked, looking him up and down like he'd just grown a second head.

"I mean, I don't see it anyway. Unless someone opens the door."

She smiled softly.

He returned her smile with one of his own. "I don't ever come in through the front door. I only catch glimpses of it when people come in. So. So you can leave it, if you want."

She nodded. "If you really are okay with it."

He held his hands out and when she handed it over, he opened the door and put it back on the door. "See? Good as new."

There was an awkward silence between them, Bell made a move like she was about to turn away, then turned and looked at him. "Do you know Aretha Gilbert?"

He nodded. "Yes. She used to substitute when I was in elementary school. Why?"

"A group of us are getting together tomorrow to work on her house. Her roof needs a lot of help. Mr. Carson is providing supplies and I think he'll ask some people to help, but whatever help we can get would be really appreciated."

Drake folded his arms. "Is this your way of asking me to help?"

"Um. Yes?" She bit her bottom lip.

"Do you ever think you worry too much about everyone else?"

"I think people worry far too much about themselves and not enough about everyone else," she replied simply.

"I hadn't thought of that." He nodded. "Alright. I always liked her, and if I can help out Zack then I'd better. What time are you meeting?"

"First thing. But I don't know exactly what time...maybe come by at nine?"

"That's really early," he sighed. "What if I'm a little late?"

"It better be, so you can make lots of cocoa for everyone." She gave him a hesitant smile.

Secret Santa

Drake chuckled. "I might be able to swing that. I'll see you tomorrow, then, in my grungy clothes. I'll even drag Chris along for the fun."

Bell's brown eyes lit up, and her beautiful smile widened. "Thank you, Drake. See you in the morning!"

He watched her carefully walk to her car. Drake ran his fingers through his hair and walked back inside, forehead pinched in confusion. He had scolded Bell, kicked her out, only to turn around, apologize, put the wreath back on the door, and now…

"How did it go?" Chris asked, leaning against the bar where Drake usually stood.

"Uh, good. I guess." He tilted his head. "I agreed to go help her fix Ms. Gilbert's house tomorrow."

A smile slowly crept across Chris's face. "Look at you. Is your chest hurting?"

"No, why?"

"I think your heart may have grown a size or two." Chris chuckled.

"Shut up," Drake chuckled, rolling his eyes. "And you're coming with me. Be sure to be ready by nine!" He nudged Chris out of the way, Bell lingering in the back of his thoughts as he returned to getting the tavern ready for the evening rush.

Over the past couple of years, they had only seen each other through casual run-ins. She would come in sometimes for lunch, he would see her randomly at the grocery store, but they'd never actually spent time together. Why he would choose to do so now, when she had so carelessly brought up his dad like she knew him? Maybe he could finally get a peek into who Bell really was, and most importantly, why he continued to agree to spend more time with her.

※ ※ ※

Bell made it back to her car and leaned her head against the headrest, heaving a sigh of relief. "Alright, Mr. Mistletoe. I know you're here." She straightened and looked to her right, jumping when her supervisor appeared beside her.

He had grown to a human size to help blend in with his surroundings but hadn't hidden his pointed ears. His brown hair poked out from under a green beanie, and he wore an oversized brown coat. She'd never seen him looking so…well, human. She missed his green suit and red glitter bowtie.

He cleared his throat softly. "How did you know it was me?"

"Why else would Drake have come out and apologized?" she raised her eyebrows, pressing silently for an answer.

"Actually, that wasn't me. He did that on his own."

"Oh…but taking the wreath back—"

"Also him. I may have stopped you from getting the wreath off the door, and I might have influenced him to say yes to helping you with Aretha's house." Mr.

Secret Santa

Mistletoe tugged the front of his coat down so the neck moved under his chin. "This is your third year working on him. You know you can't return to the North Pole until you help him." He gave her an apologetic look.

Bell felt her heart sink. This was the news she had been dreading. She lowered her hands and picked at her fingers. "I understand," she answered softly.

"Bell, you are a great Secret Santa elf. You've done some amazing things. We miss seeing you at the North Pole. You can't come home until your list is officially blank."

"I know. I miss home too, and I promise I really am doing my best." She looked at him.

"Of course. And from here on out, I won't intervene unless you truly need me. Promise." He gave her a big grin. "Merry Christmas, Bell!" He tapped his nose three times and disappeared.

Bell slumped back against her chair. One more year to get this right. She couldn't help but remember what she'd said to Mrs. Flowers—maybe all this time she'd been approaching Drake the wrong way. Maybe they just needed the friendship with each other. Maybe that's all it would take to melt Drake Pine's heart.

CHAPTER FOUR

Bell couldn't contain her excitement Saturday morning. She scurried out of bed, dressed in jeans, a Christmas t-shirt, and tennis shoes, and threw her long brown hair up into a ponytail. When she was ready, she threw on her coat and gloves and grabbed the muffins from the day before she'd brought home just for this morning, then drove right over to Jamie's. She left her car running and jogged up to the front door, pausing for a moment to look up at the sunny sky. It was warm enough she shoved her gloves in her pocket.

"About time you got here," Jamie said as she opened the door.

"I didn't even get a chance to ring the bell!"

"That's because I was watching from the window." She shut the door behind her and smiled. "It's the perfect morning for working!"

"We're definitely lucky, after the weather we've had. Though, it could only be better if I had noticed her house sooner. We could've gotten this taken care of before the cold hit." Bell led the way back down the sidewalk to her car.

Secret Santa

"Even you can't be perfect," Jamie laughed. Jamie climbed into the passenger side and her eyes widened. "Yummy! Muffins! I ate, but I'm not passing up one of these." She grabbed one out of the bag and took a big bite.

"Leave some for everyone else," Bell laughed.

They arrived at Aretha's before the others, and Bell rubbed her hands together. "I guess we go tell her the good news. You can take my car if you need to take her anywhere." She took the bag of muffins and slid out of the car. "Come on, Jamie!"

"Coming!" Jamie dusted the crumbs off the front of her coat and trotted alongside Bell until she swallowed her food. She rang the doorbell and pulled her hand-crocheted, green scarf a little closer around her neck.

Bell smiled to herself. She'd given it to Jamie for Christmas the year before, and she loved seeing Jamie wear it.

The door opened. Aretha Gilbert wore a scarf over her white hair, a coat, sweatpants, and slippers. "Yeah?" she said loudly, leaning heavily on her cane.

"My name is Bell."

"Yeah, I heard the bell. That's why I answered the door." She frowned. Her coke-bottle glasses made her eyes look gigantic.

Bell smiled. "I'm Bell," she said louder and put her hand on her chest.

"Well, why didn't you say so?"

Jamie grinned. "Some people are coming to help you, Mrs. Gilbert."

"With what?"

"Your roof." Bell pointed overhead. "And any other repairs you might need."

"I'm fine." She shook her head.

Bell shrugged. "We already have people coming. Just tell us where to start, or let us come in and check everything."

For a moment, the frail old woman looked like she might shut the door in their faces.

Bell winked softly, and tears swelled in Aretha's eyes. Aretha nodded. "Okay."

Bell waited for her to shuffle back, then followed her in. "It's cold in here!" she exclaimed.

"The heater has been broken nearly a week."

"A week?" Jamie gasped.

"My husband always fixed things. Now that he's gone…" her voice broke.

"Oh, Aretha." Bell took the old woman's freezing hands. "We're going to get you warmed up, and then we're going to make this right." She rushed to the couch, grabbed the afghan off the back, and wrapped it around Mrs. Gilbert's thin shoulders. "Jamie, maybe you could take Mrs. Gilbert to your place or the bookstore to warm up?"

"That's a great idea! I would love to." She put her arm around the woman and helped her down the porch stairs. "We'll crank up the heat and have cookies and talk about books. I bet I've got some you might be inclined to read. Meanwhile, everyone will take care of everything. It'll be

Secret Santa

like coming home to a whole new house!" Jamie got her settled in the passenger seat of Bell's car just as Drake's truck pulled up.

Bell stared. She really didn't expect him to show, especially not before Mr. Carson.

He parked and walked toward Jamie with a smile and a wave. The smile died as Jamie said something Bell couldn't hear, then he dashed back to his truck and grabbed something off the passenger seat.

As Jamie started Bell's car, Drake hurried back to the passenger door with a steaming styrofoam cup in each hand. Bell spied a tremulous smile on Mrs. Gilbert's face as she took the cocoa, and her heart swelled. She'd grown to recognize that heart-warming feeling—Aretha's name was disappearing from the book. Best of all, Drake had been the final piece.

Jamie drove off as Mr. Carson pulled into the driveway and a few other cars parked on the street.

Drake hauled a rolling cooler up to the porch. He gave her a big smile. "Hello. Jamie just told me Mrs. Gilbert's heater is out. I can put in a call to Henry and get him over here, and I think Chris just pulled up with his wife."

"First of all, I can't believe you actually brought hot cocoa," Bell grinned.

"Well, what can I say? I do my best." He opened the cooler, poured hot water into a styrofoam cup, mixed in three scoops of cocoa, and handed it to Bell. "So how long has Mrs. Gilbert's heater been broken?"

"Almost a week, apparently," Bell sighed.

Lichelle Slater

"Man." Drake shook his head then turned to Mr. Pole and his son, Jeremy, walking up to the house. Jeremy was the same age as Alaska. "Andy. Mind checking out the electrical?"

Mr. Pole nodded. "Absolutely. Jeremy, maybe you can help Mr. Carson and Alaska get the stuff for the roof?" He nudged Jeremy, who apprehensively walked over to where Mr. Carson was busy putting up the ladder.

Jeremy's name was also in Bell's book, but she hadn't had time quite yet to hunt him down and see what it is he could possibly need. Children rarely showed up on the Spirit List. Of course, the Poles were relatively new to Owentown, and as Bell watched Jeremy's father usher him toward Mr. Carson and his two sons, it dawned on her that maybe what he needed was a really good friend. Maybe she wouldn't have to intervene at all.

She watched Mr. Carson assign Jeremy and Alaska to work together and carry the two-by-fours to stack them close to the house, and the packages of shingles at the bottom of the ladder. Mr. Pole grabbed his toolbox and headed inside to assess any electrical issues.

Bell assigned Chris to investigate the basement, his wife Heather took charge of vacuuming, and Bell directed others who showed up to hunt down anything that needed to be cleaned, repaired, or replaced—like dim light bulbs, dusty fans, and any place Mrs. Gilbert wouldn't be able to reach. She armed them with rags and cleaning sprays, brought in a box of additional supplies, and put herself to work in the kitchen. Jamie had promised Mrs. Gilbert a good-as-new house, and Bell planned to deliver.

Bell was heading to the bathroom with her own tote of cleaning supplies, the main floor now completely clean, when she ran into Drake standing in the hallway, staring uncomfortably at the light switch.

"Hey, Bell." Drake said, shifting his stance.

"You afraid that light is going to eat you?" she teased.

He smiled. "Nah, I'm more afraid of the power outlets." He pointed to one low on the wall. "But to be serious, it looks like we may have electrical issues. I noticed this burn mark on the wall." He crouched and put his finger against a dark spot on the ivory and green wallpaper above the power outlet that looked like flames at one time had licked it, leaving behind a shadow of a small fire. "I pulled off the faceplate, and then came over to this light switch." He stood up again and showed her the box he'd taken out of the wall. "See these wires? How they're all black?"

Bell leaned closer. "I'm going to assume the outer sheath isn't supposed to be melted?" she said, giving him a smile that was more of a wince.

He shook his head. "Right."

"Can you fix it?"

He shook his head. "I'm not an electrician. I know we have to shut down the power to the house to fix it, but they need the electricity to run the saws and all the other stuff they're doing on the roof."

"Is this something that has to be fixed right now?" she asked.

Lichelle Slater

"I'm going to say yes. I mean, they probably got burnt from a power surge, and she's really lucky her house didn't catch on fire." He pointed his eyes to the burn mark on the wall again. "Let me see if I can hunt down Mr. Pole, he was here somewhere."

Bell smiled up at him. "I think he was in the basement. Did you get a muffin?"

He smiled. "Yeah. Three." He rubbed the back of his neck. "Hope you don't mind."

"Not at all! I'm glad you enjoyed them." She glanced over her shoulder. "Maybe I can find the right tools to help out with that wiring. My adopted father built things all the time. He specialized in robotics, so I think I may be able to help somewhat."

In reality, her adopted father was more than a toymaker; he was Santa's top robotic-making elf, specializing in anything electronic. Her heart swelled as she remembered the quiet moments when he sat down with her in the empty shop after all the bustle of Christmas and would show Bell all about how to make different kinds of toys. He had even helped her make herself a racecar for her eleventh birthday.

"Really?" Drake asked, eyes widening in impressed surprise.

"As long as I don't find any snakes tangled in the wires, I think I can do this."

He laughed. "You're afraid of snakes?"

She shuddered. "We're all afraid of something! It was the Abominable Snowman when I was little, though."

Secret Santa

Drake couldn't help but laugh again. "Oh, yeah?"

"And I had a crush on Jack Frost." She nodded.

"Well, aren't you peculiar?"

"I don't like him anymore!"

"Then who do you like?" he grinned.

Bell hesitated. "Uh…no one. I should find stuff. You should fix that."

She blushed madly and turned away; more embarrassed than the time she'd accidentally redirected him down a muddy road after he'd just washed his car. Her intention had been to redirect him down a dirt road over the summer to drive past the farms and see the baby animals and see people having fun out on the lake. That plan, like all others, had failed. She prayed this one didn't.

❄ ❄ ❄

Drake stared after Bell. She hadn't answered his question, and at the back of his mind he wondered why she would be so embarrassed to tell him. Maybe it was because she liked someone he knew, or didn't like anyone at all, or…nah, she couldn't like him. He was a hater of everything Christmas. Why would that attract her?

He shook his head and trotted down the stairs after her. He found her outside talking to Mr. Pole, who gestured for them to go back inside. Drake had to side step a ninja role, as Alaska and Jeremy were apparently reenacting some popular ninja show.

Bell stopped walking when they reached the area Drake had been working. "Mr. Pole noticed a few other areas in the house with the same problem," she said, glancing at Drake.

"Yeah, electricity is a fickle thing and wiring can be dangerous," Mr. Pole replied. "Especially in a house this old. I better get to work cutting wire." He stepped past Drake. "Thanks for the heads-up. Let me know if you spot anything else."

Drake blocked Bell.

She looked up at him with a blush to her cheeks—or it could have just been from the cold. "I was going to go back to cleaning the bathroom," she said.

"I actually had a thought," he said. It had just come to him. He wasn't sure why he had blocked Bell from continuing after Mr. Pole, but for some reason he wanted to talk to her. Until she spoke, he wasn't sure about what. Then the idea came. "You wouldn't happen to store Christmas decorations in the trunk of your car?"

At first, her nose wrinkled in confusion, and then understanding dawned on her face. "No, but I imagine Mrs. Gilbert would have some in the basement." She practically sprinted inside. She trampled down the stairs in her excitement and started scouring the shelves for the Christmas decorations.

Drake couldn't resist a little smile. How could this grown woman still feel so excited about Christmas? Especially someone who lived alone without kids of her own? What sort of magic did she still feel in it?

Secret Santa

He noticed some boxes stuffed in the corner of the basement, and with some rearranging of the piles, he realized the tall box was a tree. "Hey, I found the tree!" he called.

"Oh good! I think I just found the ornaments. But I'm not tall enough to reach them," she said, huffing with effort.

Drake turned to see her standing on her tippy-toes, reaching as far as she could and just barely able to touch the box with her fingertips. He chuckled. "I got it." He walked over and reached up over her to grab the box. "Here you go." As he handed her the box, he realized again just how beautiful she was. Even though her red shirt was now covered in dust and she had a smudge across her left cheek, Bell had beautiful brown eyes. There was also a child-like spark of joy coming from her, which made her smile seem even brighter. He swallowed and let go of the box. "I'll grab the tree. Did you find any other boxes marked Christmas?"

"Yes. This one is lights." She pointed to the next box over. "I hope there are some thin lights we can just put in the windows. It will be too big of a hassle to get the lights up on the house while the others are working on the roof."

He nodded. He grabbed the box and set that down, and the next box over was labeled "X-Mas Décor." He set that on the floor as well, so he could carry the tree up first. "After you," he said to Bell, stepping back to let her by.

After all four boxes were successfully opened, Drake had to figure out how to put together the Christmas tree.

"Man, this thing is old," he said, the musty smell of the old plastic tree wafting from the branches as he rearranged them.

"I think it's cute. She's got all sorts of ornaments in here. Look at this one!" She held up a foam stocking, which had clearly been made by a child. "And this!" She held up a paper snowflake.

"Does she have kids?" he asked. "I mean, shouldn't they be helping her out with stuff like this?"

Bell shrugged. "Maybe they live far away. Or they didn't have a good relationship?"

He frowned, thinking of his own mother. They rarely talked. Every time he tried, she would always bring up him making use of himself and his college education, leaving the bar and town behind like she had, and just starting over. It angered him to think she could so quickly forget his father and leave it all behind. Each phone call ended suddenly, and his attempts to communicate became more infrequent until they were pretty much nonexistent.

"Did you used to decorate the tree with your parents?" Bell suddenly asked.

"Yeah, it wasn't much different from this. We didn't have the money to get a pre-lit one. In fact, we used to go find our own Christmas tree and chop it down, until Mom finally confessed she was tired of vacuuming the needles every day." He chuckled. "That settled it. Dad got a fake Christmas tree that year. It was sad to lose the tradition of chopping it down, but we quickly grew to like not being out in the bitter cold arguing over which tree we liked the best."

Bell smiled. "That must have left some good memories with it."

He looked over at her when he finally got the tree to stand upright. "What about you? Or did you just have a pine tree growing in your house that you kept decorated all year?"

She laughed. "No, pine trees can't grow inside houses. I thought you would know that?" she teased.

He attempted a smile.

"We always had real trees when I was growing up," she said. "I don't now, because I didn't even think about seeing if we could get real ones around here. When I was younger I never asked where the tree came from. I guess I always just thought there was a man who delivered the trees, like the mailman delivers mail." She gave him another one of her half-embarrassed smiles.

Drake glanced back at the tree. "This is the first year I've even put up a Christmas tree since Dad passed. I guess two Christmases isn't too much, but I can't even remember if I helped him decorate it that year."

"Two Christmases can feel like an eternity when you're reminded of someone you miss," Bell said softly, arms folded gently as she looked at the crooked tree.

Drake watched her from the corner of his eye, and opened his mouth to try and say something, but Chris interrupted, and he was mildly grateful to avoid the uncomfortable conversation of loved ones being dead.

"You two slackers," Chris said as he stepped into the

room. He breathed hard but smiled at them. "Great idea." He gave them a thumbs-up. "It looks like Mr. Pole is replacing some of the wiring as soon as the roof is done, which it almost is, and Henry is fixing the heater—easier than your fix, Drake. All it needed was a new part! Then I'm thinking everyone should come over to the Red Dragon for lunch?" He looked right at Drake.

"Sure. You want to leave and start making something? What are you thinking?"

"White chicken chili," he grinned, rubbing his hands together. "With chips and cheese and bread and stuff."

"Is it really time for lunch?" Bell looked at her watch.

"Yeah, almost," Drake answered. "Chris likes to sneak his way out of work."

"Hey, I object to that. Heather is here, cleaning the bathrooms. I was helping Zack with the lumber and shingles, and the chili has to simmer for a while before it's ready to be eaten."

"Yeah, yeah," Drake laughed. "Just get out of here. I'll give Heather a ride to the tavern."

Chris rolled his eyes and grumbled under his breath as he left.

Drake opened the box labeled, "Christmas Lights." It didn't take long for Bell to magically untangle the white lights for the tree, and she began draping them while he started framing the windows with the small colored lights. By the time he was done, she was once again on her tiptoes trying to finish off the strand at the top of the tree. Drake couldn't resist a grin again, and leaned close against

Secret Santa

her side, brushing her arm as he reached up to help her wrap the lights. He didn't need to say anything, she didn't either, but she didn't readily move away from him. Bell handed him the Christmas topper next—a little paper angel, glued crooked, and covered with glitter. Together, they began decorating the tree.

"I can't wait to see Mrs. Gilbert's face when she comes home," Bell said, finally taking a step back to assess their decorating. "It's perfect."

Drake stepped back beside her, but all he saw was a crooked tree with old, faded ornaments and a crumpling angel at the top. "It'll do."

"Don't you understand, silly?" she smiled. "These are all her memories. Ornaments made by her children throughout the years, times she spent with her family cooking Christmas dinner, making treats, hearing their laughter and arguing, longing for all of that to happen all over again."

"It sounds painful."

"Memories can be painful." She stepped closer to him. "But they also bring so much joy. If you focus only on the pain of the world, you will drown in it. But if you can look at this—" She opened her arms to the meager Christmas decorations. "—and remember the joy and feel happiness, then maybe you can make it through another year. Maybe you can tolerate life and being alone."

Drake suddenly wondered if she was talking about Aretha or herself. He rubbed his cold nose. He wasn't sure what to say, so he stayed quiet while he looked at the bright lights.

"Well, that does it," Mr. Carson called as he walked into the house. "Should be fixed for now, but I'd like to get in the attic just to make sure she's got enough insulation and no leaking."

"Great!" Bell said, smiling. "Does anyone else need help with something?" she called, shoving the protective newspapers back into the boxes.

Something clicked, and the house started to smell like dirt as the air slowly began to heat through the furnace.

"Power's back on!" Mr. Pole called from somewhere at the back of the house.

"Furnace is fixed!" Henry called from the basement.

"House is cleaned!" Heather smiled as she hopped down from the steps, three women behind her.

Drake leaned over and plugged in the Christmas lights. The small colored lights twinkled amid the simple decorations and filled the living room with a warm glow. Though she wore a huge smile, Bell looked like she could cry.

Drake thought he finally understood why Bell was the way she was, or at least partly. She was alone, just like him. Believing in the magic of Christmas gave her hope and encouraging people in the town to help each other brought her joy. Being with people, helping them, that's what helped Bell get through the years of being alone. Maybe she wasn't so bad after all.

"Thank you all so much for spending your morning getting this all done for Mrs. Gilbert. She's going to be so happy!" Bell said. "Drake has also offered to let us all go over to the Red Dragon Tavern for some lunch."

"We sort of wanted to stay and see the look on her face," Mr. Carson said, putting his hand on Alaska's head and ruffling it.

Bell grinned. "I think that would be a very appropriate thing to do. And then we can help you put all of your tools and scraps away and head out to get food."

"Speaking of which, someone just pulled into the driveway," Heather observed, pointing through the window.

Everyone hurried to gather into the living room.

Aretha walked in and put her hand on her chest, tears swelling in her eyes as she looked at her home and the Christmas decorations. "Oh my goodness. I haven't put up the tree in years."

"It was all Bell," Drake said.

Bell laughed, playfully nudging him. "The Christmas decorations were definitely Drake's idea, and he helped just as much."

Aretha was so excited, she could hardly contain herself. She wanted to know what repairs had been made, and who had done what. She walked around the house to personally admire every detail of the work that had been done. Drake watched Bell as they walked around the house with the sweet old widow.

Finally, she stopped back in the living room, the house now heating up nicely. "Thank you all so very much. I don't even know what to say. For you to take time out of your own busy lives to help a little old lady…" She patted her chest, choking up with tears.

Jamie hugged her.

"This is very exhausting," Aretha finally laughed. "I think I'll go lay down for a little while, if you don't mind."

Slowly, everyone gave her a big hug and walked out. Drake headed for the door, pausing to look back in the living room where Bell stood holding Aretha's wrinkled, arthritis-ridden hands. "Please don't hesitate to call for help," she was saying. "I put everyone's numbers on the door. It doesn't matter which one you call, we've all agreed to be here if you need us for anything. You understand?" she said almost firmly. "For anything, Aretha. Even if you just need someone to come sit with you."

"Bell, I couldn't have asked for anything better."

"Will you have family here for Christmas?"

Aretha sighed. "I'll be here, but both my boys are busy with their own families, and it is just too far and hard to travel."

Bell frowned. "Well, that won't do. You should come to the town Ch…" The words faded. "Well, on second thought, I'm not sure if we're having a town Christmas party. The school flooded." She shook her head. "In any case, I will come here for Christmas, so you won't have to be alone."

She smiled. "I'll hold you to it."

Bell laughed. She gave Aretha a gentle hug and soft

Secret Santa

kiss on the cheek, finally turning to leave. She made eye contact with Drake and pink began to cover her cheeks. "I thought you'd left."

"I was going to, but for some reason didn't," he confessed. "You're coming to lunch, right?" he asked.

She nodded softly.

"I'll see you over there, then." Drake nodded. "Heather, I'm your ride!"

❄ ❄ ❄

Bell slid into the driver's seat and sat for just a moment.

Jamie nudged her. "I can't believe you got Drake here, *and* he helped you decorate the tree!"

"He did that all on his own. I didn't do anything," she said softly. She smiled and looked at Jamie.

Jamie must have recognized the look on her face, because she started squealing. "You're head-over-heels for him!"

"It doesn't do me any good! He hates me, and Christmas." She put the car in reverse and headed out of the driveway.

"I don't know. Today, decorating the tree with you, I don't think he really hates Christmas as much as you think he does. And he definitely doesn't hate you. Did you see the way he looked at you?"

"Like I'm an idiot?" She headed toward the tavern.

"No. He sort of stares at you like he's...I don't know, trying to figure you out." Jamie shrugged. "I mean, you are a tough nut to crack with your mysterious stories."

"Mysterious stories?" Bell exclaimed.

"Yeah! You tell stories about growing up and your past, but never yet have I heard you say where you're actually from." She twitched her brows.

Bell rolled her eyes and looked at Jamie. "Canada."

"Which part?"

"Let's go eat." She shut off the car.

"See! You're avoiding the question even now!"

"I'm hungry!"

Jamie shook her head. "You don't get to escape this time. Where are you actually from?"

Bell looked at Jamie, confused by her sudden curiosity. She'd always been pacified with "Canada" and never pressed further. "Nunavut," she answered and quickly stepped out of her car.

Jamie hopped out right after her. "That doesn't sound like a real place."

"It is. You can look it up and everything." She held the door open.

Jamie pulled out her phone and began researching it.

"I can't believe you don't believe me," she mumbled, following Jamie to a table to take a seat. Drake was already at work carrying trays out to the few people who had helped and set bowls of chili before them. "What do you think would make him really happy this Christmas?" she asked in a low voice.

Secret Santa

"Ever thought about inviting his mom and brothers?"

Bell shook her head. "That is not my place. I tried last year, but...I don't know what their relationship is like now. He never brings them up. I'm lucky I even found out he had brothers."

Jamie nodded. "I could have told you."

"And yet, you didn't. After lunch, I'm going to go home and shower, and maybe I can get to the bakery and get something made today."

"You still have half a day. You'll have plenty of time to get things done."

"I don't suppose you would want to help?" Bell grinned widely.

"I have my own shop to run," Jamie reminded jokingly.

Bell chuckled.

"So what's your plan of attack for Mister Tall Dark and Handsome?" Jamie asked.

Bell arched her eyebrow. "Oh, I was thinking of buying some treats, a collar..."

Jamie snorted. "What?"

"I was thinking about that cute little King Charles puppy at the pet store." She glanced at Jamie with an innocent look.

"I was talking about Drake, you dork."

Bell laughed. "I know. Jamie, I don't know. I have such...mixed feelings about him. I mean, don't get me wrong, I absolutely think he's handsome, but for as long as I've known him, he pays no interest to me. So, I will be his friend, I will invite him to all things Christmas, and probably drive him nuts, and that will be that. Still single after Christmas."

"You could be more bold instead of beating around the bush."

"Oh really? How do you propose I be more bold than sticking a Christmas wreath on his door?"

Jamie rolled her eyes. "Actually ask him out? Tell him you find him attractive."

Bell shook her head venomously. "Absolutely not."

"Why!"

"Because...because I can't! I just...I don't know. It's easy for you to say that because you're already married."

Jamie scoffed. "I'm the one that proposed to Andrew, Bell. I'm also the one that asked him out on a first date."

"Now *he* is tall, dark, and handsome."

"Don't you know it?" Jamie grinned. She pulled her phone out of her pocket and looked at the lock screen on her phone. It showed her standing with her arm around her husband Andrew in his uniform as he shipped off for deployment. Andrew was a handsome African-American, with a large smile and kind green eyes. Despite his height and muscles, he was the biggest teddy bear Bell had ever met. "I miss him," Jamie said longingly.

Bell reached out and squeezed Jamie's knee. "He'll be back before you know it."

Jamie nodded and put her phone back in her pocket.

Drake caught Bell's gaze and smiled with a wave toward the bar. "Hey, I'll get you some food."

Secret Santa

"Aren't you going to eat too?" she called over the slight clamor.

"Of course. Just give me a minute."

"See?" Jamie whispered. "You two are so smitten."

"Drop it, Jamie," Bell sighed. "He, me, we, isn't going to happen." Bell found a seat by one of the windows and rested her coat on the back of the chair. "What are you in the mood to eat?"

"Really?" Jamie asked. She rolled her eyes, grabbed Bell's coat in one hand and her wrist in the other and dragged her to a four-person table in the middle of the room. "If you sit at a two-person table, he can't sit beside you." Jamie draped Bell's coat on one chair, then sat across from her.

Bell couldn't resist a smile. "Thanks for looking out for me. I just…oh, that was fast, Drake."

Drake set a mug of cocoa in front of Bell and one in front of Jamie, and then the bowls of steaming white chili. "Do you two want something else to drink?"

Bell licked her lips. "This looks amazing. Maybe some water? And you're going to sit and eat with us, right?"

"Of course," Drake smiled. "I just have to make sure I'm still running the place. Unfortunately, this is the busiest I've been in a while." He nodded to the two of them and slipped through the kitchen door.

"Don't say a word," Bell interrupted before Jamie could get anything out.

Jamie closed her mouth, just smiling, and leaned back in her chair.

Drake returned a few minutes later and set their drinks on the table before choosing the seat next to Bell. "Sorry about that. Chris is cooking the food, so I had to get everyone's drinks done."

"We totally understand," Bell said.

They sat for a moment in silence.

Jamie glanced at her phone. "Oh, look at the time. I forgot I have a thing." She stood up.

Bell opened her eyes wide at Jamie. She really couldn't be leaving just for the sake of her and Drake talking? "What thing?"

"Oh, you know." Jamie winked unapologetically. "I'll grab my lunch to go, no worries, Drake." She walked to the window and called to Chris, asking if she could get her meal to go.

Bell sighed and faced Drake. "She is sly as a fox, that one. Better watch out."

"It could be worse."

"Yeah?"

He paused and thought for a moment, then shrugged. "She could have left you with a real dragon."

Bell laughed at the unexpected reference. She folded her legs and leaned her elbow on the table. "I've been meaning to ask you about that. Some say there is a treasure buried in the cellar. They say you have a little dragon handed down from father to son through the ages." She raised her eyebrows with a curious grin.

Drake smiled his half-smile. "Yep. But it's supposed to be a family secret." He put his finger to his lips.

Secret Santa

Bell chuckled and took a drink of her cocoa. "What do you do in your spare time?"

He shrugged. "Nothing. Just the bar. You?"

"I spend as much time as I can out in the community. After I close the bakery for the day, I volunteer at the after-school reading program, or take treats and play games at the retirement center. Just different ways to stay busy."

"You don't just go home and get off your feet and watch a movie?"

She shrugged. "What's at home? I live alone, so if I go out and do things with other people, then it doesn't feel so empty."

"Drake, your order's up!" Chris called.

Drake got to his feet with a short, "Excuse me."

Bell filled her cheeks with air and slowly exhaled. Why did she have to be so awkward?

This time, when Drake came back, he asked about why she loved Christmas so much.

Bell had to think before she answered. "I guess I love Christmas because it's the one time of year everyone tries to be a little better for the sake of someone else. It's not about the presents, or Santa, or lights. It's about the magic in the air, the feeling of joy and love, knowing even the worst of us have a chance of changing." She blushed. "That's why I love Christmas."

"Huh. I didn't expect that answer from you. I figured you liked it because of the treats, the parties, all that kind of stuff."

"Don't get me wrong, those are a lot of fun too, but that's not the whole reason I enjoy it."

They began eating. Now and then one would come up with a question that was easy to answer, like what their favorite color was, favorite movie, until they'd both finished eating and it was time for Bell to go home for her shower, so she could get back to work and open for at least half of the day.

"Thanks for staying today," Drake said.

"Well, I had a good time eating lunch with you," Bell smiled.

Drake stood and started gathering their plates. "You're welcome to come by any time you want." He looked at her. "I didn't mean to actually banish you from here."

Bell smiled. "Then you will definitely be seeing me again."

She drove herself home for a much-needed shower after the morning of work. When she'd finished, she twisted her hair into a French twist while it was still damp and sat on her couch to check her book. She knew it was still early to hope, but she couldn't help it. She opened the book and turned to "Gilbert, Aretha." The black lettering of Aretha's name slid from the page and twirled into the air, disintegrating and leaving the page completely clean.

Bell squealed and jumped up. "First one out of the book! Yes!"

After a celebratory dance around the living room, Bell pulled on her coat and headed to her bakery to finish the second half of the day baking Christmas treats.

Secret Santa

CHAPTER FIVE

Bell walked into the bar the next morning, carrying a plate of muffins she'd made just for Drake, and looked around. Not only was it vacant of customers, Drake was nowhere to be seen. "Drake? Are you here? Your door was open."

"Coming!" he called from some back corner of the tavern. He finally appeared, tying his bar apron around his waist. Clearly, he wasn't expecting to see her, because his eyebrows twitched upward, and his green eyes looked over her dress. "Back for more breakfast?"

"I was actually stopping by to give you some fresh muffins." She set down the plate, which held four muffins and a small plastic container of homemade cranberry jam and pecan spread.

"You're not here trying to get me to go to church with you, right?" His gaze hinted toward her dress.

"No. I just thought you would like some breakfast. Oh, and a tin of cocoa." She pulled a huge can from her purse and set it on the counter. "Since I've been drinking all of yours."

Secret Santa

"You've had, like, two glasses."

Bell shrugged. "Then I'm planning on coming by for more."

Drake stared at her in silence for a good minute before he finally shook his head. "You really came over this morning just to bring me breakfast?"

She nodded.

"You do know I'm smart, right?"

"What's that supposed to mean?" she frowned.

"I can see what you're doing." He leaned his arms against the bar. "Come on, Bell. You're not fooling me. You put a wreath on my door, you have me come help with Aretha's house, now you're bringing me muffins and cocoa for breakfast? What's next? Caroling?"

Bell bit her lip, but that didn't stop her smile from spreading. "Actually…" She hadn't been planning on it, but with him suggesting it, Bell realized this would be a fabulous way to reach out to the Pole family.

He rolled his eyes and straightened. "Find someone else to be your Christmas project, Bell."

"Oh, come on. What harm is it to go sing to a couple of families and elderly people?"

"I don't do that."

"What? Sing? Or go visit people you haven't seen in a while?"

He folded his arms. "Both."

"I hear you singing all the time, so *that* is a lie." Bell wondered if she was giving him a motherly look and relaxed her face and lowered her hands so they weren't on her hips.

"Why do you even bother?"

"Because no one actually wants to be alone on Christmas, even if they pretend to." Bell watched him, silently hoping she wasn't pushing him too hard.

Drake slowly exhaled. "Don't be offended if I don't come."

"I won't be. That's entirely your choice. But I'm going to keep inviting you to things, so don't be offended by that," she winked.

He finally cracked the smallest of smiles. "Deal. Where are you meeting and when?"

"Jamie's bookstore at seven o'clock."

"Alright. Thanks for stopping by." He pulled the plastic off the top of the muffins and smelled one of them.

She smiled. "Have a good Sunday! See you later!"

"Maybe, Bell. I said maybe!" he called as she walked out the door.

She waved to him through the window and climbed in her car to head to church. Drake was certainly an interesting person. The more she talked to him, the more she wanted to be around him. Maybe Drake started off as a project, and she still had responsibilities to get him off the Spirit List, but with every interaction, Bell wanted to be around him more.

At church, she slid into her typical pew beside Jamie and gave her a side-hug.

Jamie stopped singing and leaned over. "Where have you been?"

Secret Santa

"I stopped to give Drake some breakfast." Bell grabbed her own hymnbook and flipped the pages.

Jamie's smile broadened. "Drake, huh?"

"Shh. I also invited him to come caroling with us tonight at seven."

"We're going caroling?"

"We are now."

Jamie grinned and started singing again, and Bell caught a little laugh between words.

After the service, Bell joined a group of women in the foyer, all of them talking about how good Betty and her family were doing, and how great it was that they'd all come to church. Emily brought up that she'd finally opened her handmade soaps and candle shop, and that everyone needed to stop by. Everyone politely said they would, while Bell knew most wouldn't. Mrs. Brown bragged her husband had been given a promotion, and the gossip continued.

Bell, however, noticed Amanda Skye cradling her two-month old, arguing with her three-year-old that it was time to go, and calling for her five-year-old to come back—he was running down the hall. Normally, this would look like any other scene with a family, but it was the look in Amanda's eyes that made Bell leave her group and walk over. Amanda looked like she might burst into tears at any moment.

Bell crouched down onto Becky's level and held her arms out. "Hello, Becky. Mind if I help get you to your car? It's so cold outside today!"

"Brr," Becky said, wrapping her arms around herself and pretending to shiver.

"That's right!" Bell picked up Becky and looked at Amanda. "I hope you don't mind."

"No, not at all. Thank you. Adam! Please, let's go home!"

"I wanna stay with Dad!" he yelled back.

"Dad will be out in the car in just a minute! Please come here." She started marching toward Adam, who let out a squeal and turned to run, but was caught by Mr. Merrick, the owner of the local grocery store.

"You need to listen to your mother, Mr. Adam."

"But-but I don't want to!" Adam whined.

Mr. Merrick crouched and spoke softly to Adam.

Bell watched from afar as Adam sheepishly approached his mother, head bowed. "I'm sorry," Adam said.

Amanda mouthed, "Thank you," to Mr. Merrick and led the way back out to the car.

"Where is Steve?" Bell asked, not meaning to be nosey.

"He's speaking with the bishop," Amanda said softly, opening the sliding door of the van. She helped Adam climb into his seat in the back and lay little Charlotte down in her carrier.

Bell walked around to the other side of the car and got Becky buckled in.

"He just got laid off," Amanda said, so softly Bell almost didn't hear.

Secret Santa

"Dad is taking a nap?" Adam asked innocently, struggling to buckle his seatbelt.

"No, honey, he's just taking a little break from work, like you do from school." Amanda smiled and reached out to help, but Adam yelled that he could get it on his own.

Bell closed her door and walked around to the other side of the car.

Amanda finally closed her door and ran a hand over her face. "I just don't know what to do."

"I won't pry, but if there is anything at all I can do to help, please let me know. I don't have my own family to get gifts for, so I really can help."

Amanda shook her head. "We have their gifts already. But we have bills, Christmas dinner to buy, we just got this van, and Charlotte a new car seat…We do have some savings left over, but still…"

"You worry." Bell took her hands. "Are you looking for some work until Steve can find something?"

Amanda wiped at her eyes. "I don't know who will let me work with the kids. I can't leave Charlotte all day with a babysitter. She's too little. Adam is in preschool, but that's only a half-day. Who will hire someone for half of a day? And then I would have to pay someone to babysit Becky too." She shook her head.

Bell smiled. "What if you helped me in the mornings at the bakery? This is my busiest time of the year, and I just can't keep up with baking all day and trying to manage the front. You could bring Charlotte, and maybe Becky can have a little area she could play in the back."

"Oh, I don't know."

"I would love to have an assistant during the Christmas season," Bell insisted. "It's my busiest time of year, and I know it's only going to get more nuts. I'm having a difficult time trying to keep up on the baking and the selling, preparation, cleaning, and everything else that goes with Christmas. You would be a huge help."

Amanda could no longer hold back the tears. She hugged Bell tightly. "Thank you for doing this for me."

"Of course. Just come over after you drop Adam off at school." Bell gave her a squeeze and let go. "See you tomorrow."

Amanda nodded and climbed into the passenger seat. "Thank you. Thank you so much."

Bell waved and put her hands in her coat pockets. She spotted Jamie hurrying down the stairs and waited for her to catch up.

"I invited all of the ladies to join us for caroling, and we're all going to spread the word. My place at seven! Drake or not, we're going caroling!"

"If Drake doesn't show up, we'll go sing to him first," Bell smiled.

Jamie laughed. "Hey, is Amanda okay? I noticed you made her cry."

They stopped in front of their cars.

"I asked if she wanted to come work for me during the mornings. It takes a lot this time of year for me to get things done, and I could really use any help she can give."

"And her husband lost his job. No need to beat around

Secret Santa

the bush."

"I figured she wouldn't want me spreading that. How did you find out?"

She smiled. "Word gets around. I was thinking maybe I could host a silent auction for them."

Bell nodded. "That's actually a really good idea. They have savings, but who knows how long he will be out of a job? I can donate any goodies you want, just let me know when you need them." She rubbed her hands. "I'm freezing. I'm getting in my car."

"Hey, what are you doing for the rest of the day?"

"I'm going to visit Aretha and play games. Want to come?"

Jamie shrugged. "Might as well. I was just going to sit at home and watch TV. It would be good to see her too." She promptly walked to the passenger side of Bell's car and climbed in. "You can drop me off after!" she called, closing the door.

Bell chuckled and climbed into the driver's seat.

❄ ❄ ❄

Drake spent the day pouring over his books, double-checking to see that his reports were accurate—sales were declining. The depressing numbers were reinforced by the fact only two people had shown up at lunch. He knew there was another bar in town several blocks away from the town's center, and that must be where all of his business was going. He needed a way to get people back, and he'd been trying to rack his brain to figure out how.

He leaned back with a groan and rubbed his head.

"Your brain is going to explode if you keep trying to think," Chris said as he walked through the door.

Drake looked up at him and sighed. "Yeah, well. Chris, we need to figure out how to get people coming in, or we're going to have to close down."

"You always say that."

"Yeah, well, look at the numbers." He turned the thick binder to Chris. He knew he could do it on a computer program, but the binder was how he learned to do everything, and paper didn't lie or accidentally do an automatic formula wrong.

Chris sat beside him and started looking over the pages. He pursed his lips. "Man."

"I'm sorry," Drake said.

"Hey, don't worry about it."

"Can you think of anything we can do to help generate more business?"

Chris licked his lips and looked around the bar. "You aren't going to like what I think."

"Just tell me."

"Well..." He looked back at Drake. "What's the whole reason you run this place?"

"For my dad."

"In memory of him, right?"

Drake nodded.

"Well, maybe it's time to stop doing things in memory

Secret Santa

of him. This bar is a part of him, right? A part of you? Just like that barn out back. You literally live upstairs. You already have him here. You need to step out of his shoes now and start fitting into your own. Make this bar yours."

Drake shook his head. "I don't think—"

"You know how, Drake. You know what will actually get people here. You just don't want to change to do it."

"Why should I have to change?"

"You're the marketing expert. You tell me."

Drake frowned.

Chris smiled and patted him on the shoulder. "I bet Bell has some Christmas decorations you could use." He stood up. "I'm going to start coming up with a new menu. If we could hold a re-launch, that would be awesome."

"No. We aren't a spaceship, we aren't 're-launching' the tavern. Or doing a re-opening either, which is actually what it should be." Drake said.

"Maybe you could come up with some pretty fliers," Chris continued. "And how much would it cost to paint the walls? I bet I have paint in my basement, actually."

"We aren't changing the look of the bar." Drake climbed to his feet and slammed his binder shut. "We aren't changing anything!"

Chris eyed Drake. "If you don't change something, we're going to keep going downhill." With that, Chris walked into the kitchen.

Drake clenched his fist and glared at the binder. Chris was right, and Drake knew it. He had known it for a while. Now he had to fix it. He ran his fingers through his hair and stared at the pictures on the wall behind the computer. One of those pictures showed an elderly man holding a small child. Drake was that child, and the elderly man was his grandfather, his dad's dad, of whom his dad rarely spoke.

Drake got a little idea. He sat at the desk and typed the password in to unlock his computer, then began looking through the files of stories his dad had written down. He remembered one thing: his grandfather was Irish. His dad had built this place to resemble that heritage, hence the black, white, orange, and green tiling underneath the bar, and the carvings in the dining room.

He finally got up and walked into the kitchen, where Chris had just finished chopping up potatoes to make French fries. He hopped up onto the counter. "I have an idea."

Chris frowned at him. "Your butt is sitting where I'm trying to prep food."

"I'm not on your cutting board. Listen, I was thinking about what you said. Dad wanted this place to be a tavern, right? Taverns serve food."

Chris stared at him blankly. "Uh." He gestured to the potatoes like Drake was an idiot.

"Well, right. I just mean, I looked up my family's heritage. We're Irish."

"You're still not giving me enough information here."

"I want you to revamp the menu with Irish influence. We need a better recipe for fish and chips, stew, lamb, even the nachos even need to change. We'll add sausages, sandwiches, all that stuff." He jumped down and began pacing. "We don't have money to revamp the look of the dining room, and I like it except the booths could have the fabric replaced. We might have to do that when we get more money. I think I've got some paint down in the basement, and I can go into a little more debt to hire a professional cleaning service to get the floors done. I can spend tonight and tomorrow morning scrubbing all the scum that's built up on the lights and molding over time."

Chris slowly smiled. "Wow. I haven't seen you this fired up in a long time. But don't go into debt. I can help out, and I can pay for new paint. That stuff in the basement is so old the lids are rusted."

"You know what else?" Drake felt the excitement flittering in his chest. He faced Chris. "I'm going caroling tonight with Bell."

"Wait, what?"

"It's a great marketing technique! If people see me out and about instead of cooped up in here all the time, they'll realize I still run the place. Maybe if they see me, they'll remember Dad and how awesome he was and want to start coming back."

Chris nodded. "I'll do some research on Irish food and start a menu."

"Keep the menu small, too. Like, one page. Maybe a separate lunch and dinner menu? I'm going to come up with some mixed drinks that might help attract some new customers, too." He turned to head into the dining room. "Chris, thanks for being honest with me."

"No problem. I got your back."

Drake smiled and glanced at the clock on the wall. He had an hour to kill before he needed to go caroling. He pulled out a pen and paper, started going over his current drink menu, while writing down the ingredients in each drink. He would compare the ingredients to see which were similar enough to be removed, and what he could add to fill in gaps. This would also help with his inventory, because he wouldn't have to purchase liquors he didn't sell.

By the time he got the list made, he heard Chris call from the kitchen, "Yo, aren't you supposed to be caroling?"

Drake glanced at the clock. It was five after. "Crap," he mumbled. He grabbed his coat. "Call me if you need me!" he yelled over his shoulder. Drake had to tiptoe-run through the piles of slush and snow, but he finally rounded the corner to Jamie's bookstore, just in time.

Bell spotted him, and her eyes brightened. "Hey, Drake! I'm glad you showed up."

Drake cleared his throat and coughed. He was more out of shape than he cared to admit. "Hey. I figured it would be a good idea to come and see people." He took a breath and nodded. The group was mostly women, but three of them had brought their husbands, for which he was relieved.

Jamie raised her hand. "Alright, everyone! Let's start from that house on the corner and work our way through the streets! We'll keep going until we're too cold to sing

Secret Santa

anymore."

"And then you can come over to the tavern and have some hot cocoa, courtesy of Miss Bell." He winked at her. "Or something a little stronger if you're up for it."

"Do we know what we're singing?" one of the men asked.

"Whatever we feel like, darling," the woman with him responded.

"'We Wish you a Merry Christmas' is always a good one," another woman suggested.

"And we can always throw in the classics, like 'Frosty' or 'Rudolph,'" Bell said.

"And 'Santa Claus is Coming to Town,'" Drake nodded.

Bell laughed. "Can't forget that one."

Everyone else just stared at Drake a moment, clearly remembering how much of a Grinch he'd been for so long, before they started walking down the street. Drake silently watched Jamie talking to Bell about the latest letter she got from her husband, Andrew. He tried not to eavesdrop, but it was impossible, since Bell fell into step alongside him. Jamie explained he was really vague, just someone mentioned the squadron might be returning home sometime around Valentine's, which was almost an entire month earlier than they'd initially been told.

"That's fabulous news," Bell said.

A man Drake thought looked vaguely familiar fell back to walk alongside him. "It's good to see you joining us, Drake. I don't know if you remember me. I was pretty good friends with your dad. We used to get together at the tavern and you'd run around the room while we drank and talked."

So that's where he knew this guy from. "Oh, right! You're...Tim?"

"Tom," he laughed. "But close enough. I know losing your dad was hard on you. People around town will be happy to see you."

Drake nodded. "When Bell invited me to come, I thought the same thing. It's been a while since I just walked around town. I guess I sort of hated all of the sympathetic looks I got."

"I don't blame you," Tom said.

Drake remembered going caroling with his family, when they were all together. They would take plates of sugar cookies, fudge, and his mom's homemade caramel, and deliver them to a few people they knew. Drake remembered it got so cold one winter his bottom lip went numb and he couldn't feel it as he sang. That was the same year they'd started a snowball fight on the way home and his brother Dustin fell on a patch of ice and broke his arm.

The small group arrived at the first house, and they all approached the door.

Jamie pushed her way to the front and rubbed her hands. "We're singing 'We Wish You a Merry Christmas' first!" She knocked on the door and stepped back. The door opened, and Jamie cued them to start singing.

Drake glanced at Bell from the corner of his eye. She

Secret Santa

had a beautiful voice, and he couldn't help but to listen to her as they sang. After the first song, someone called out "Silent Night!" and they sang that too.

The couple thanked them graciously, and they started toward the next house.

"Bell, I heard you're hiring Amanda to work for you," one of the women said.

Bell nodded. "I am. I could use the help."

"You manage every year without it. I think it's very sweet of you to help them out right now in their time of need. But what happens after the Christmas season?"

Bell shrugged. "I plan on keeping Amanda on as long as it takes for her husband to find a job, or however long she wants to stay."

The woman's brows pinched in disapproval. "You don't have to rescue them single-handed, you know? And short-term help won't help in the long run."

Bell smiled politely. "Martha, do you have a job for Steve? Or for Amanda? Either of which is long term and good enough for them to support their family? I may not have something permanent, but every little bit helps. Steve will find something, but until that happens, I am going to help them because it's the right thing to do."

Martha blushed, and her husband mumbled something to her under his breath as they stopped at the front steps of the next house.

As they moved to the third house, Bell finally looked at Drake. "You're being quiet tonight," she said.

"I enjoy people watching," he smiled. "I don't really

know how to contribute to the conversations. I don't know what's going on with the Petersons, or the Richardsons, or the Smiths. I don't know why gas prices are high, or how long it takes to change out a radiator."

"Not one for gossip, hm?"

"Nope."

Bell nodded. "Me neither. But it really helps me know what's going on in town. I like to be a little nosey around Christmas, I guess. I like to see who I can help as discreetly as possible."

"Oh, so you're the town's Secret Santa?" he smiled.

She winked.

Snow started to flurry around them as they stopped to sing another song.

"You know," Drake said as they walked across the street, "you have a beautiful voice."

Bell laughed. "Why, thank you, Drake. I love to sing, especially Christmas songs. In fact, I used to go to the symphony. They do a sing along to The Messiah every year. It's fun to go, even if it's just to listen to an entire symphony hall singing."

He nodded. "I guess. We used to go caroling every year on Sunday night." He looked at her. "But I have a feeling you already knew."

"I did not." She crossed her finger over her heart. "Cross my heart."

He chuckled. "Well, we did. We'd deliver treats and sing. My whole family would go together. When we were younger we used to complain, but as we got older it was just a part of what we did. We also used to go cut down our own Christmas trees. Mom would make a huge dinner on Christmas Eve, and my grandparents would come out with my mom's sisters and their families."

"Do they still talk to you?"

Drake shrugged a shoulder. "Not really. My brothers will sometimes call and we will meet up to go fishing or camping over the summer. They've got their own families and they get busy."

"What about Christmas time?" she asked. "Do you still get together as a family?"

Drake licked his lips and glanced at her, a burning ache deep in his chest growing. "I uh didn't get invited last year. I think I've burned that bridge with my mother." He sighed. "I got upset with her for how quickly she recovered after my dad's death. She was dating someone last year around Thanksgiving and I told her I wouldn't come out to any family events if she was with someone other than Dad."

He remembered that conversation. He'd stormed out of Thanksgiving dinner—their first dinner without his dad. His mom had brought a complete stranger to sit at the head of the table, and Drake couldn't stand it. He stormed out of the house and his oldest brother, Matthew, had to chase him down and try and talk some sense into him. Matthew agreed that it was tough to have her boyfriend there, but that they still needed to support their mother. Drake argued he couldn't just let it go. If she really cared about him, or any of them, she wouldn't be dating someone. It hadn't even been a year since their father's death, not to mention she would put a stranger at the head of the table, where his father sat!

In spite of all of that, he missed them. All of them. He had lost touch with his mom after that incident, expecting her to call and apologize and invite him to Christmas, but she didn't. His brothers told him to give her time, but Drake knew how stubborn his mother could be.

Drake suppressed the unpleasant memories as they finished caroling. He'd certainly think about his family a few more times before Christmas, but he wanted to enjoy his time out with Bell.

"Everyone ready to warm up by the fireplace with some cocoa?" Drake asked, looking at them.

"I've been waiting all night for it," Tom laughed. "Only thing that kept me going!" He received an elbow in the ribs from his wife for that comment.

Once they made it into the tavern, everyone found seats close to each other, and Chris walked out from the back with a tray of already prepped hot cocoa.

"Got any schnapps?" Tom asked, leaning to Drake. "Maybe peppermint schnapps?"

"Actually, we do." Drake headed to the bar and grabbed some from behind the counter. "Here you go."

"Good. I like this with my hot cocoa." He poured a little in and stirred it with a candy cane.

"My dad used to make that," Drake said, recalling the memory of his dad making the same motions.

"Yeah, I'm the one that gave him the idea," Tom

laughed. "Anyone else want to try?"

Another man, Drake had learned that night went by the name of Billy, reached out to take the liquor and added some to his own cocoa before handing it back to Drake. Drake returned it to its place on the shelf, then took a seat beside Bell.

Bell squirted some of the canned whipped cream on top of her cocoa, but the top exploded and the cream went everywhere. She gasped and looked at Drake. "I'm so sorry! I swear, everything I touch breaks!" She grabbed a napkin to wipe her hands.

Drake used his own napkin to wipe a clump off her leg. "Yeah, I remember the ice cream incident. Are you always accident-prone?" he asked.

"Well, sometimes."

Jamie nodded intently behind her.

Drake smiled. "So what good cheer are you going to spread next, Bell?" he asked.

"I don't know. We sang to the Shepherd family tonight, and I think they need some cheering up." She added in a low voice, "I've noticed their son, Milo, has been having some struggles lately, and I wonder if they've got medical bills. I don't want to get too involved, but I'm worried about them. Jamie is planning a silent auction for another family, I wonder if we should do something similar for the Shepherds."

"But you don't like to be nosey," he winked.

She pursed her lips. "If I don't help, who will? Someone has to know what's going on with other people in town. How else are people supposed to spread the cheer and joy of Christmas if they can't serve those around them?"

Drake thought a moment. He took a sip of his own cocoa, forced to admit she had a good point. "Touché," he finally answered.

Bell was a curious creature, indeed.

Then something else she said caught up to him, and he set his mug down too quickly, almost spilling it. "Wait, you're holding a silent auction?" He leaned across Bell to look at Jamie.

She nodded. "Yeah. I haven't quite talked to everyone yet, but I was thinking we could get some great stuff. We could do a swap too with toys, clothes, electronics."

"You'll need a place to hold it, right? This is a tavern. You could hold it here!" he smiled. "Chris and I were talking just this morning about redoing the menu and making this Irish tavern a wee more Irish. The auction would be a good time for people to come in and sample the new food."

"That's a brilliant idea!" Jamie gasped. "How much time would you need to put it together?"

"Chris!" Drake called.

"Yeah?" he called from somewhere out of view.

"How long do you need to come up with the menu?"

Chris walked back to the front and pulled up a chair. "Maybe a week? We aren't exactly slammed for business," he gestured. "No offense," he quickly added, looking at Drake.

Secret Santa

Drake shrugged.

"I figure I can look up some recipes, make them up, but we'd still need people to taste and see what they like before we make it set."

"We're talking about using the silent auction on Saturday to do that," Jamie said.

Chris glanced between Drake and Jamie. "We're doing a silent auction?"

"Hosting it," Drake added. "And we could have people sample the new items."

Chris slowly nodded. "I think I can get it done by Saturday."

"Can you get your auction pulled together by then?" Drake asked.

Jamie scoffed. "Never underestimate a woman." She straightened and sipped her drink with a smirk.

"Alright. Saturday is the silent auction." Drake smiled, leaning back.

Bell had a gleam in her eye as she sipped her cocoa and watched him over the top of her mug. He wondered what she could be thinking.

Jamie grabbed a pen and notebook from her purse. "We will need to come up with a list of people to contact," she mumbled to herself. "I'll donate some books, Chris and Drake are doing snacks. I can contact someone about making a wreath, or something…"

One by one, the crowd thinned out, each stopping to thank Bell for the opportunity to serve, to thank Chris and Drake for the delicious food and warmth, and then it was just Chris, Drake, Bell, and Jamie sitting at the table.

Drake finally climbed to his feet. "I should start cleaning up." He grabbed a bucket and began setting the empty mugs inside.

Bell lingered and walked over to him. "Thank you for coming today. It was fun spending time with you."

Drake gave her a grin in return. "I appreciate you asking me. I actually had fun. I didn't think I would. Made me remember some good things with my family."

"Those are the best."

They stood in silence, looking at each other, Bell fiddling with the end of her hair until she straightened. "Well, I guess I should go."

"See you tomorrow for your breakfast cocoa?" He couldn't resist grinning at her.

She laughed. "Deal! I'll see you in the morning, then."

Drake watched her leave and stared after her. That is, until Chris smacked him on the back of the head with a towel. "Hey! What was that for?"

"Dude! Just ask her out!"

Drake rolled his eyes and picked up the tray. "She's not my type."

"Oh? She's pretty, happy, and smart. Yeah, totally not your type."

"I heard that!" Drake called back.

"You were supposed to! I wasn't exactly being discreet." Chris leaned against the counter. "But seriously. Why not ask her out?"

"I barely know her."

Secret Santa

"That's the point of dating. You've known her for two years, and you know enough to know you're attracted."

"Whoa, I never said that."

Chris raised his eyebrows.

Drake sighed. "Look, it's just this time of year. It's all romanticized. I don't date new people around Christmas."

"You don't date anyone around any time."

He turned on the warm water and poured the dish soap into the sink. "I just don't want to risk ruining anything. She's nice. What if we start dating, and it doesn't go well? Or she gets too attached? What if she—"

"Drake," Chris interrupted, "you're overthinking. Look, ask her or don't, but I know you're both attracted to each other." He tucked the dishtowel on the hook above the sink. "Everything is cleaned, other than those in the sink. Want me to help?"

"I got it. You go home to Heather."

Chris patted him on the back and left, leaving Drake alone in the comfortable silence.

He couldn't help but think about Bell. She was just like him. She was alone at Christmas too. She didn't live with any family. Drake remembered what she said the day before, about being lonely and alone especially around Christmas, and he realized she helped those in town as a way of having a family.

Maybe he and Bell weren't so different after all.

CHAPTER SIX

Monday morning came all too soon. Bell dressed in her typical leggings, long shirt, and sneakers, then headed out to go to Drake's for breakfast. After all, he had invited her the night before. As she walked, she scanned the pages of her book, and she smiled. Aretha's name was gone, as were Betty Johnson, Jeremy Pole, Zack Carson, and now William Lewis. Bell hadn't even had a chance to visit with William, but his name no longer appeared in her book. Thirteen individuals still on the Spirit List, and only seventeen more days to help them all. She could manage.

She imagined Amanda and Steve would be off the list by Christmas pretty easily, and she'd stolen the chance at church to watch Kristi. She'd hoped Kristi's date with Drake would go better, but Kristi remained in her book, and the one word—"lonely"—was still written beneath her name.

"I wonder who else in town might need a friend," she muttered, climbing into her car and staring at her book. She flipped through the pages slowly: Dorothy Erickson was busy at the post office, and tired of grumpy

Secret Santa

customers, while Logan Strong had been having car issues. Nancy Tibble had nothing written below her name yet, but these people weren't quite the right ones.

Bell filed through the names again, finally stopping at Brian Eilin. She tilted her head. Had she seen his name before? It wasn't uncommon for names to suddenly appear on the Spirit List, but still, it was rare especially if the list had already been given to the Secret Santa elf. Maybe his name had been there all along and she just hadn't taken time to see it.

With a groan, she put the book in her pocket and turned to the Red Dragon. Once inside, where it was warm, she asked Drake, "Hey, do you know who Brian Eilin is?"

He set her mug of cocoa down and sat across from her. "Brian..." He glanced at the ceiling. "I feel like he's someone I went to school with. Oh! Yeah, Brian! He was on the debate team, or drama, or something like that. Super shy, but I remember him being nice. Why?"

"I was helping Jamie put together the list of people to invite to the auction Saturday," she lied. "It was a name I hadn't heard."

"Yes. If I remember right, his dad owns the mechanical shop on the opposite end of town."

Bell wanted to take out her book and write it down, but if Drake saw that, he would definitely think she was strange. So, she winked and hoped that was enough magic to write "mechanic" in her book. She would have to see if she could get Brian to help out with Logan's car issues.

Drake finished his coffee. "I hate to have you drink your cocoa and run, but I'm going to start a deep clean of this place to get it all ready for Saturday. It's long overdue."

"Don't worry about it. I'm supposed to meet Amanda at my bakery anyway."

"Oh yeah, she's working for you now. Cool. Look at you, business woman."

Bell rolled her eyes with a gentle smile. "Have a good day."

"Until we see each other again."

That got a laugh out of Bell and she left grinning like a fool. Oh boy, Jamie was right.

When she got to her bakery, Bell went to the back office (a space she never used) and started piling things in the corner, so there could be a little bit of space for Becky to safely play. She glanced at her phone to check the time. Amanda would be there any minute, and the office was definitely not childproofed for a three-year-old.

She put her hands on her hips and took a breath. "Alright, magic. Do your thing." She winked, and the boxes quickly stacked, the random tools filed into an empty box at the top, and the dust swirled around her and settled into the garbage can by the back door.

Bell dusted her hands and grinned when she heard a knock. "Perfect timing."

She hurried to the back door and opened it.

Becky immediately ran in, and Amanda sighed. "Sorry about that. She's really excited to be here."

Secret Santa

"No worries, I promise. Do you have a playpen for the two of them?"

"Yes." She patted the large rectangular thing hanging from her shoulder. She set Charlotte down in her car seat.

Bell guided her to the office and helped her set up the playpen, then set Becky inside with books and some large toys.

Amanda smiled as she looked around the back of the bakery. "So, this is where the magic happens?"

"All of it," she nodded. "I would like to have you run the cash register. Follow me." She guided Amanda to the front of the store and started teaching her how to use the credit card machine, and how to do cash.

"It's a lot easier than I anticipated," she said, relief evident on her face.

"You're quick at picking up on things. I'll get to baking and decorating. I have three batches of cupcakes ready to frost, and some cookies to get in."

"Do you need help with any of that?"

Bell looked at the racks of cupcakes. If business continued to be well, maybe she could keep Amanda on throughout summer. An extra set of hands would make decorating a lot faster indeed, even if Bell was particular with how they looked.

"I'd love to show you how to decorate the cupcakes," she finally answered. She pulled out the hot cocoa cupcakes and set them on the counter. She loaded up a piping bag with frosting, and a cupcake corer to punch a hole in the middle. "First things first, we need to get a hole in the middle of the cupcake, all you have to do is this." She demonstrated how to push the device in and drop the remnants into a large bowl. "I use the middle pieces to make a dessert similar to a bread pudding, so keep all of them you can. Go around and do that, and I'll follow behind with this ganache. When that's done, we put the frosting on top."

Amanda worked better than Bell could have hoped. She was accurate, fast, and listened to every direction. When they were through filling the cupcakes, Amanda watched Bell with the piping bag swirl the frosting expertly on top and place a mini candy cane in it.

Bell was thrilled to see Amanda try and imitate as best she could, doing a considerably good job. When they finished the cupcakes, Amanda began loading them into the display case beside the fudge and muffins, while Bell got the cookies out of the oven and into the blast freezer.

She had no idea how big of a help Amanda would be until customers came. Bell was able to bake, mix, decorate, and get all the desserts finished and loaded into the display case, all while Amanda ran the front, sold everything, greeted customers, and she completely rocked it!

Charlotte fussed about an hour and a half into the day. Amanda excused herself to go feed her, and Bell took over again. But she had no stress. She'd already loaded all of the morning desserts into the display, more dough was rolled out and cooling, and another batch of cupcakes was baking.

Secret Santa

Amanda returned with Becky on her hip and a smile on her face. "Mind if Becky helps me up here?"

"Sure! Becky, you can't touch the treats, though," Bell said with a smile.

Becky shook her head.

Bell stepped back and watched Amanda hand Becky some money to put in the drawer after helping a customer, and she smiled. This arrangement could work out nicely.

"Well, I just put the 'Closed for Lunch' sign up," Amanda said.

Bell wiped the last of the crumbs in the garbage and shook her head. "I can't believe how fast that went. You're an enormous help. Amanda, I seriously can't thank you enough."

"I can't thank you enough, either. This was a lot more fun than I thought it would be."

"Do you want to leave the playpen set up here?"

"Sure!"

"Can I help you get the girls to the car?"

Amanda shook her head. "I got it, but thank you. You go enjoy your lunch!"

Bell hung her apron and headed out to get some lunch. Unfortunately, the Red Dragon was closed, and she could see Drake scrubbing the top of a light, standing on a ladder. The edge of his shirt was lifted enough she could see his side and the bottom of another tattoo on his ribs she didn't know he had.

She found herself wondering where else he could have tattoos, and immediately blushed. She quickly looked around to make sure no one had seen her blatantly staring before she hurried down the street to Jamie's bookstore to snag her for lunch.

"So what mischievousness are you up to this Christmas?" Jamie asked as she opened a box and started pulling out new books. Jamie and Bell had grown pretty close the past year. What started as exchanging meals had grown into a tight friendship they both needed.

Bell shrugged and flipped through the holiday-themed adult coloring book from a display on the counter. "I have no idea what you're talking about." Bell wrinkled her nose at the cheap pine tree candle and pushed it away. "That needs to go. You need a better candle."

"I like it. Smells like Christmas."

"Smells like wax. You need to get one that actually smells like Christmas. Like…like cranberries and cinnamon!"

Jamie walked past Bell with her arms full. She leaned close to Bell. "You're avoiding my question, so I'll ask another. Have you asked him on a date yet?"

"Who?" Bell felt obligated to ask.

Jamie rolled her eyes. "Bell, come on. You aren't discreet." She carried the pile of new books over to the romance section. She pushed the books into their new spot and stepped back to take a look at how they fit in with the display. She unfolded a small stand and put it up, then set one of the books on it. "There we go."

"Look, I don't have any intention of asking him on a date."

Secret Santa

"Bell. He helped fix Aretha's house, early on a Saturday. He went caroling with you too. He *wants* to be around you, I just don't get why you can't see that." Jamie grinned. "Maybe he's too tall, handsome, and damaged for you."

Bell returned the holiday coloring book to its display and pulled out another stack of books from the box to bring to Jamie. "He's not damaged. And if you say he is, then we all are."

Jamie raised her eyebrows at Bell.

Bell grabbed a few books from the top of the stack and started shoving them on the shelf, feeling her blush creeping up on her cheeks. "Besides, I'm totally not—I mean—he's not my type."

"How do you know what his type even is?" Jamie faced Bell with one hand on her hip and her shoulder leaning against the bookshelf. "And what's up with you inviting him to everything this year if you don't like him?"

Bell stopped and looked at Jamie with raised eyebrows, trying to stare her down. However, she relented and sighed. "Jamie, I know I'm not his type. Look at me. Look at him. He owns a tavern, has tattoos, a beard—"

"Woah, back up. Tattoo*ssss*? He has more than one?"

Bell felt her face grow hot with a brighter blush this time. She finally rolled her eyes under the pressure of Jamie's look. "I *happened* to be walking by the tavern this morning on my way *here*, imagine that, and he was changing light bulbs and…" She shrugged, picking at her fingers. "I noticed his shirt was up, and he's got a tattoo on his ribs."

"Not that you've been stalking him or anything," Jamie teased

"Jamie! I have *not* been stalking him! Besides, do I look like his type?" Bell gestured to herself. She had French braided the top of her long brown hair and pulled the whole thing into a loose ponytail. Her makeup was simple, just some eye shadow and mascara to highlight her brown eyes. She wore green leggings with thin white stripes, red sneakers, and a long red shirt with her ornament necklace dangling around her neck.

Jamie looked her up and down. "You are definitely Christmassy. But that doesn't mean he wouldn't like you."

"Don't guys who run bars typically go for the bad girls? Or the cute, flirty blondes?" She rolled her eyes and walked back to the box.

"Not always." Jamie shrugged. "Maybe you need to read something to help you figure out how to approach him. I think I've got just what you need." She walked back to the romance section and ran her finger along the spines, paused at one cover and glanced at the back. She looked at Bell, looked her up and down, then shook her head and turned to the shelf across the row and looked up and down the "proper romance" section. "Ah ha. This one is cute." She walked over to Bell and handed her a book. "Proper romance is more your style."

"See! You know I have a style! Why wouldn't he?"

"Maybe he does, and maybe that style is someone like you. Maybe *you* are the one making the wrong

Secret Santa

assumptions." Jamie raised her eyebrows at Bell.

"Whatever." She rolled her eyes. "I don't need a book to help me." Bell did find Drake attractive, but the rules of the Secret Santa forbade her from pursuing him.

The song overhead changed, and Jamie stopped. She drew a shuddered breath and hurried to the front. Bell finally realized why—it was playing "Baby It's Cold Outside," Jamie and Andrew's song.

Bell strummed her fingers on the shelf. If she could get Andrew home for Christmas, Jamie would be fine. It would be a miracle, and take a lot of work, but certainly Bell could manage that. She was a secret Santa elf, after all! But if she could get a soldier home, and not help Drake…

"Want to do lunch?" Bell asked.

"I literally ate before you walked in. I had my homemade peanut butter sandwich. Sorry."

Bell shrugged. "I think I'll grab something from the diner before going over to Emily's. She's got that new soap store," she said, walking back toward the front, noting the song had changed to "Rockin' Around the Christmas Tree."

"Sounds like fun, I guess." Jamie looked over at her when she finally came into sight.

"Yes. I'm going to get you a new Christmas candle."

Jamie shook her head. "You're impossible."

Bell smiled and leaned across the desk. "But you still love me."

"Only because I have to." She slowly smiled and then

shook her head with a giggle. "Why do I put up with you?"

"Because you have to," she repeated."

"Why not eat at the Red Dragon?" Jamie grinned.

She rolled her eyes. "Because Drake has it closed. He's cleaning it."

Jamie's smile seemed to only get bigger and she twitched her eyebrows.

"I'm not…you know, I only know what he was doing because I have to pass the tavern to get here." She tossed a harmless wad of crumpled paper at Jamie. "I'm going to go eat, you troublemaker."

Jamie laughed. "Let me know if you find anyone else to volunteer at the auction!"

Bell ate her sandwich while walking back down the street, past the bookstore, tavern, and her own bakery. Emily's shop was on the road just north of Bell's bakery. By the time she arrived, she'd finished her lunch and wiped her hands on her pants.

Bell put on a big Christmas smile before walking in. "Good afternoon, Emily."

The building was a half-circle, with wooden shelves carefully placed in front of the windows, and circular tables strategically placed around the store. Candles were organized by scents, and soaps ran along one wall. Bell could smell the peppermint cocoa candle burning on Emily's desk.

Emily grinned and jumped to her feet behind the cash register. "Merry Christmas! Would you like to look at something specific? I've got any scent you can think of. Well, almost."

"Yes, please. Jamie needs a new candle at the bookstore. She has a pine tree one, but it's gross. She really wants something Christmassy. Maybe something with a little bit of cinnamon, a little bit of cranberry. I love the one you're burning right now."

Emily grinned. "I have a whole Christmas section right here." Emily walked around to one of the table displays, each item with its own beautiful glittered label. "I personally love this the most. I call it, *The Most Wonderful Time.*" She pulled the lid off and let Bell smell it.

It smelled like sweet cranberries, a touch of pine, a dash of cinnamon, like sitting at home in front of the fireplace with a book in the peace of Christmas morning. "This is perfect!" Bell said. "I'll actually take two of those, so I can have one at home." She looked around. "Your shop is beautiful. How has business been?"

Emily carried the two candles to the counter. "Um. I thought it would be a little better, to be honest. Some people have come in, but I think more out of the kindness of their heart. Not what I was hoping it to be around Christmas. We only have a couple more weeks, and I really thought people would be buying more last-minute gifts."

"I run a small business myself, and I know how difficult it is to market when you're just starting. Am I intruding if I ask if you need any help?"

"Actually, that would be a huge help," Emily said. "I

know I make good products because I've been doing it for a long time online, but a storefront is a whole different game."

Bell pursed her lips in thought. "Well, it so happens we are doing a silent auction on Saturday. Would you be willing to donate something for that? It would be a good way to get some visibility in the community and show off your quality products."

"Absolutely! I could do an entire little basket with a bath bomb, lotion, and candle." She immediately went back to the Christmas candles, grabbed one, and then the lotion and bath bomb from their respective locations.

Bell had taken the opportunity to pull out her book and jot down "marketing" under Emily's name in her book. She put it back in her pocket just as Emily returned to the counter. "I know I have some great resources I used when I first started. Obviously, the most important thing is getting the word out, and you've definitely been talking to people. Maybe I can help you design a flyer to put up around town? You could do a little sale to try and get people in."

She nodded. "I love that idea. But I wouldn't make you design it alone."

"Maybe after work today I can come over and see what help you can offer?"

"I'd love that." Bell nodded. "I'll see you after work!"

❄ ❄ ❄

Secret Santa

The day felt like it would never end. Drake trudged down the stairs, scratching his cheek. His shoulders still burned and his back ached, but as soon as he stepped into the dining room, he felt an immense sense of pride.

The tavern hadn't had a deep cleaning in years. In fact, the last time he could recall scrubbing everything down was just before his dad passed. The lights seemed to shine brighter, and the wood glistened.

"Holy smokes, what did you do in here?" Chris said in amazement, turning in a slow circle.

Drake gestured with his arms wide. "Right? It looks pretty good."

"What time did you start working?"

"Uhh, I think seven?"

"In the morning?"

"Well, considering it's not seven at night yet…"

Chris shook his head and let out a low whistle. "Man."

"I went to the grocery store after eating lunch, just to get out for a little while, and I overheard Mr. Taylor on the phone telling someone his tools got stolen."

"Mr. Taylor, the guy that does the woodwork stuff?"

He shrugged. "I think. I'm going to go see if maybe I can help him put in a security system, see what got stolen and if maybe my dad had any of those tools I could loan him."

Chris stared at Drake.

Drake raised his eyebrows. "What?"

"Who are you and what did you do with Drake Pine?"

He rolled his eyes. "I'm being serious."

"I just…never thought I would hear that from you. Bell, yeah, but you? No offense."

Drake shrugged. "Want to come?"

"We opening for dinner?"

"Oh yeah…" He looked around the dining room. "You run the show until I get back. I shouldn't be too long." He walked to the back and grabbed his coat. He sighed and rolled his eyes and looked at Chris. "You're staring."

"I got this!" Chris saluted, hung his coat, and started pulling out food.

Drake vaguely remembered where Mr. Taylor lived. He'd gone to Mr. Taylor's house a while ago to drop something off but didn't have the address anymore. He drove into the neighborhood he remembered, but after driving around for fifteen minutes, couldn't remember which house he lived in.

He finally parked and walked to a nearby house and knocked on the door.

A woman answered and looked him up and down. "You aren't the cable repairman."

"No. I was actually looking for Mr. Taylor?"

"Ah, well he lives further down the street. The old blue house with the broken trailer on the side." She leaned out the door to point for emphasis.

"Thank you." He turned to leave.

"I don't know what you're planning on doing, but he's not a very pleasant person. Just giving you a fair warning."

Secret Santa

He nodded. "I'll be wary."

He climbed back into his car and drove down the darkening street until he found the old blue house with a broken trailer on the side. He parked in the driveway and walked to the door. Only, when he pushed the doorbell, it didn't ring. He frowned and knocked.

"If you're here to steal more stuff, I don't have anymore!"

"I actually wanted to come help you with that," Drake called through the door.

It opened, and Drake felt his lips part in surprise. Standing before him was a man he recognized from years ago. When Drake and his father had built the tavern and barn, they had borrowed tools from Mr. Taylor. Drake hadn't recognized him in the store, possibly because he'd had a beanie on and now he didn't.

"What?" the man grumbled.

"I'm sorry, I just recognized you. I don't know if you recognize me, but I'm Drake Pine."

Mr. Taylor's gray eyes finally opened wide enough to see him. "Drake? You're Thomas Pine's youngest boy, aren't you?"

"Yeah, that's me."

"Well, what are you doing here? Come in!" He leaned heavily on his cane as he shuffled aside.

"I overheard you at the store, that you had some stuff stolen."

"Yeah, I went to go out and finish the jewelry box this morning, and someone had gotten into my garage and stole my Dremel and chisels. I don't know why they'd steal them. Not like they're going to use them. Might try and sell them, I guess."

"I actually went and bought a camera security system for you. Would you like me to help you put it up?"

Mr. Taylor studied him. "You'd do that for me?"

"Of course."

"Before you even knew who I was?"

Drake shrugged. "It's the right thing to do."

"Your dad would be proud of you." Mr. Taylor patted him on the shoulder. "I won't say no. What do you need from me?"

"Got a ladder?"

"Yep. Come out this way." Mr. Taylor walked through the kitchen and out the door into the garage. "So how does this security system work anyway?"

"I'm going to install a screen on the inside of your house. You can put it by your door or in your room, or even in your garage, if you want. You can also get the app for your phone if you're not home and something goes off."

Drake hoisted the ladder and dragged it out front. He wouldn't have light for very long, so he needed to work as quickly as possible. He'd brought his own screwdriver and other tools to mount the equipment. It took an hour to get the two cameras mounted on the front of the house, and he put in the last screw as it was getting too dark to see anything.

"Alright, let's get it all running." He sat the screen in

the mount, started it up, and spent the next thirty minutes showing Mr. Taylor how to use the screen.

"So, these are always on? And I can watch them here?"

"Yeah. From what I know, it keeps all the footage and then dumps it at the end of each month, unless you want to save it somewhere else. You can also check them any time from your phone. When were your tools stolen?"

"Last night some time," he shrugged.

Drake shook his head. "Well, I hope we can figure out who it was. Maybe it was just some teenagers playing a prank. In the meantime, I know my dad used to have a chisel set. He carved a lot of the wood in the tavern when he made it, I'm sure I can dig it up."

"Oh, I couldn't take those from you, Drake."

"Mr. Taylor, I haven't touched them in years, and I probably never will. I never learned how to do any sort of woodworking. They'd be better used in your hands than sitting in the garage collecting dirt."

Mr. Taylor smiled and gave a little chuckle. "I was worried how I was going to get that jewelry box done. It's for my granddaughter. It's the only thing she asked for this Christmas."

"Hey, why don't you come back with me and look through my dad's tools? You can take whatever woodworking tools you need."

Mr. Taylor shook his head quickly. "No, no. The chisels will be fine."

Drake nodded. "Alright. I'll get them and bring them to you tomorrow. I've got to get back and help Chris with the tavern, our dinner started a little while ago and I'm sure we've got some customers."

Mr. Taylor shook his hand. "Thank you, Drake."

"You're welcome. I'll see you tomorrow."

Drake waved before climbing in his truck and heading back to the tavern. He walked in to see Chris look up, each burner busy cooking, the oven timer going off, and he'd just dumped a tray of dishes into the sink.

"Oh boy am I glad to see you! We have fifteen customers!"

"Why didn't you call me?" Drake hurriedly washed his hands before tying on his apron.

"You were busy!"

"I could have come back." He stepped out into the dining room and smiled immediately at the men sitting at the bar. "I apologize for being late. I was helping Mr. Taylor install a security system. It appears someone has stolen his tools." He started washing the mugs and glasses in the sink behind the counter.

"That's too bad."

"I know him. Why would someone steal his tools?"

"Probably some kid thinking it's worth something."

"Kids these days have no respect for anyone else's stuff."

Drake smiled to himself. He stacked the washed glasses on the drying rack, then went to the nearest table. "Good evening, ladies. How are you doing tonight?"

"Ah, you're here!"

"We're great."

Secret Santa

"Can I get another drink?"

Drake lifted the glass. "What were you drinking?"

Drake moved his way through the dining room, visiting each table to check on their needs, grabbing more drinks, collecting dirty dishes, delivering completed orders. It took a few minutes for everything to get back into a rhythm, but it felt amazing to actually be busy.

He'd just cleared off a table when he heard Jamie say, "About time you showed up. Where have you been, Bell?" He looked to the doorway to see a flustered-looking Bell standing in the doorway, trying to smooth her hair.

"Sorry, I stopped to help Tina Michaels," Bell replied.

Jamie sighed. "You're one of a kind."

"I thought we were doing dinner at your place."

"Well, I accidentally might have burned it…"

Drake walked over. "Hey you two. Come on in. Anything I can get you to start?"

Bell and Jamie sat at one of the tables close to the bar.

"I'd actually really like a Diet Coke," Jamie said. "And what desserts do you have?"

Drake glanced at Bell. "Your best friend is a baker."

Bell laughed. "I actually sold out of everything today. I don't even have leftovers to eat for breakfast tomorrow!"

"Hey, you have second breakfast after you have it here?" Drake said playfully. "What are you, a hobbit?"

Bell's eyes lit up and she smiled brightly. "You just made one of the best references ever."

He grinned. "I'm cool that way."

"Can I just have some water? Maybe juice too.

Raspberry lemonade?"

He jotted it down. "Got it. And take your time choosing your order." He handed them menus and started away.

Bell groaned as she stretched. "I saw Emily today. Oh, and I got you an early Christmas present." She set a small paper bag on the table with a reindeer head looking upward and a bright red glittery nose.

Jamie opened it and laughed. "A new candle, huh? I told you my pine tree one was fine." She opened the lid and took a sniff, her eyes widening.

"See? Isn't that better? Now, I just need your help figuring out how to help Emily market them."

Drake listened carefully while filling up the glasses.

"Bell, you're asking the wrong person about marketing," Jamie scoffed.

Drake carried the drinks over to Jamie and Bell. "Hey, sorry to interrupt, I couldn't help but overhear you saying something about marketing?"

Bell nodded. "Emily Hayes opened a new little soap and candle shop and isn't getting the business she thought she would around Christmas time. I guess she used to do online sales only and was doing pretty good and she thought she could open a physical store too."

"I actually have a degree in marketing. It's what I went to college to do."

Bell gasped. "Really?"

He nodded. "I wouldn't mind meeting with her."

"You have no idea how amazing that would be! I tried

Secret Santa

to give her some resources after work today, but I just couldn't figure out the best way to help her. We have different fields and I don't have resources in the soaps and candles world."

"Yeah, a lot of marketing is knowing your kind of customer and figuring out how to reach them. I'll go over tomorrow morning."

Bell smiled and grabbed his hand.

He felt something between them wash over him, like a warm wave. Goosebumps sprung up all over his arms, and he couldn't help but smile back.

"Thank you so much," she said. "You have no idea how big of a help this will be."

"No problem," he replied.

She held on for a little while before finally letting go. "Sorry," she apologized, cheeks turning pink.

"Don't worry about it." Drake made his way to the next table.

The whole rest of the night, he couldn't help but glance Bell's way. At one point, Jamie got up to talk to someone by the fireplace, and Drake noticed Bell pull a book out from her pocket. She smiled brightly and danced in her seat before tucking her book back in her pocket.

Strange girl, Bell Winter.

When they'd both stood and started putting on their coats, Drake nodded and waved to them both. Bell pushed her lips to one side of her face and walked over to him. "Hey, I have a question for you."

"Oh no," he blurted before he could stop himself.

She smiled. "I promise it's an easy one."

He rested his hands on his hips. "Alright. Shoot."

She shifted under his gaze. "I know you're really not into the whole Christmas thing, and that's completely fine, but I was wondering if maybe…Well, see you haven't ever come down to my bakery and I thought maybe you would want to come and make cookies with me? I'm getting them ready for the elementary school, I always bring cookies for their big read-in, North Pole Day they do."

He was taken back. "You really want me to help you with cookies?"

"Yes." She gave him a big, hopeful smile. "I do have to warn you, though. My bakery is all decked out in Christmas."

Drake was about to refuse. Why spend time with Mrs. Claus, the queen of Christmas? Not to mention finishing the revamp of the tavern for the auction, plus getting his own marketing scheme together, and now Emily's too. But an, "Okay," slipped out of his lips before he realized it, and then stood awkwardly while it dawned on him that he'd just agreed.

Bell's eyes lit up. "Thank you, Drake. I'll see you Thursday morning? Eight o'clock?"

"That early?" He shook his head. "Everything you do is so early."

She twirled the end of her hair around her finger. "I'm sure you can make it over there by eight." She patted him gently on the arm. "Have a good night!"

Secret Santa

Drake carried a tray of dishes back to the sink in a stupor.

Chris glanced at him. "You alright?"

He leaned against the counter. "I'm making Christmas cookies with Bell Thursday morning at her bakery. At eight in the morning." He felt his forehead tighten as he furrowed his brows.

Chris dropped the spatula he was using to try and flip the hamburger patty, and just stared at Drake. "What?"

"I agreed to make cookies with her."

"Christmas cookies?"

"Christmas cookies."

Chris put the back of his hand against Drake's head. "You feeling okay?"

"I don't know, man," he chuckled. He batted Chris away and shrugged off the counter. "Maybe you and Heather can come too?"

"Nah uh, no way. This is for you and Bell only."

He shrugged. "It was worth a shot." He smiled and returned to his duties.

He couldn't remember the last time he made Christmas cookies. His mom would make them, though she always let he and his brothers help decorate. Drake felt couldn't figure out if he was tingling with excitement or dread at the thought of spending all day with Bell making cookies, but he hoped they would have at least a little bit of fun.

CHAPTER SEVEN

Tuesday seemed like it would never end. Bell had closed the bakery early to try and run into Kristi on her way home from work. She managed to follow Kristi to a pizza place two streets away from the city center. Bell strummed her fingers on her steering wheel, wondering what to do. The only way she could think of helping was to set Kristi up with someone. She'd checked with Heather just that morning to see if she'd been doing anything with Kristi, and according to Heather they'd done a lot of things. If Kristi was still lonely after being with friends, she definitely needed love.

Bell pursed her lips. Where was a single guy when you needed one? She climbed out of her car and looked through the front window of the pizza place. Bell had magic, but not the kind that would summon anyone to a location on a whim. They needed to already be on their way somewhere. Then, she could only give them an idea to change directions. She couldn't make them follow through.

She stared at the book in her hands and winked with every bit of magic she could hope for. Brian had to be close. He just had to be.

Bell looked around and walked slowly into the pizza place, keeping her eyes on passing cars or people walking down the street—which were few and far between. She numbly ordered a small pizza (if she needed to eat pizza for dinner to get Kristi hooked up with Brian, she would do it).

Her stomach sank when Kristi got her pizza and headed out to her car. Kristi set the pizza on the front seat and climbed into the driver seat.

Bell looked around almost frantically. Where was Brian?

Then she spotted him parking his car across the street. He and his three friends climbed out of their car, laughing. They started across the street.

Bell winked as quickly as she could, and Kristi tried to start her car.

"Come on," Bell whispered, winking yet again. Brian just *had* to see her!

Bell held her breath when Brian looked Kristi's way, and walked over to her car.

"Small cheese for Bell?" the guy behind the counter called.

Bell hurried over to him. "How much?"

"Seven thirty-two."

Bell started digging through her purse for her wallet, finally found it, and then started trying to count out her cash. By the time she got exact change and grabbed her pizza, Brian had moved his car over to Kristi's and attached the cables to jump them.

Bell stepped outside with a smile on her lips and breathed a sigh of relief. She watched Brian hook the cars together, and Kristi sat in her car and turned the engine. Bell headed back to her car, and heard, "Try it again." Bell gave a wink of Christmas magic and heard Kristi's car start.

"Thank you!" Kristi gushed to Brian. "How can I ever make it up to you?"

"It really was nothing. I promise," he assured her.

"But you have no idea how much I needed that. I had a rough day at work today, and this was just the icing on the cake."

"Hey, I got an idea. Speaking of cake, how about we go to Bellisima and get a dessert to go with our pizza?"

"Tonight?" she asked.

Bell climbed into her seat. Whatever happened, she'd started everything. She leaned her back against the chair. If she was going to keep the two of them going, she needed to get back to her bakery, so they could come get dessert! She started her own car and hurried back to the bakery.

She parked and turned the lights back on inside. She pulled out the leftover cupcakes and cookies from the day and replaced them in the display case. She didn't have much left, but it was something. She'd just settled the cookie sheet in the back counter when she heard her door open.

Bell curiously walked out to see Emily. "Oh hey! How

are you?"

"Well, Drake came by today. He spent all morning going over different ways to market and gave me some awesome resources. He did suggest I change locations."

"Oh? Why is that?"

"Apparently, I'm in the 'old' part of town, and there isn't a lot of traffic in the area itself anyway. He showed me that the store just next to mine was a child's clothing store, a scrapbook store, and a photography business. The store on my other side used to be a video rental store, and then a music store before it was whatever it is now."

She nodded, trying to stay interested as she saw a car in her peripheral vision pull up. "So where are you thinking of moving the store?"

"I've got to look. I just wanted to come by and thank you for having him help me. I've got a long way to go, and I told him I'd pay a little for all of his advice. He actually tried to refuse, just saying he was doing it to be nice, but how can I take advantage of that?"

"I don't know," Bell grinned. She knew Drake would go visit Emily, but spending so much time with her? And refusing to be paid on top of it? Her heart swelled.

Emily looked over her shoulder when Kristi walked in. "I should go. See you, Bell! Thanks, again!"

Bell waved. "Bye, Emily!" She looked at Kristi. "How are you, Kristi?"

"I'm sort of freaking out." She gave a nervous laugh and looked through the front window, wringing her hands and shifting from one foot to the other. "I just ran into

Brian. Well, he sort of saved me, my car wouldn't start, and for a thank you he's on his way over here and I don't know what to do. I've always liked Brian, ever since school, and apparently he's still single."

"It so happens, I have cupcakes left just for you guys," she grinned.

Kristi gave her a nervous smile.

"Relax. Just be you, Kristi. Take a breath," she coaxed.

Kristi drew a slow breath.

Brian pulled up and walked in. "Hey! I made the guys stay in the car."

"Well, pick what you want."

"Nah uh, my treat."

"I'm supposed to be thanking you!" Kristi smiled.

"Yeah, but I can't let you pay. But you can give me your phone number, so we can go on a proper date." Brian bumped her gently with his shoulder.

Kristi grinned and nodded. "I can manage that."

Brian looked at Bell. "Can I get the chocolate cupcake? What would you like, Kristi?"

"The hot cocoa cupcake."

Bell grabbed one of each, boxed them carefully in their own containers. "Anything else?"

"I think I better get the rest of your cookies, so they don't get mad at me for getting something without them." Brian nodded his head toward his car.

She put all ten of the cookies in a small bag. "If you want to take the last two cupcakes, you can have them both for the price of one."

Secret Santa

"Hey, I'm cool with that," Brian grinned. "You want two, Kristi?"

"Sure."

Bell rang them up and watched them leave. Her heart did flips as she watched Kristi give Brian her phone number, and Bell let out a sigh. She hoped she and Drake looked that cute together.

She quickly shook her head. What was she saying? They hadn't even been on a date!

"Stop it, Bell Winter. You're being ridiculous." She hurried to the front and locked the door, closed the blinds, and flicked off the light.

All she had to do was get the dough ready for she and Drake for Thursday. That wouldn't be a date, but a service project. Just hanging out with a friend, helping him feel a little Christmas spirit. That was the whole point of being his Secret Santa elf, after all. And maybe Drake would have fun.

Maybe it was okay she liked him.

CHAPTER EIGHT

Drake stood outside the bakery, staring at the cutesy pink font above the bakery. Bell wasn't kidding. She had painted a big holiday scene on the biggest window to the right of the door, and each of the windows had garland and colored lights framing them. He could see a Christmas tree inside, and even more decorations. He could only hope she didn't have Christmas music playing. He knocked on the front door, and waved to Bell, who looked up from the dough she was rolling out in the back.

She dusted her flour-covered hands on her apron and hurried through the kitchen doorway, lifted the counter, and unlocked the front door. As soon as she pushed it open, Drake heard the Christmas music playing. "Good morning! I almost thought you weren't going to show."

He stepped inside and looked around. "You weren't kidding about the place."

"I spend more time here than at home, so I figure I should make it just as inviting." She locked the door and led the way to the back. "You can hang your coat on that hook, and I have a spare apron you can wear." She held up a plain green apron.

Secret Santa

Drake hung his coat and scarf and smiled a little when he saw the apron. It was a huge contrast from the Christmas one she wore. "What, no elf apron for me?"

"Uh, I actually have one if you want to wear it."

He chuckled and put the green one on. "This will be fine. So, what are we working on?"

"Sugar cookies and gingerbread cookies." She gestured to the sugar cookie dough rolled out on the counter. "Oh." She leaned over and grabbed her phone, turning off the Christmas music. "Sorry, I forgot. What do you want to listen to?"

"It's really fine if you want that on," he said. "I mean, this is your place."

"You sure?" Her brown eyes searched his.

He shrugged. The Christmas music was actually the perfect addition to the situation, but he wasn't going to tell her that. "Nah, it will be in the background anyway. What do I get to do?"

Bell smiled, hit play, and set a container of cookie cutters in front of him. "You get to cut out the sugar cookies while I start the gingerbread cookie dough. Just put them on that cookie sheet when you're done."

Drake started looking through the cookie cutters—Santa, reindeer, tree, elf, ornament, sleigh. There were so many different kinds that he decided to start by doing ten of each. "So tell me about you, Bell. Why be a baker?"

"My mom was the greatest cook ever. She used to make the cookies for the…family Christmas party."

Drake didn't miss the hesitation but said nothing as

Bell continued.

"Everyone loved them. When she passed, I decided that's what I wanted to do." She turned on the blender and returned to his side to roll out another batch of sugar cookie dough.

Drake paused, as he set his second Santa on the cookie sheet. "She passed?"

Bell nodded. "Both of my parents. They died in an accident when I was twelve."

"Oh. I'm so sorry, Bell. I really—"

"It's not a big deal," she shrugged.

"Yes, it is. I yelled at you for not getting what it was like to lose a parent, and I didn't know you'd lost yours. I'm really, really sorry."

She gave him a weak smile. "It was a while ago. I just know they're in a better place, and they're still with me no matter what." She gave him a big smile. "What better way to carry on my mom's memory than opening my own bakery? The sugar cookie and gingerbread cookie recipes are hers. Everyone loves them."

"Yeah?" Drake snagged a scrap of the sugar cookie dough and popped it in his mouth. He'd always been a sucker for sugar cookie dough. "My mom used to make sugar cookies around the holidays," he said, reminiscing. "This dough tastes just like hers." He smiled.

"That's great!" Bell leaned over and grabbed the elf cookie. "Why stay at your dad's tavern?"

"Same reason you have the bakery," he said. "I remember him building it, and I helped him build the barn.

Secret Santa

It's hard to give up something you know was built by your dead father."

"But you haven't always lived in Owentown. I mean, you went to college, right?"

"Yeah, for that marketing degree I never use."

Bell's cookie sheet was already full, and she picked it up to put it in the oven. "You went to school for marketing and you now you run the tavern."

He grinned. "Funny how priorities change, huh?"

"What were you hoping to do with it?"

"I don't know. Work somewhere in a big city, have a desk job, be in charge of big promotional things." He shrugged.

Bell started laughing and Drake lifted his gaze. "I'm sorry, I just can't see you wearing a suit every day sitting behind a desk."

He gave her a crooked smile. "Right?"

She smiled. "So, do you date anyone?"

Drake watched her stack her second cookie sheet on the baking rack. "Why did you want me to come today? You're faster than I am." He set another cookie on the sheet. He still had three more to go before he filled it.

"I've been doing this every day for a long, long time," she smiled. "And I noticed how you skillfully avoided that question." She winked.

"No, I'm not dating anyone." He wiggled the cookie cutter and picked up another reindeer. "You asking me on a date?" he half-teased, half-scolded.

She grinned. "Isn't this one?" She wadded up the

scraps of sugar dough and set them in a bowl to the side.

Drake lifted his eyes.

"I'm joking, sheesh." She laughed and dusted the countertop with a little bit of flour before scooping out the gingerbread dough.

He wasn't sure she was joking. After all, it really was sort of a date. Even if they were making cookies for the elementary kids it was still just the two of them. The weirdest part was he didn't mind. He'd never been around anyone as happy as Bell. She seemed to be happy every time he saw her, except the night before when he yelled at her. She had even been happy when talking about her deceased parents.

There was a knock on the back door and Bell glanced up at the clock. "Oh, that's Jamie. It's open!" she called.

Jamie opened the door, letting in a gust of cold air and snow. She quickly stomped her feet and shut the door. "I got the sprinkles you wanted, and cocoa. I was thinking we could stop by Betty's for lunch and…" Her words faded when she finally looked up from the bag in her hand. She stared directly at Drake, then shifted her gaze quickly to Bell and back. "Uh, hello."

Drake smiled. He could only imagine how he looked covered in flour up to his elbows, rolling out a new batch of dough. No one really saw him outside of the bar. "Hey, Jamie."

Bell cleared her throat. "Jamie?"

"Yeah, sorry. I just can't believe you managed to get him out of the bar. And what sorcery did you use to get

Secret Santa

him to help you make *Christmas* cookies?" Jamie had never been one for being subtle.

"It was rather easy," Bell said.

"Yeah, she's only had to stalk me for the past two years," he threw in.

Jamie smacked Bell's shoulder. "I told you to stop doing that."

Bell's eyes widened. "Jamie!"

Drake laughed. "So, you *have* been stalking me?"

"No!" she answered, maybe a little too quickly. "I really just want to get to know more people around town. I only see people if they come into the bakery, or if I see them at the diner. I really don't get to get out socially, and—"

"Relax, I was joking." Drake plopped a glob of dough in his mouth to eat while he set another cookie sheet full of uncooked sugar cookies on the baking rack. "Hey, I'm catching up to you. Better pick up your speed." He pointed to Bell with his ornament cookie cutter. He quickly pushed the dough together and started rolling it out again to use as much as possible.

He pretended not to notice Jamie give Bell two-thumbs up before she turned and headed back to the door. "I'll let you two spend the rest of your day together. Have fun!" she sang and hurried back out into the snowstorm.

"I'm really sorry about her," Bell sighed.

"That's Jamie for you."

"How well do you know her?"

He laughed. "Have you never lived in a small town

before? Besides, I went to school with her. Pretty much almost everyone who grew up here still lives here. They may or may not go off to school and seek a career, but most of us end up coming back."

"So, you knew her through school? She never told me."

"Yep. She prodded me into my first kiss."

Bell tilted her head. "You kissed her?"

"No," he laughed. "No, she goaded me into it. I think it was one of the girl's choice dances, and we were behind the school."

"I never see you do anything together."

"Yeah…" He heaved a sigh. "I kind of drifted away from everyone when my dad passed. I used to be really close with Jamie, Chris of course, and Brad. There was another girl, Bridgette, but she moved off and started a family of her own somewhere out of state."

"Huh. I guess I didn't think about that."

"That I'd have friends?"

"No, that people tend to stay where they grow up. You're falling behind again." She grinned and held up a tray of gingerbread cookies.

"Now, I think you've got to be cheating. How are you humanly that fast!" He flicked some flour at her.

She gasped and gave him a mischievous grin before she grabbed a handful and tossed it at him, hitting him in the shoulder, which also splattered him across the face. She put her hand over her mouth, eyes wide.

"Oh, so that's how you want to play?" He grabbed a

handful of his own.

Bell quickly set the tray of cookies on the counter and scrambled around to the other side. "I'm sorry," she laughed. "I didn't mean to get it on your face!"

He dropped the flour and strolled over to her casually and calmly. "You had to know it would do that."

"I swear, I didn't." She stifled another giggle as she grabbed a hand towel and reached out to wipe the flour from his face.

Drake seized the opportunity to reach out and rub his flour-covered hand all over her face. He started laughing while Bell stood for a moment, wrapping her mind around what just happened. Soon, they were both laughing. Bell leaned against him, catching her breath. Drake felt his heart skip a beat. He wasn't supposed to like this girl, yet here they were covered in flour in her bakery, with her leaning against him. He smiled at her softly. This felt good.

Bell handed him a towel, still giggling now and then. "You have a little something right here." She touched his cheek.

"Yeah? You've got something here." He rubbed his hand down her cheek, again smearing it with flour.

"Drake!" she laughed. "I just stopped laughing." She clutched her side.

Drake couldn't help but laugh again. He took the towel from her and wiped it across his face, not actually caring if he got anything off or not. He handed it back to her, grinning like an idiot. "I suppose we should finish the cookies?"

"No more interruptions, Drake." She swatted him playfully with the towel and winked. "You said caramel is your favorite flavor, but what's your favorite Christmas treat?"

"You know I don't like Christmas." He returned to his position at the sugar cookies.

"Pshh. That doesn't mean you can't enjoy the treats. You look like…a fudge kinda guy."

He raised his brow. "What, you can read minds now?"

She shrugged. "I don't work in a bakery for nothing!" she sang as she skipped to her display case and returned moments later with a square of parchment paper and a piece of deliciously dark fudge sitting on top.

Drake couldn't deny his mouth watered just looking at it. "It's only nine thirty in the morning."

"My mom used to say, 'Life's too short. Eat dessert.'" She held up the fudge.

He smiled. "You should put that saying on your window." He accepted the fudge and took a bite. The goo melted in his mouth, the sweetness trickled down his throat, and he couldn't help but close his eyes. "Holy cow."

"Told ya." Bell resumed her position at the gingerbread cookies.

Drake no longer cared that it wasn't lunch, or even ten yet. The fudge was the most delicious stuff he'd ever tasted. "Bell, you could sell this stuff."

"I already do," she laughed.

Secret Santa

"No, I mean production. Everything I've tasted is delicious. With the right marketing, you could get people from out of town who would stop by and get your treats." He bit another piece.

She glanced up from her dough. "I bake because I enjoy it."

"But everyone should taste this stuff. I mean, seriously," he said through another mouthful. "I could put my marketing skills to work. You could bake a bunch of treats, bring your hits, and I bet we could set up somewhere in the city and have people try it. If they try it and taste how good this stuff is, they'd be willing to drive and get it."

"I'm doing well enough for myself, I really don't mind."

Drake gave her a confused look. "You don't want it to be more?"

"Not really." She shrugged. "I know how to run a little shop. I just hired Amanda and have been working with her the past couple of days, but she's my first employee. I didn't even know how much paperwork it was to figure out how I'm supposed to hire someone! I can't imagine adding more people and all of the extra work…" She shook her head. "I like being my own boss of my own little bakery in a small town."

"I can understand that," he nodded. "You know…" He walked to her side of the counter. "Today really hasn't been that bad. I've actually really enjoyed it."

Bell stifled a giggle.

"What? Didn't think I could have fun?" He rested his fists against his hips.

"It's not that. You've got fudge on your nose."

"Here?" He tried to reach his tongue up and lick it off, which only managed to make them both laugh. He eventually used his thumb to wipe it off, then wiped his thumb off on his apron so he could keep working on the cookies. "This has been a lot of fun."

"You're welcome. Thank you too."

Finally, they set the last cookie sheet in the oven. They wiped off the counters and stood side-by-side to wash the dishes—in spite of how much Bell protested. With the dishes done, cookies in the oven, and kitchen clean, Drake hung up his apron.

He always attributed his distrust for Bell to the fact she was so nice. People weren't just nice to be nice. At least, not from what he'd experienced. After his dad died, people showed up out of the blue pretending to be nice, pretending they were friends with his father, pretending to care, and then they disappeared out of the blue too. But there stood Bell, wearing a long green Christmas shirt over her white and red striped leggings, looking like an adult-sized elf from the North Pole.

"I've got an idea," he said. "When the cookies come out, they have to cool, right? Why don't you come over to my place for lunch, and then I can come back and help you decorate them."

Bell stared at him, eyes wide.

"What?"

Secret Santa

"I just...I figured you would be done."

He scoffed. "Decorating is the funnest part!"

"Funnest, huh?"

"Yep." He gave her his crooked smile.

She nodded once and removed her apron. "Deal."

❋ ❋ ❋

Once the cookies were out of the oven, the two bundled up and made their way through the snowstorm, down the street to Drake's tavern. Bell reached out for the door, but Drake grabbed it and pulled it open for her. Bell hesitated only a moment before escaping the snow. Her heart was doing flips, or was it her stomach? Maybe she was just hungry. Being with Drake all morning had been eye-opening. He wasn't the grumpy man she'd always thought he was. He could actually have fun and had a heart-melting smile.

Bell shook her head and walked over to the bar, while Drake headed into the back for a moment. "Hey, do you have hot cocoa?" she called.

She heard a light chuckle before he returned, the teakettle in one hand and tin of cocoa in the other. "Read your mind." He placed them on the counter beside her. "You can go sit by the fireplace until you warm up, if you'd like. And any thoughts on what you'd like to eat? Want to look over the menu?"

She accepted the menu from his hand and glanced over

the lunch section. "Is Chris back there?"

"Yeah, he was already prepping for our lunch rush."

Bell glanced up at him, aware of the sarcasm in his voice. "I just got an idea for the silent auction!"

"What's that?"

"We get the kids at the school involved! When we hand out the cookies, we give them flyers to have them make their favorite Christmas treat. They will be taste-tested, and the winner will get to have a day baking with me! All of their treats can be sold at the auction. That will get more people here too!"

She watched his brows lift. "That's a brilliant idea."

She couldn't hold back a clap of excitement. "I've got to tell Jamie."

"Go ahead and call her. Should I get you a burger?"

"Oh, that sounds perfect! And your fries with the garlic rub?"

"Got it." He chuckled and headed to the back.

Bell quickly called Jamie and told her the brilliant idea.

Jamie gasped. "Brilliant! That's absolutely perfect! What a great idea to get people there! I can make some flyers while I'm working today. Hey, how's your date with Drake going? Just say yes, it's awesome, or no, it isn't."

"I'm at his tavern right now for lunch," she flushed. "And then he volunteered to come back and help me decorate and deliver the cookies."

Jamie squealed so loudly on the other end of the phone, Bell had to pull it away from her ear.

Secret Santa

"You're going to make me go deaf!" she laughed, putting her hand over her mouth when other patrons in the tavern gave her the side-eye. "I'm trying not to get my hopes up," she added in a whisper.

"Bell, that's what Christmas is all about! Get your hopes up! Let them be dashed or come true. You don't know what's going to happen if you don't try."

"I know. I do have to say, I never saw this coming. Oh hey, he's coming back. Let me know if you need help with anything else for the auction."

Drake set down her food and had his own plate of food. "She thought that was a good idea, huh? I could hear her squeal all the way back in the kitchen."

"She's very dramatic," Bell chuckled. "That didn't take long at all."

He rolled his eyes. "Turned out Chris sort of figured we would be back around lunch and actually had these ready, believe it or not." He shrugged. "I swear stuff around here just seems to happen." He shook his head.

"Christmas magic," Bell winked.

"Ah, right." He scoffed. "Should have known."

"Emily was really excited about the information you gave her," Bell said, munching on a fry.

"That's good. She's actually got some good stuff, it's just getting it out there in a market already saturated with that sort of product." He smiled. "Wow, that sounded weird to say. Made me sound smart."

"You are smart, weird-o." Bell wanted to smack herself on the forehead. Who was she!

Drake's smile broadened. She loved it when he smiled that big. "I guess my secret identity has been revealed."

"Not if it's not who you wanted to be."

He tilted his head, clearly confused. "Huh?"

"Well, who do you want to be? Do you still want to be that marketing guy? Or do you want to run the tavern? Or, maybe you could even balance both. You only open for lunch and dinner, you could use mornings to do your marketing on the side, you know. Especially since it's mostly online now, right?" She took a bite of her hamburger that was probably a little too big.

Drake nodded. "True." He started eating his own lunch. "When we're done with your cookies, we're delivering them, right?"

Bell smiled. "Yep. Still committed to coming?"

"Of course," he replied simply.

"Cats or dogs?"

He lifted his gaze and smiled. "Why does it have to be limited to a cat or dog?"

"Because you can't have a pet dragon. They will burn the tavern down."

"Shh, we don't want Zathora to hear, remember?" he whispered, eyes glancing down toward the basement.

Bell almost snorted her drink out of her nose.

The friendly conversation didn't end there. They continued to talk all the way back to the bakery, all the while decorating, and even after Drake volunteered to drive them.

Bell leaned her back against the passenger door of

Secret Santa

Drake's truck, the trays of cookies laid across his back seat, and she pursed her lips. "Alright. Favorite song?"

"Oh man. That's like trying to ask you what your favorite book is."

"Hm." She tapped her chin. "Depends on the genre."

"Bingo."

"Fine. Favorite type of music?"

"That's easier. I love old, classic rock. Bon Jovi, Journey, that kind of music."

She nodded. "Completely makes sense."

"I'm guessing your favorite thing to read is…romance?"

Bell laughed. "Actually, not my favorite, but I do love fantasy. Could you imagine how cool it would be if dragons were actually real?"

Drake looked at her. "The thought of being burned to a crisp doesn't make me want them to be real."

"Not all dragons breathe fire, and not all are greedy."

He chuckled. "If you say so. My turn. Favorite movie?"

Bell tilted her head as she thought. "Hm."

"Not Christmas related."

She laughed. "Oh, bummer! I was going to say The Grinch. Fine, let's say…I don't know! I think my favorite go-to movie is Princess Bride, but I also absolutely love Star Trek."

"Really? I sort of figured you for a Pride and Prejudice kind of person."

Bell made a face. "I actually don't like Jane Austen,

but don't tell anyone else. Especially Jamie. She will have my head!"

Drake laughed. "Your turn."

"What do you do during the day? When you're not at work?"

He shrugged. "Nothing. I've been trying to teach myself the guitar but decided I'm just really not good at it."

"Everything is tough when you're learning it."

"Do you play a musical instrument?"

She licked her lips. "I've always wanted to learn to play the piano," she admitted.

The stopped at Jamie's bookstore. "I'll run in and grab the flyers," Drake said.

Bell watched him, smiling at nothing in particular, letting out a soft sigh. When he returned, she felt the familiar fluttering in her stomach she got whenever she was near him. He set the stack of flyers on the seat between them and glanced at her.

"What?"

She blushed. "Nothing. I was just thinking how fun this day has been."

"Even though neither of us has really gotten any work done," he winked and started driving again.

She shook her head. "This is way better than work."

"You did the same thing you always do."

"No, I didn't. I had you there." She blushed and started fiddling with her fingers. "I just mean, it was nice to not be alone in the bakery working on the cookies, of course."

Secret Santa

"Of course."

"I didn't have to talk to myself while I baked. I mean, you answer back, which is great."

"Yep." The corner of his lips tugged. "I do respond. Do you respond to yourself?"

"Only sometimes." She nodded.

Drake chuckled, his smile finally breaking through. "You're an interesting person, Bell."

She felt her heart flutter again. "You're not too bad yourself, Drake."

They stopped in front of the school, and both lingered in the truck a moment. Drake finally grabbed the flyers and climbed out. Bell followed his example. She grabbed two trays of cookies, and Drake grabbed the other two trays.

Bell watched Drake hand out cookies to the preschoolers. He was a much warmer person than he let on. Watching him with the littlest kids made her heart melt. He crouched so he was on their level, smiled at them, and asked them what they thought Santa might bring them.

When they had managed to successfully give away all of the cookies and flyers, they climbed back into his truck, and he looked over at her.

"What?" she asked. "Do I have frosting on me?" She looked all over herself.

"No, you look fine." He smiled. "Kind of like a human-sized Christmas elf, to be honest."

She ran her hand over her knee, not embarrassed in the

slightest. But he'd been looking at her, and that made her heart do flips. "I'm really glad you came. It would have taken me a lot longer to get them all delivered."

"How would you like to go ice skating with me after the silent auction?" Drake asked. She stared at him, watching his face shift into apprehension, dread, and then worry. "I mean, you don't have to if you don't want to," he added quickly.

"Are you kidding? I haven't been ice-skating in probably three years! I would love to!"

Drake smiled. "So, why hot chocolate all the time?" he asked, starting the car.

"Coffee is gross. Tea has no flavor. With cocoa, you can add anything you want! Candy canes, marshmallows, you can flavor it with raspberries, nuts, and lots of other things. It's delicious." She shifted in her seat, so she was facing him.

"What are you planning on doing for the rest of the day?"

She stretched. "It's pointless to open my bakery for the rest of the day, but I was going to get some more dough prepped for tomorrow."

"Does it ever get boring to you? Baking the same thing over and over?"

"Not even a little bit. Besides, Saturday is the auction, so I've got to come up with something a little different than I usually make."

"And what are you doing for dinner?"

Bell glanced at her phone. "Well, today is Thursday, so

Secret Santa

it's my day to cook. Jamie and I switch off sometimes, so we can eat together. What are you doing?"

"I think I'm going to start making some new logos for the tavern. See if I can get a kick start on that marketing you mentioned earlier." He stopped outside of her bakery, putting his truck in park. "Thanks again, Bell."

She softly bit her bottom lip, leaving her hand on the seat beside her; far enough away she hoped Drake would touch her. "I'll see you on Saturday."

"See you then. Oh, don't forget your trays!" he called when she slid out of the front seat.

"Right, duh." She blushed, now embarrassed. She quickly grabbed them and waved, watching as he drove off. She hugged the cookie sheets to her chest and turned to look at her bakery. This was everything she'd always wanted.

She hummed as she walked inside and felt a warm tingling coming from her pocket. She pulled out the Spirit List. Although Kristi and Brian had just met, set up by none other than Bell herself, both names were now out of the book. To top it off, Paul Taylor was gone as well. Twelve more days until Christmas, and still ten people on the list. She needed to stop flirting with Drake and start working on everyone else!

But even as she began making a list of what to bring for the silent auction, she couldn't help but daydream about Drake.

Chapter Nine

The sunny morning light penetrated the front windows. Drake and Chris had stacked the tables on the far right wall and lined up the chairs to face the bar. Knowing children would be coming, Drake covered the liquor shelf with a dark green curtain. Chris had worked hard all morning to get the finger foods ready, while Drake had coordinated with Jamie where the items for sale would be placed (on a row of tables to the left of the entrance) while the kid's treats and tasting would happen at the bar.

"The only thing that would really set this all off would be decorations." Jamie faced Drake.

His stomach clenched, and he looked around the place. "Yeah, I guess you're right. But I don't have any. I threw them out last summer. I doubt you've got some in your trunk."

"Bell might have some more."

He nodded solemnly, looking around the tavern again.

"You know, I should have been a better friend," Jamie said. "I know how close you were with your dad, and I should have been there for you when you were going through his passing."

Secret Santa

"How could you do that?" He studied her. "I pushed everyone away. I thought it would be easier for me to deal with it on my own than let people in to share the pain. That's not something I've ever been good at."

"At least you let Bell in," Jamie grinned.

The door opened, and Bell stepped in.

"Were your ears burning?" Jamie laughed.

Bell gave her a confused look. "What?"

Drake chuckled. "We were just talking about you. Wouldn't happen to have any decorations in your trunk, would you?"

She blushed. "Well, actually, I do. I just finished helping Tina decorate her house, and have a bunch still left."

Drake laughed. "Of course. Can I take that plate from you?" He held his hands out.

Bell handed him a plate of peppermint goodies. "Let me just go get the box."

He didn't miss the dramatic thumbs-up from Jamie to Bell. He set the plate on one of the tables and followed Bell out to her car, parked in the lot on the side of the tavern. "Think this will be successful?"

"Honest opinion?"

He felt his stomach sink.

Bell reached into the back seat of her car and handed him the box of decorations. "In my opinion, yes. We're going to have the community pull together to earn money for two different families, and they're going to show up to support you."

Drake didn't want to move from in front of her. He loved how she smelled like peppermint, the way her eyes sparkled, how every time he looked at her, he just wanted to be closer. He felt the tug between them, the desire to drop the box of Christmas ornaments, grab her by the waist, and kiss her.

But someone honked their horn as they pulled in.

Drake lifted his gaze and spotted Tom waving from his open window. "Morning, Drake!"

Drake smiled softly and stepped back to allow Bell to walk. "Morning, Tom! I guess we better get in and start putting some decorations up, huh?" he asked Bell, eyes shifting between her gaze.

She nodded, locking her door behind her. "Yes, we better."

Drake and Bell took charge of hanging the silver tinsel from the bar, using some heavy magnets to prevent the tinsel from sliding off. Drake couldn't resist the urge to touch her hand and would "accidentally" leave his hand in the way so their fingers would brush, and each time they did, he felt a spark between them.

"That's it," Bell said, dusting her hands off on her legs.

Drake looked around, pulled out of his trance. People had already started gathering, kids were lining up their baking creations, and the auction table was starting to fill. "Wow. Time flies, huh?"

Bell gently bit her lip. "Guess so."

He reached out and put his hand on her cheek, moving his thumb across her skin.

Secret Santa

"Dirt on my face?" she asked.

"Nah, an eyelash." He pulled away, grinning sheepishly. "Got it."

"I'm so excited to see you all here!" Jamie announced to everyone starting to gather in the bar. "We'll get started in about five minutes!"

Drake nodded a hello to Emily, who had set a gift basket on the auction table and found a seat toward the back. There was also jewelry displayed, gift boxes with "mystery" men's socks inside, toys, puzzles, gift cards, and other fun items. Chris entered from the back, a tray of appetizers carefully organized: pretzels, stuffed red potato bites, mini stout pies, dip and delicately sliced bread, and more.

The tavern was soon packed, people standing at the back and kids sharing chairs.

Drake nodded to Jamie and stood in front of the crowd. "Welcome everyone to the Red Dragon! I'm excited you're all here for the purpose of helping raise some money for the Skye and Shepherd families. Jamie and Bell organized this—"

"I didn't do anything," Bell interjected with a little laugh. "Just the taste-testing."

He smiled. "Okay, well she only offered the grand prize."

Everyone laughed.

"But I'm thrilled to have you here. Chris is passing around some items from our brand-new menu, so don't hesitate to taste it. All of it is safe for the kids too. I'll turn the time to Jamie to explain how the day is going to go." He stepped aside, intentionally stopping close to Bell.

Jamie rubbed her hands eagerly. "Like Drake said, we're going to auction off some items, and taste others! If you don't want to necessarily purchase anything, you can leave some cash in that jar on the table, which we've already got some money in. We're going to auction items while Chris walks around with items from Drake's new menu. Bell will also taste the creations you've brought and should be done within an hour hopefully. Bell, what's the first thing we should auction?"

Bell grabbed a box and carried it over. "Looks like this has a superhero mug in it." She held it up for the audience to see.

"Okay, let's start with five dollars?" Jamie asked, looking at the crowd with a tight smile.

Drake could feel what she was feeling: fear this whole thing was going to crash and burn. They'd spent a lot of time and effort putting this whole thing together, and if no one bought anything, the Skyes and Shepherds would have nothing for Christmas.

But a boy jumped from his seat, waving his hand with excitement. "I'll pay five dollars!"

"Ten!" an older boy said.

The first boy turned to look at his parents and raised his eyebrows expectantly.

After some back and forth, the superhero mug sold for thirty dollars, and then Bell tasted the first item—a white cookie with chopped Kit-Kats baked in it. She complimented the little girl who made it, then sold the next item.

With each item they sold, the crowd got more excited and they sold for more and more money. Finally, Bell finished tasting the items brought and looked at her piece of paper with a score sheet on it. The last of the items had been sold, and Kristi was taking the cash and writing it down, then putting it in the moneybag Drake had brought.

"Alright, the winner of the bake-off this Christmas is the white cake peppermint cookie," Bell said. "Who made that?"

A boy, about eight or nine years old, was prodded to his feet by his parents, his mouth hanging open as he shyly walked forward.

Bell leaned down and looked him in the eye, holding out her hand for him to shake. "Your cookie was delicious. How would you like to spend a day baking with me?"

He nodded, finally smiling, and shook her hand enthusiastically. "I can't believe I won! My mom and dad love my cookies, but I just thought they were being nice."

"What do you want to be when you grow up?"

"I want to cook. I don't know what yet, but I want to be a cook," he nodded.

"Well, I'm glad you won, then! Maybe I can talk you into being a baker, huh?"

He grinned. "Maybe."

"I'll talk to your parents and I'll see you next Saturday morning!" She gave him a playful salute, to which he saluted back.

Jamie stepped in front of the small crowd. "Thank you for coming, everyone!" she grinned. "Be safe driving home."

Bell stepped forward quickly. "And thank you so much for helping to support your neighbors and friends. We know they'll be thrilled to receive some extra help at Christmas."

Slowly, the group climbed to their feet. A few went over and gave Bell and Jamie hugs, and shook Drake's hand. Drake got a lot of compliments about the new foods, and more than a handful asked when the new menu would start. Drake hadn't felt this sense of neighborly support since his father died. Of course, he couldn't help but feel it was his fault for pushing people away, and to see a few familiar faces that morning helped him feel maybe he could finally get the tavern back on its feet.

"How much do you think we've earned?" an elderly man asked Bell.

"Well, it's too soon to tell. We haven't finished counting it yet," she answered with a laugh.

"Let us know when you do. I think it would be great to know." He gave her a handshake and limped with his cane out the door.

As the crowd began to thin, Drake stared rearranging the dining room. Jamie and Bell sat at one of the tables and began counting. "Need help with the money?" he asked, setting another chair down.

Jamie held up a finger until she was finished counting,

Secret Santa

and then looked at him. "I'm counting, and Bell is double checking. We've got this."

He shrugged and set the last table in place. "I'll go help Chris with the kitchen."

Chris walked out. "I'm done. It wasn't too much to clean up."

"And just so you know, the food was awesome," Bell threw in.

"Yeah, almost everyone liked it," he grinned.

"So new menu launches tonight at dinner!"

Chris made a face. "You gonna do lunch before you go ice skating?" He nudged his head toward Bell.

"Ah, right. Because otherwise, it will be a dinner thing…" He looked over at her.

Chris cleared his throat and walked over to the table. "Hey, Jamie, let me help count. Let's get Drake and Bell out on their date."

Jamie jotted something down. "Good idea! Get out of here, you two."

Drake looked at Bell and shrugged. "Lunch first?"

"Oh, please! I'm famished! I totally forgot to eat breakfast."

"Let's head over to the diner, then. You can see Betty. It's been a long time since I've actually eaten there." He motioned for her to follow him through the back of the tavern and out to his truck.

"So, you live upstairs?"

"Yeah."

"Not very big."

"I'm only one guy," he chuckled.

She nodded. "Good point." She climbed into the car and they drove down to the diner.

The drive was short, and Drake was mildly surprised at how comfortable he was just sitting in the car with Bell, both of them not really having much to say during the drive. Drake climbed out of the car and held the front door open for Bell, who thanked him as she passed, and they sat at a booth against the front window.

She ordered a French dip sandwich, while he decided to try the spicy chicken sandwich.

He looked up at her. "So...what do we talk about?" he laughed, his nerves moving between making his heart skip and choking him.

"I don't know. To be honest, I'm a little nervous."

He sighed in relief. "I am too. I mean, it's been ages since I've been on a date. You?"

Bell's smile was stiff. "Uh. Well, would you believe me if I told you this is my first official date?"

"You? No way."

She nodded.

"Well, at least we know each other, somewhat. And besides, we're only going ice-skating. Wh—"

She reached across the table and clamped a hand over his mouth. "Don't finish that sentence. Don't jinx it."

He chuckled, unable to contain it.

Bell's cheeks grew red and she sat back down. "I'm so sorry. That was probably really awkward for you."

"No." Drake said, still chuckling and shaking his head.

Secret Santa

"But it was really funny."

"Oh good." She finally gave him a smile. "I was thinking about what you said yesterday, how you once really liked painting. They do these fun paint events where you go to dinner and learn to paint a picture at the same time. Is that something you'd want to do?"

He shook his head in disbelief. "Do you remember everything about everyone? You really are the most…amazing person I've ever met." Drake's eyes locked with Bell's as he stared at her in wonder. He blinked as he remembered he hadn't answered her question yet. "Yeah. I would actually like that a lot. We have nothing going on so far next week."

Bell's smile widened. "Sounds good to me."

"That makes me remember," Drake said. "A couple of years ago I painted a big dragon for my dad, so he could hang it up in the tavern. It was a huge canvas, actually quite good, from my own biased opinion," he grinned. "But I tossed it out with a bunch of stuff when he died so I wouldn't have to remember. I think someone picked it up with all the stuff I set out, but I'm not sure. I regret it so much now and wish I hadn't gotten rid of it."

She tapped her nose. "We can find it."

Her smile made his heart flip. He'd do anything to see her smile like that all the time.

❈ ❈ ❈

Bell had braided her hair into two braids—one on each side of her head—and she nervously fiddled with one of them before pulling a warm hat over her ears to keep her warm while ice-skating. She couldn't believe she was on a date with Drake. A real date. She could hardly contain the excitement and nervousness bubbling in her chest and stomach.

"Okay, name this song." Drake hit play and the music started.

Bell scoffed and playfully smacked his arm. "That's easy. 'Bohemian Rhapsody,' duh."

"You're good."

"My turn." She grabbed his phone and found a song, smirking.

The music started, and he rolled his eyes. "Seriously?" He looked at her. "That's the best you got? It's 'Phantom of the Opera.'"

"I didn't think you would know musicals!"

"Who wouldn't know that one?" he laughed.

She held his phone. "You know, I don't have your number in my phone."

"Well, you better put your number in my phone, then."

Bell added it in. Did she really think she would still be here after Christmas? If she got Drake off of the Spirit List, she would be able to go home to the North Pole. Some part of her argued against it. Was she really silently hoping Drake wouldn't be off the list this year, so she could stay in Owentown?

They parked and walked to the booth that rented the

skates. The man in the small hut smiled. Bell recognized him as one of the men from caroling, and she'd seen him in church too. "Hello, you two! I don't think I've ever seen you ice skate, Bell. And it's been a long time since I've seen you, Drake. What sizes can I get for you?"

Bell glanced at Drake, who motioned her forward. "Eight and a half, please."

The man reached down and produced two gray skates that were rather worn. He looked at Drake. "Guessing eleven for you?"

"Twelve, please," he smiled.

"Someday I will perfect my art of choosing the correct size." He handed Drake the skates and Drake handed him the cash. "Just be sure to bring them back when you're done. Have a good time, you two!"

Drake and Bell took a seat on the bench beside the homemade ice rink. Bell couldn't get the grin off her face. She felt like a little kid again, when she used to put on her white skates and take off across the pond with the penguins. No penguins lived outside of Santa's village, it was much too dangerous, but they were rather delightful to have as friends inside the village, and they loved the ice rink.

Drake had his skates on in no time and he smiled at her. "Ready yet?"

Bell straightened. "Yes, I think I am. Go easy on me. It's been a couple of years."

"It's been a while too. I guess we'll figure out just how good we are at doing this." He stepped carefully out onto the ice and turned to her. "You coming?"

"Of course. I'm just a little nervous. It's a lot further to fall being a…" She'd almost said 'human,' but had been lucky enough to catch herself.

"Adult?" Drake finished. He held out his hand. "Even if you do fall, at least we will both go home with bruised rear ends."

Bell took his hand and slowly slid one foot across the rough ice, and then the other. "Not nearly as smooth as I remember ice being."

"It will be once you get going." He didn't let go of her hand.

Of course, Bell may have been gripping rather tightly. She'd never skated as a human, and the fear of falling was real. She didn't know how injured she could get. Of course, when she'd first become a human sized person, that had taken some getting used to, but she'd adapted rather quickly to every other task. This was a little different, since it wasn't something she'd tried yet.

Drake started sliding a little faster, pulling her to keep up. "It's better if you go faster."

"I know." She finally gave him a nervous smile and started pushing her feet outward from her body, the skates cutting into the ice and propelling her forward. The ice was a little rough and bumpy from being used and not being groomed, but it didn't take long to start skating at a comfortable speed for the two of them.

Bell realized after a few minutes they still held hands, and she felt her heart swell. Throughout her years as an elf, and even as a human sized one, she'd always wanted someone she could spend time with on a daily basis.

Was Drake that person?

"You're staring at me," Drake grinned.

"I'm sorry. I was just thinking about…well, about you. Thank you for asking me to come skating with you today."

"You weren't staring at my dashing good looks?"

Bell laughed, and her cheeks burned with a blush. "That too."

Drake tilted his head. "I have an idea. We should race around the rink, and whoever wins has to pay for hot cocoa."

"Wait a minute, shouldn't it be the loser has to pay for cocoa?" she said.

"Well, I figure I'm going to win, and I'm the one that's paying on the date, so…"

"Oh really?" Bell arched her brow. "Challenge accepted." She took off without waiting for Drake to say go.

"Cheater!" he laughed and hurried after her.

Bell tried to stay on the outside of people, passing where there was more room—as everyone seemed to try and crowd in the center. Drake suddenly cut across the ice rink back to where they started. "Hey!" she protested. "I was winning!"

"But I actually won," he laughed.

Bell gave him a playful shove, unintentionally catching him off-balance and causing him to slip and land in a pile of snow. She gasped and put both hands over her mouth.

Drake, however, burst into laughter.

"I'm so sorry!" she apologized, reaching her hand out to try and help him back to his feet.

"It's alright." Drake tugged her hand, pulling her into the pile on top of him. His laughter faded, and his smile softened. He reached out and put his gloved hand on her cheek. "You're beautiful, Bell."

Bell blushed. "Thank you. You're not so bad looking yourself," she winked.

He grinned. "Oh really? Not too bad, huh?"

"You're handsome. Is that better?"

"A little." He chuckled and helped get her back to her feet, then climbed to his own. "Now I need cocoa more than ever." He took her hand and they walked the short distance to one of the benches. "You go ahead and sit, I'll go get the cocoa."

Bell sat down and watched him from behind as he went back to the skate rental and got them each a big cup of cocoa. He returned shortly and sat beside her, handing her a foam cup of steaming chocolate goodness. Bell rested the heels of her ice skates against the ice and watched people of all ages slide across its surface. It made her think of home. They had a permanent ice rink beside the ornament decorating shop and in front of the reindeer barn. Whenever the elves got a break, they would take to the ice, build snow castles, have snowball fights, and whatever other snow activities they could do. Moments like this made Bell homesick.

Secret Santa

"What's on your mind?" Drake asked, interrupting her thoughts.

She looked at him, quickly putting on a smile. "I was just thinking. Where I come from, ice-skating is something we always do. It feels like our rink was so much bigger, but I was also smaller."

He chuckled and rested his arm across the back of the bench. Bell couldn't help but shift and lean against his warmth, silently trying to justify her actions. For a moment she wondered if this was what she was supposed to do in this situation, but then Drake confirmed it when he put his hand on her shoulder and pulled her a little closer, making her stomach do backflips.

"This brings memories for me too," he replied. "We used to come here, my brothers and I, and play hockey or just mess around. Dad would always warn us we could do whatever we wanted, just as long as we got home in one piece, so Mom wouldn't have a heart attack."

"How many brothers?"

"Two." He smiled sadly but nodded. "When we lost my dad…it was the hardest thing I've ever gone through. We sort of distanced ourselves. Mom moved so she wouldn't have to be reminded of him every time she woke up. Even just seeing people in town made it hard. But spending time with you these past few weeks, you've really made me think. You've reminded me how magical Christmas is, the joy I feel when I do something for someone else without expecting anything in return…" He smiled and looked down at her. Drake took her hand and pulled her off of the bench. She staggered a step and bumped into his chest. He gave her a soft smile and reached out to touch her cheek.

Bell blushed, uncertain if the cold hid it. Her heart fluttered. She had known in the back of her mind that she was developing feelings for Drake Pine but dismissed those thoughts whenever they came. This time, however, she entertained the thought Drake had feelings for her too. He looked at her in a way she'd only caught him doing once before, and he looked away quickly. This time he held her gaze—his eyes were soft, his lips in a gentle, crooked smile.

He leaned closer and her heart began pounding so hard she thought he would be able to hear it.

There was a muffled splat, and Drake's brows shifted as he turned around. Only then did Bell see the snowball planted onto Drake's back and the kids standing a few feet away.

Bell started laughing.

Drake put on a determined face, crouched, wadded up a snowball, and threw it at the offending group of kids, who had previously looked scared half to death. The group easily dodged Drake's shot, and one of them shouted, "Snowball fight!"

Drake grabbed Bell and pulled her in front of him as a rain of snowballs flew their way.

"Hey!" Bell laughed. She ducked, but a few still hit her shoulder and side. She wiggled out of Drake's grasp and crouched to make her own snowballs. She'd been an

Secret Santa

expert snowball fighter at the North Pole during the Carnival of Snow.

"You were supposed to be my shield!" Drake protested with a laugh, scrambling to get his own snowballs ready. A snowball hit the side of his head just as he stood up, and he made a face. "That just got in my ear!"

"No head shots!" a kid scolded, punching a smaller boy in the shoulder.

The boy pouted. "It's not my fault he stood up!"

Bell straightened, cradling a pile of snowballs in her left arm so she could use her right to throw them, hitting all three of the boys in quick succession.

"Ah!" someone behind the two boys yelled. "Get Bell!"

Drake started throwing his own—in a much less sophisticated way. He stayed crouched behind a mound of snow and just threw the snow at them instead of making proper snowballs.

"Not cool!"

"There's more of us than you!"

"Then you should be winning!" Bell called back with a laugh.

When they ran out of snowballs and sort of gave up making more, they decided to mutually stand down. Bell dusted off her hat and shoulders while Drake rubbed his ear.

"We should do that again," she said.

He grinned like a kid on, well, on Christmas morning. "Yes, that was fun. I think we should turn in our skates and go warm up."

"We could go to my house," she offered, gesturing across the park to a cute brick cottage with a sloped roof and Christmas décor visible even from where they stood. "I've got treats."

"Of course you do," he smiled. "Alright then."

They turned in the skates, put their boots back on, and walked down the shoveled path to the other side of the park.

"I don't think I've had a better snowball fight," Drake said. "As kids, I'm pretty sure we just grabbed chunks of ice or the most dense snow we could find."

"We used to have teams and competition at the Carnival of Snow," Bell said.

"What's that?" He glanced at her.

"It was a huge carnival," she said.

"Obviously to celebrate snow," he added.

She nodded. "There were all sorts of treats themed to the snow, funny music, everyone just enjoying themselves." She walked up the steps.

"Was it to celebrate the first snowfall or something?"

"No. More of a kick off to the winter season." She opened the door and stepped inside, leaving it open for Drake to enter.

"You like snow that much?" He stepped to the side, so she could close the door. He unlaced his boots and stepped out of them, placing them on the rug while his eyes scanned her home.

"Where I'm from, it's always winter."

Secret Santa

"Where are you from?" he laughed. "The North Pole?"

She added her own quick laugh, knowing it would have been impossible for him to figure it out. "It definitely felt like it." She hung her coat on the peg and crossed the room to light the fireplace. The fire slowly lit, and Bell stepped into the kitchen to grab the s'mores cookies she'd brought back from the bakery. "You know, I've never asked if you prefer coffee or tea over cocoa. I just assume everyone loves cocoa."

"It's growing on me," he grinned. He leaned across the bar. "Your house is cute."

"Thanks, I like it. It's cozy. Where did you live growing up? You didn't all live above the tavern, right?"

He shook his head. "We lived over in the Bird Addition. That little neighborhood—"

"That's got all the streets named after birds," she finished. She poured two glasses of milk.

"Right. But that was a while ago and I haven't been back since."

She nodded. "We can sit on the couch." She walked around the couch, to the coffee table, and set the plate of cookies down. She turned to grab the milk, but Drake was right there with the glasses. "Thank you." She took a seat.

He sat beside her and studied her face. "This was a lot of fun. Next week we can go do that painting thing?"

"I would love that. Why don't you find which picture you want to paint?"

"Or we could do it now."

Bell took out her phone and pulled up one of the

places. She scooted closer so Drake could see her screen, and he scooted a little closer so they were touching. She wanted to stay like this forever.

But time was against them. They'd chosen a night to go to—Wednesday—just as Drake's phone buzzed, letting him know it was time to go prep for dinner.

Bell reluctantly stood, letting him get to his feet, and accepted his mug from him. "I had a really great time."

"Me too. Seriously one of the best days ever." He leaned over and kissed her softly on the cheek. After lacing up his shoes, he waved goodbye and walked out the door.

Bell shifted the mugs into one hand and placed her hand on the cheek he had kissed. He kissed her cheek. That had just happened. Slowly coming out of her daze, she quickly dumped the mugs in the sink and spun in a circle while squealing with joy.

✹ ✹ ✹

Drake flopped down in the armchair in his apartment. He was exhausted. The dinner had been a huge success, busier than they'd ever been, not to mention his date with Bell had been an equally huge success. This month had definitely been his best. Ever since he started going out with Bell to things in the community, ever since he started seeing people and talking to them, they'd started to come back to the tavern. It helped, of course, that Chris's new

Secret Santa

menu was a hit, and people also loved the new drinks.

He stared at the phone in his hands. He'd been contemplating for a while how he should reach out to his mother, and what he should say. Christmas was creeping up on them. Surely she already had plans. He finally shook his head and mumbled, "Just do it. You're an adult." Finally, he touched her name on his contact list in his phone. He ran his tongue over his teeth, his heart freezing after each ring. The third time caused his stomach to drop, knowing the next would lead to voicemail.

"Hello, you've reached Lacey, please leave your message and phone number and I'll get back to you as soon as I can."

Drake wasn't sure if he should leave a message or just hang up and give up. When the phone beeped, and the answering machine began recording he stuttered out a message. "Um. Hey, Mom. Lacey. Mom." He closed his eyes. "I just…I w-wanted to talk to you. Just give me a call. If you want. I completely understand if you don't. Or…yeah. Bye." He hung up and leaned back in his chair. He exhaled heavily and ran his fingers through his hair. "Well, what did I expect? Really?" He shook his head and pulled off his shoes.

He'd had a busy day and just needed a shower. He wanted a nap too but held out hope more people might show up for dinner.

Drake had just started towards the bathroom when his phone rang. He paused, pulled it off the desk and continued towards the bathroom. "Hello?" He leaned over and turned the bath water on to warm it up a little.

"Hey, Drake. It's Mom."

Drake felt his throat tighten. "Hey," he said softer.

"Sorry I didn't answer, I was on the phone with Michael and didn't look to see who it was. How...how are you, Drake?"

"I'm actually doing okay. I'm still running Dad's tavern. We just revamped the menu and mixed drinks, business is starting to pick up too. And I've sort of started dating someone."

"That's great news."

There was an awkward silence.

Drake spoke first. "I'm really sorry about last Thanksgiving. I know I should have been more sensitive. I didn't mean to distance myself from you and the family. That was never my intention, and then...when no one really talked to me after, I figured you didn't want to talk to me. So, I wasn't going to press the issue."

"You're just like your father."

He smiled shortly. "Yeah. Guess I am. So how are you and Brad?" He rubbed the back of his neck.

"Uh, well..." He heard noises like the phone being moved and then a door closing. "He proposed. I know you don't approve of him, but I want you to know how happy he makes me. He doesn't replace your father and he never will. Brad makes me...so happy. He makes me laugh and he loves me and respects me, and he reminds me so much of your father. It's actually almost like your father picked him for me. I've prayed a lot about this."

Secret Santa

"Mom," Drake interrupted when she paused. "I'm not mad at you. I'm really glad you found someone that makes you happy. I miss Dad so much, I never paused to think how you were feeling. I've been really lonely here, and I understand why you left. I understand why you started dating."

"Drake…" Her voice hitched.

Drake rubbed his eyes and cleared his throat. "I know you probably already have plans for Christmas, but…if you don't, maybe you could come out here. We wouldn't have to do the town party, we could just have our own. Or we could do the town party. Or none at all." He felt like an idiot, barely pausing between phrases, but he didn't know what to say to fix what he'd destroyed. His mom didn't answer, and his mouth went dry. "Mom?"

"I'm sorry." She sniffled. "I've been waiting so long to have this conversation with you. I should have been a better person and called you after you left last year. I should have called you that Christmas, on your birthday, and all the times in between."

"I told you not to that day." He sat on the edge of the shower to plug the tub and let it fill with warm water.

"But you're still my son. You were always the closest with your dad, sometimes even closer than he was with me. I didn't realize how much his death hurt you until that Thanksgiving. I should have told you. We should have talked. I should have called you."

"I shouldn't have overreacted even then." He smiled softly.

She gave a little bit of a laugh. "We've all been emotional. We do have plans for Christmas, but I'll see what I can do about maybe switching them."

"Okay. I would love that. Again, no pressure."

"Thank you, Drake, for calling. Thank you so much."

"You know I love you, right Mom?"

She laughed. "Yes, I do. And you know I love you?"

"To the moon and back, as you used to say." He smiled.

"I'll call you when I know what we're doing."

Drake took a deep breath and slowly let it out, a huge weight falling from his shoulders. "Sounds good. Bye, Mom."

She hung up and he put the phone on his bathroom counter. He hadn't felt this good in a long time. Now there was one big problem: if his mom came for the Christmas party, there needed to be a party.

Secret Santa

Chapter Ten

Bell had spent all morning on the phone, reminding people to meet at Jamie's bookstore. When she'd received confirmation from everyone she could reach, she finally left. Amanda met her at the bakery to get some work in before they closed for an extra break starting at eleven thirty. Bell was so distracted, she accidentally put the peanut butter frosting inside of the hot cocoa cupcakes and had to dump out a dozen when she finally realized her mistake.

"Have you ever heard that saying, a watched pot never boils?" Amanda asked.

"I'm sorry. I'm just so excited, I can't stand it!" She wiped her damp palms nervously on her apron. "Setting up this surprise is something I've been dying to have happen, and the week before Christmas is almost too perfect to ask for!"

She giggled. "You're amazing, Bell."

"All I did was plant the idea in someone's head. I have absolutely no power to do anything else," she insisted.

"Yes, but you still gave them the idea." Amanda darted over to Becky, the three-year-old had found an enticing-

Secret Santa

looking stack of boxes to attempt to climb. After saving Becky, Amanda's phone buzzed. Amanda glanced at Bell. "Mind if I answer?"

"Not at all! Go for it." Bell set a new batch of peanut butter cupcakes in the display case—the real ones this time—and grabbed the new hot cocoa cupcakes, half of what she planned on, due to her earlier error.

"No way!" Amanda almost shouted. "Bell, Steve got two calls for interviews!" she announced, hurrying to the front of the store.

Bell gasped. "That's great news! Good luck, Steve!" she called into the receiver.

Amanda laughed and turned away. "I'm so proud of you, Steven. You've been working so hard on that. I know. Okay."

Bell glanced at the clock for the millionth time. She could swear time wasn't moving.

Eventually, the minute hand did edge closer and closer to eleven-thirty, but Bell couldn't stand it anymore and ended up closing up fifteen minutes earlier than she should have. She helped Amanda bundle up Becky and Charlotte before heading over to Jamie's bookstore.

She noticed a couple of people enter, and grinned to herself. They were just as excited!

She stepped inside and walked over to Jamie's counter. "Hey, do you need help restocking anything?"

Jamie looked up from her computer with a wrinkled nose. "Aren't you supposed to be at work?"

"I already sold out of my treats for the day. Want an

early lunch? We could head over to Drake's."

She shook her head. "I'm trying to expand some of my marketing. I talked to Emily about the information Drake shared with her, and I'm going to give the online stuff a shot."

"Good." Bell leaned against the counter, intentionally leaning close to Jamie's computer screen.

"What are you doing?"

"Nothing."

"Bell." She frowned. "You're making me uncomfortable."

"Well, I'm antsy. I…I sort of need some advice," she said softer, glancing down one of the aisles of the bookstore, which now had three people in it.

"With what?"

"Drake." She bit her lip and met Jamie's gaze.

"Okay." She leaned back. "And?"

Bell sighed. "Jamie. I went on a date with him Saturday, like an official date that he asked me on."

"I know."

"Well, we're going to a painting thing this week, and…" This idea was failing. She hoped she could get Jamie out of the bookstore long enough for people to enter without Jamie growing suspicious. Jamie had said herself sales were steady, but a sudden influx of customers would definitely draw attention. "Is it too much to ask him to make gingerbread cookies with me Thursday? The retirement home is doing their annual event."

Jamie smiled, the hint of sadness keeping her lips from

pulling all the way upward. It was an event Jamie and Andrew had attended together in the past. "As long as your date goes well Wednesday, you should be fine Thursday too."

"But he does run the tavern. I mean, his place of business is really quite busy right now, and I'm pulling him away to do dates. Isn't that selfish?"

"Well, the gingerbread thing is in the afternoon."

"But they serve lunch."

Jamie shrugged. "If you're important to him, he will figure out a way to make it work. Or he waits two weeks and you guys get past Christmas and start doing other dates."

Bell hadn't noticed Jamie's eyes wander from her own, despite the five people that had entered and moved into the children's books section. The door opened again, and Jamie was about to look when Bell leaned even closer. "Jamie, I really like him," she whispered. It was the truth, not just a distraction. "What if we don't work out and I've ruined Christmas for him all over again?"

"You've been on two dates. You aren't in a relationship," Jamie laughed. "Just have some patience." She looked back down at her screen.

Bell nodded and finally put her feet back on the floor. Even if they did their date Wednesday, another one Thursday, Jamie was right. They would have to see if they worked for each other, Christmas or not. She drew a breath. They needed to slow down. Or at least, she did. They'd only just started dating. She nodded to herself.

The door opened again, and Bell's lips parted.

Jamie looked up and followed her gaze.

Drake had entered, carrying a small bouquet of yellow flowers. He smiled. "I couldn't find any hyacinths. Seems they don't sell those in bouquets, and that they're more of a spring flower? So, I hope these work for today."

"I don't even know what to say. These are amazing. I've never had someone give me flowers." She reached out and accepted them. "Thank you." She reached an arm around him and gave him a hug. She locked her gaze back on Jamie, giving her a huge smile.

Jamie said, "Aww! Aren't you two the cutest!" with a big smile of her own. She got up and walked around the counter. "You joining us for an early lunch at your place?" she asked Drake.

Bell let go of Drake. "Actually, Jamie, I have to ask you. I don't have a present for you this Christmas yet. What one thing would you want above anything else?"

"You know that. I want Andrew to come home. But, to be reasonable…" She glanced up, tilting her head with a thoughtful hum.

A deep voice behind Jamie responded, "Who says you have to be reasonable at Christmas?"

Jamie went rigid at the male voice, then spun around, spotting the tall man in camouflage standing just behind her. "Andrew…"

He grinned and held out his arms. Jamie ran to him and jumped, wrapping her arms and legs around him as she showered him with kisses. "What are you doing here!" she exclaimed. "You aren't supposed to be home for another two months!"

Her husband laughed. "I guess you could say it was a little Christmas miracle." He pulled her closer.

Jamie looked up, and her husband followed her gaze. "A mistletoe! You owe me a few more kisses." He dipped her and kissed her again.

Everyone came out of the rows of books and started applauding. They were friends, family, and community members who had gathered together to welcome Andrew home, and to support Jamie as well.

Andrew slowly made his way around, giving a firm handshake to each person individually, or a hug to the family members, until he reached Bell. He wrapped her in a long hug. "Thank you so much," he whispered.

"Of course," she said, trying not to get choked up. "You spend the day with each other and have a lot of fun, okay?"

Jamie nudged Andrew out of the way and pulled Bell into a rib-crushing hug. "Bell, I can't believe you did this for me," she cried. "Thank you." She squeezed Bell's hand.

"I barely did anything, but it was the only thing I could think of that would make you happy again. I had to contact a million people before I found the one man with the right authority." She let go of Jamie. "Go have fun."

Jamie leaned to her ear. "Do whatever you like with Drake. You're right. Christmas is a time for miracles, and you might as well try and make him yours."

Her heart did a flip. "I will."

Lunch was spent at Drake's, then Bell finished the rest of the day at her bakery. She'd just finished cleaning up and locking the back door at the end of the day, when she heard someone softly clear their throat.

She turned around and laughed. "What are you doing here, Drake?"

"Well, I know you and Jamie usually switch off doing dinners. I was thinking maybe you and I could do dinner tonight?"

"Don't you have a tavern to run?"

He shrugged. "Yeah? Dinner will be completely free, and I know it's a terrible date because I'll be busy, but—"

"It's better than eating alone. I would love to."

Drake smiled.

"You trimmed your beard," she observed, noting how short it was now, nice and close to his face.

"You still like it?"

She nodded. "I actually prefer it this way over it being longer, to be honest." She reached out and ran her hand over it. "Makes you look younger."

"Ah, well you should see me without it. I'd look like a baby. Baby face Drake."

She laughed. "We can't have that!"

Drake put his hand over hers, still resting on his cheek. "No, we can't. Could you imagine telling people you were dating a high school student?"

She wrinkled her nose. "You think you look that young?"

"It's been a while, so I can't promise. I can't carbon date my beard either."

Bell laughed again.

Finally, he lowered their hands and entwined their fingers. "You drive me over and we'll do an informal dinner. What will you do tomorrow night for dinner?"

Bell pulled out her Spirit List. She'd been planning on visiting Nancy, but if Drake wanted to do dinner instead, she would have to reschedule the dinner. Emily's name was gone now, as well as Jamie, the Shepherd family, Skye family, Logan Strong, and Dorothy. To her pleasant surprise, Drake's name was beginning to fade as well. She'd never seen a name fade so slowly, but it was amazing to watch.

"I think I can find something to do for dinner tomorrow," she finally answered.

Drake poked his nose over the book. "I've seen you carrying this around. What is it?"

"Oh, it's nothing important." She tried to close it, but Drake stuck his finger in the pages.

"Nothing, huh?" he teased and pulled it from her hands. "Shall we see?" He opened the book. Bell tried to grab it, panic tightening her throat. Humans weren't supposed to see the book. What if he saw his own name? But Drake was much faster than her, and much taller.

"Let's see here. Nancy Tibble. You even have her address in here?" His brows pinched and he gave Bell a confused look.

Bell finally got a hand on the book before he could

continue reading her scribbled notes. She pulled it away. "I keep track of things during the year. I like to make sure everyone in town is taken care of during the holiday season."

"Is my name in there?" He arched his brow.

Bell panicked. If Drake saw his name, what would he do? What would he think? But what if he flipped through and found his page? "Yes, actually," she answered with hesitation. "I have a list of everything I've invited you to do." She opened his page and showed him the things she'd written down. Luckily, they were little things, like caroling, making cookies, ice skating..." She had the dates and a short description of what they'd done. "It's more of a journal," she said. "I write down little things you say because they are important to me. Your birthday, so I can tell you happy birthday in March. Favorite music, so I can keep an eye out for tickets or something, those sorts of things. I don't know. I like to write stuff down, so I don't forget it. Because...well, because you're important to me, Drake."

Drake smiled softly. "You're important to me too, Bell." He leaned in and kissed her cheek. "Let's go eat. I'm starving."

"Do you always eat while you work?" She pushed the book back in her pocket, the panic slowly fading from her chest.

"Only when there's a pretty girl to distract me," he winked.

Secret Santa

✼ ✼ ✼

The rest of the week was a blur. Drake took Bell to the painting dinner night, temporarily hiring two kids home from college for Christmas to wait the tables, and Chris got Heather to come in and help run the register for the date.

And then the next date too, during lunch, which luckily wasn't as busy. Bell had invited him to the retirement home to make gingerbread houses. They'd split up—she helped an elderly man, and he helped an elderly woman. In fact, there were quite a few volunteers that afternoon.

But Drake couldn't leave it at that.

On the way home, Drake took Bell's hand. "I want to go and get a Christmas tree tomorrow. A real one to put in the barn for the Christmas party. Want to come?"

"I would love to come get a tree with you." She gave his hand a squeeze and then his words sunk in. He watched her eyes widen and she gasped as she turned to face him. "Did you just say Christmas party?"

He grinned.

She put her hands over her mouth. "Does this mean…?"

"It would be selfish of me to stop the town Christmas party. Everyone has the right to enjoy Christmas. The party isn't about me or my dad, it's about spending time with people."

"I'm so excited, I can't…I don't even know what to

say!"

"I have to tell you the barn hasn't been cleaned in like three years."

"Who cares? Cleaning is easy! And I'm sure the city council has Christmas decorations. We can do a potluck thing for the dinner and desserts. Your eyes are glazing over."

"Oh, sorry." He shook his head. "I was just trying to recall how we used to set it up. And you don't have to help me clean the barn."

Bell smiled. "Ever think maybe I want to spend time with you?"

"I'm beginning to catch onto that," he admitted. "Considering how much time we've spent together this week." He brought her hand to his lips and kissed the back.

"This is so new to me," she said.

"Me too." He stopped the truck in front of her bakery.

"I'll see you tomorrow night, then, to chop trees," she said as she climbed out of his truck.

"I'll see you at nine in the morning!" he grinned.

"Well look who's a morning person," Bell giggled.

The next day, he picked her up at nine in the morning, right on the dot. Bell stepped out of the house in tall winter boots, snow pants, a coat, gloves, and beanie hat with a pompom on top.

"You look cute." He opened the truck door for her.

"Thanks. You look handsome as well. So where are you taking me?"

Secret Santa

"Our secret tree-hunting spot we used to go to as kids." Drake climbed into the driver's seat, and they headed out toward the mountain.

"You do know Christmas is a week away? Won't the tree wilt by then?"

"It's not a flower," he explained. "As long as you keep it watered, it should stay pretty spry. I thought you used to have real trees growing up?"

She nodded. "All I remember is constantly sweeping the floor because the needles fell…"

"Yeah, there is that."

They continued down the road, and Bell's smile stayed on her lips. "I love being in the forest," she said. "I really should come out here more often. Look at how beautiful everything is, covered in snow."

"Where did you put your winter wonderland painting?" he asked.

She laughed and shook her head. "I hung it in my room. Though, yours should be in a museum or art exhibit. It was incredible. Where did you put it?"

"I hung it in the bar, actually. On the far left wall. Well, right as you're coming in."

"Good! I'm glad you've got it on display. You should have more of your work up, you know."

"Meh."

"What do you mean, meh? I think you're an amazing painter."

He shrugged. To him, it didn't look any more spectacular than anyone else's painting.

Bell gave him a look and shook her head. "You just don't realize it. I'm telling you the truth. You could do that in your spare time instead of learning to play the guitar."

"I guess I could." He turned them down a road hidden between the trees.

Bell leaned forward. "Are you sure we aren't going to get stuck in the snow?"

"I put chains on my tires before we came. I know what this baby girl can handle." He patted his dashboard, earning a chuckle from Bell. "I've had her for a while."

"Your truck is a she?"

"Do you not call your car he or she?"

Bell shook her head.

Drake pursed his lips. "Huh. I thought everyone did. Ah, here it is." He stopped the truck and grinned. "Just through those trees is the perfect area. See, the trick is to find one with a lot of needles so it's nice and full." He climbed out of the truck and grabbed his handsaw, hatchet, and axe.

"Can I carry anything?" she offered.

"Sure." He handed her the saw. "You never did this with your parents?"

"Nope. Like I said, I'm pretty sure our trees just got delivered. I don't have any memories of chopping down the tree or dragging it to the car or anything. This will be a new memory." She looked at him from the corner of her eyes.

"I like making new memories."

Secret Santa

"What made you want to host the Christmas party?"

He shrugged. "I guess you sort of changed my perspective this year. I started remembering all of the good times, which you said is what we should do around Christmas anyway. Yeah, there's pain. That won't go away. But neither will the good, if I don't push them away. And, I sort of called my mom."

Bell almost stopped walking. "You did?"

He nodded. "I invited her to come to the Christmas party, but they're going to her fiancé's family for Christmas Ever, but we're going to get together after Christmas."

Bell smiled bigger than ever and stomped through the snow. "I see a perfect tree for the Christmas party. See?" She pointed.

Drake followed her gaze and saw a plump, six-foot-tall, full tree. "Absolutely perfect. Okay, we're going to take that saw and get underneath, to the very bottom. We're going to saw off the bottom branches and that will give us room to reach the hatchet or axe down there." He crouched and started pushing the snow away from the base of the tree.

Bell got right down on her hands and knees next to him and started helping.

"I can't think of many girls that would do this, you know?" He looked over at her.

"Well, I'm not just any girl." She nodded with confidence. "And we're making new memories, remember?"

He chuckled. "I just...yeah."

She grinned. "You got something..." She pointed.

"How?" He frowned.

But instead of Bell reaching out to get whatever it was off, she rubbed a handful of snow across his face, then burst out laughing and tried to crawl around the tree

"Oh, you little..." Drake scrambled after her.

"No! It was a joke!" she laughed.

He snagged her ankle and tried to start tickling her but couldn't really get to her through her thick winter clothes. "I'll get you back later. Just you wait."

Bell giggled and took off her glove. "I'm sorry." She tried to wipe off some of the snow. "I shouldn't have done that. It was just so perfect."

"Yes, it was." He helped her back to her feet and they set to work getting the tree cut down.

She took turns with Drake sawing off the lowest branches, and then Drake chopped at the trunk with the axe until it finally started to tip. Bell balanced it while he finished, and then Drake dragged it by the trunk back to his truck. They set it on a net Drake had brought, wrapped it up, and placed it carefully in the bed of the truck.

Bell dusted off her hands. "Now we get to set it up and decorate it!"

They got back to the tavern and Drake scratched the back of his neck. "We have to clean up the barn before it can go in, which will take us all day, so maybe we should clean tomorrow and then move it in. Until then, I'll have it sit in the dining room of the tavern."

Secret Santa

"That's a great plan. Tomorrow morning, Aaron is coming to my bakery. He's the kid that won the taste-testing thing last Saturday. He's only going to be there for about an hour, and then I'll come over. I've got to call Mrs. Flowers too, she's got to start getting all of the decorations out of storage."

He patted Bell's knee. "You get on that."

She pecked his cheek. "Today was fun. I can't wait to see what that barn looks like all decked out for the party."

"Then I'll see you tomorrow," Drake said.

CHAPTER ELEVEN

Bell opened her door to Drake, wearing old jeans, a grubby Star Wars t-shirt with a green paint splotch on the shoulder, and sneakers. He'd come to pick her up to get an early start on cleaning out the barn.

Drake grinned. "Awesome shirt." He led her outside. "Next date, we're binge watching the whole series."

"Except, let's just skip to the good ones."

Drake laughed and held the front door open for her. "I think I can handle that."

"I didn't realize you were a fan." Bell walked out to Drake's truck parked in her driveway.

"Of course. Who doesn't love Star Wars?" He grabbed her door and opened it before she could.

"You didn't tell me it was a favorite when I asked."

He snorted. "I just assumed it was a given."

A few minutes later, after parking his truck at the Red Dragon, Drake unlocked the door to the barn. Not sure what reaction Bell would give him, he held his breath as the doors slowly swung open.

The hinges groaned softly, and Bell stepped in, holding two dust pans and two brooms. The barn was massive—

Secret Santa

the perfect gathering place. Drake and his dad hadn't built it to serve the purpose of a barn, but to be a place for celebrating events. The loft only filled half of the upper part of the barn, with a staircase immediately to the right of the door leading up. Three wide, wooden columns stood in a row on the right, and a row of four on the left. With the windows shuttered, the place looked gloomy, and for a moment Drake wondered if this would work.

He looked nervously at Bell, wondering what was running through her mind, but her eyes were sparkling, undoubtedly already imagining what it would look like covered in garland and glistening with lights. He cleared his throat. "I was thinking we could put rows of tables on the left side for the food. Right here by the door we could get racks for people's coats, and back there we can have the DJ set up."

"We could set more tables up in the loft, and a few down here for people to eat," Bell suggested, walking right in and heading for the back of the barn. "This place is amazing!" She spun in a circle, kicking up dust around her feet as she did so.

Drake relaxed. How could she be like this so consistently? So happy no matter what? "Hey, how about I turn on some music?"

"Only if it's Christmas," she grinned.

"Of course. I know you by now." He walked to the wall on the left and plugged in the Bluetooth speaker he'd brought from the kitchen. He opened up his music app on his phone and Christmas music started, kicking off the day with "Sleigh Ride." "I'm going to open the shutters and get the furnace turned on. It might take me a minute because the old thing hasn't been turned on in a long while and it might be all frozen up."

Bell tapped her feet, swaying left and right to the beat of the music. "Or two! Come on, it's lovely weather for a sleigh ride together with you," she sang.

Drake grinned. He could watch her all day. But they didn't have time for that. He quickly walked around the barn, opening the shutters and locking them open with the hooks he'd personally put up. It had been his own idea, which he was now grateful for. Surprisingly, the furnace started without any problems, and Drake returned inside to see Bell had already swept a good quarter of the floor already.

He grabbed his own broom and walked over to her. He bumped her hip with his own. "Hey, I'm sweeping here."

"We aren't going to have a hockey match over the dust," she laughed.

"Now that would be some story."

She chuckled. "You must have had some great memories in here."

He looked up and around. "Yeah, we did. We'd use it for Thanksgiving, Christmas dinner, of course our town Christmas party, birthdays, stuff like that. Dad used to rent it out too."

"That's a great way for you to get extra income!" Bell smacked his arm.

"Ow. Who are you, The Hulk?"

Secret Santa

She rolled her eyes, smiling wider. "It wouldn't hurt."

"Yeah, it's just sometimes a mess to clean up." He shrugged.

"Please Come Home for Christmas" came on, and Drake set the broom down. He held out his hands. "May I have this dance?"

Bell hesitated.

For a second, he thought she was going to say no, but she rested her broom on the ground and stepped over it. Her cheeks were pink—she was adorable when she blushed. He took her right hand with his left and rested his right hand on her lower back.

"You know how to dance for real? Because I don't," she said.

"Only a little bit. I took a ballroom class in high school, but that was forever ago." He pulled her close and swayed with her to the music. "You're doing great," he said softly.

Bell stared up at him.

Drake realized something he hadn't before. Bell felt perfect to him. There, in his arms, he imagined what it would be like knowing her forever. He had noticed how beautiful she was, but always thought she was way out of his league. Her constant happiness made him assume he was too gloomy for her. But something about being with Bell felt right, felt good. She made him happy, made him want to be better, made him actually want to listen and dance to Christmas music. He wasn't going to get on a knee and propose, but he really wanted to give the two of them a shot. Even with them in grungy clothes, covered in dust, dancing in the dim barn, all he wanted to do was stay in this moment.

The song ended, and Bell went to pull away.

Drake held onto her and lifted her chin. "Bell…"

"Yes?" she answered softly.

He leaned in to kiss her and his phone rang. He closed his eyes in annoyance.

Bell leaned back. "You better get that. It might be someone important."

"I'm sorry." He pulled out his phone. "What?"

"Oh, Drake! This is Mrs. Flowers, I just wanted to thank you indefinitely from the bottom of my heart—all of our hearts, really—for letting us host this party at your barn this year!"

Drake looked at Bell and pointed to the phone while Mrs. Flowers kept talking. "It's Mrs. Flowers," he whispered. "She's thanking me."

Bell laughed and picked up her broom to keep sweeping.

"Hey, Mrs. Flowers," he interrupted. "Would you mind taking charge of getting decorations?"

"Oh, we've already got them, darling."

"That's great. You can start setting up Monday, if you want to. Bell and I are here now at the barn cleaning it up."

"Bell is there? Can I talk to her?"

Drake looked at Bell, but she quickly shook her head. "We're actually pretty busy. Call me if you need to later, okay? Thanks."

"Oh, okay. Bye!"

Drake hung up and put his phone in his pocket. He started laughing. "Every time we get close. Are we doomed to be interrupted at every chance?"

Bell shrugged. "Possibly?"

"All I Want for Christmas is You," came on the speaker. Drake watched Bell. He could have let it go, but no. He'd come close to kissing her a few different times now, and he wasn't going to lose the perfect opportunity. He walked over, pulled the broom out of Bell's hand, making it fall, then put one arm around her waist and dipped her low.

"Not this time." He leaned down and pressed his lips to hers.

Bell wrapped her arms around his neck just as he was about to pull away and held him closer.

Finally, he let her to her feet and looked down at her. "Maybe that wasn't the ideal situation. Was it?"

"Are you kidding? You just dip-kissed me, that's every girl's dream. Especially as a first kiss." She laughed, her cheeks the adorable red color.

He grinned proudly. "We need more slow songs to keep us distracted."

"Then this barn will never be ready!"

"Then I'll get to spend more time with you."

Bell's entire face and neck turned red this time. She giggled and grabbed her broom.

"Alright, no more distractions," he said.

But the rest of the day they spent plenty of time being distracted by dancing—Drake even danced with the broom one time—until finally, the barn was clean. They had to sweep a couple of times to make sure they got all of the dust, and then they wiped down the columns, loft, and railings to make sure all of it was good to go and dust free. The sun had just begun to set when they stood in the doorway, covered in dust and smiling like fools.

"Dinner?" Drake asked.

"Don't say we're going out, because I don't have time to shower and get all pretty."

"Who are you kidding?" he scoffed. "You're pretty no matter what. But I sort of wanted to take you somewhere we don't usually go. You okay with that? I'm not pretty either."

She grinned. "That's because you're handsome."

"I thought I was only kind of handsome."

"That was before you kissed me," she laughed. "Now you're really handsome." She stepped closer, clearly hesitating before wrapping her arms around him. "I'm thinking sushi."

His eyes lit up. "I love sushi! There's a great place about twenty minutes from here."

"That sounds perfect!" She let go of him and grabbed the broom. "Come on, Drake!" She pointed forward with the broom and headed out the door.

Drake chuckled and flipped the lights off, then secured the door behind them as they left.

After they decided they really were too dirty to just

show up at a nice sushi house, Drake changed, and drove Bell to her house to change. Then, they were on the road out of town to enjoy another dinner date together.

Drake cleared his throat softly. "You know how I invited my mom to the Christmas party?"

"Yeah."

"Did I mention she's engaged to the guy from last Thanksgiving?"

"No…is that bad?" she asked.

He shrugged. "I never even gave the guy a chance last Thanksgiving, but it turns out they're engaged now. I told my mom that was great. As long as she's happy, that's all that matters, right? And my brother, Dustin, said Brad's actually a great guy and he really does seem to love Mom."

Bell put her hand on his arm. "That's good. Especially since she's your mom."

"She told me she thinks my dad hand-picked him."

She smiled. "That's sweet." Bell's brows shifted, and she pulled the small book from her pocket. She never seemed to go anywhere without it. Sometimes he wasn't sure if she got a little too involved in people's lives, but she seemed well-rounded enough.

From the corner of his eye, he saw her flip through the pages, stopping at one of them. She hummed a moment, then closed the book and put it in her pockets, the same perplexed look on her face.

"You alright?"

"Oh, fine," she quickly smiled. "I was just thinking

about someone."

"Care to elaborate?"

She paused and leaned forward. "Hey, there's a car up there. We should stop and help them."

Drake shifted his gaze forward and saw a car pulled onto the shoulder with their hazard lights blinking. "We can do that," he replied. Luckily, it wasn't snowing tonight, and the roads were nice and dry, but the air was bitter cold. When they got close enough, he pulled up behind the car but further off the shoulder, put on his own hazard lights, and looked at Bell. "Wait in the car."

She raised her eyebrow. "Seriously?"

"It's safer for you." He climbed out of the car, hearing her chuckle before he closed the door. He walked up to the passenger side and tapped on the window. Sitting inside was an elderly man, hands trembling as he tried to turn the engine over.

He looked at Drake when Drake knocked again.

He went to climb out, but Drake opened the door. "Stay inside of your car. How long have you been sitting here?"

"Oh, I don't know. Fifteen minutes? My car just started shaking and I pulled over and now she won't start."

Drake noted the inside of the car was no longer warm, and only served to protect the man from the chilly wind. "My name is Drake. I'm going to have you come sit in my truck while I look at your car, okay?"

"You don't have to do that."

"Sure I do," he smiled. "You need help, and I'm here

to help you." He closed the door, surprised at how much he sounded like Bell. He peeked around the car to watch traffic, then walked to the man's driver side door and opened it for him. "I'll help you out."

"That's very kind of you, young man." He placed one very gnarled, arthritis-ridden hand into Drake's, and Drake gently got him to his feet. "I'm glad my girlfriend spotted you. Well, she's a girl. My friend."

"Well, which is she? Just a girl or just a friend?" The man smiled.

"I'd like her to be more. We just barely started dating each other."

The man chuckled and tapped his nose.

Drake opened the passenger side of his truck, and Bell had already scooted over.

She gave them both a big smile. "Hello, sir! I'm Bell."

"My name is Lucas." The man turned to Drake and said. "I can see why you want her to be more. She's a keeper, Mr. Drake."

Drake glanced at Bell, this time feeling his own blush creep along the back of his neck. "Go on up there and I'll see if your car can be fixed." He helped Lucas into the car and closed the door. He shouldn't have told the old man his hesitation for his feelings for Bell, because now he was alone in the truck with her and they would probably talk about their relationship. Who was he kidding? Bell could hold her own.

Drake returned to the car and climbed into the driver side to turn the key over, just enough to turn on the lights and see the dashboard. The car was out of gas. Luckily, that would be an easy fix, but they'd have to drive a little while to get the gas. He took out the keys, kept the flashers on, but locked the doors before returning to the truck and climbing in.

"Looks like you're out of gas, Lucas," he said.

Lucas frowned. "How's that possible? I just filled her up…oh…I don't know how long ago."

Bell wiggled into the middle seat and buckled. "We were talking about his wife, Mary. He was on his way to get her a special treat, so they could eat it after dinner tonight."

Drake smiled. "If you don't mind, Bell, I think we should take him to get gas, then to get his special treat before we get him back to his car and make sure he gets home safe."

"I don't mind at all."

"We'll be late for dinner."

She grinned with a shrug. "Who cares?"

Drake couldn't help but lean over and kiss her cheek. Whatever magic spell Bell had put over him, he liked it. "Lucas, what's this special treat you were getting for your sweetheart?"

He sighed. "It's silly, really. She likes those little peppermints candies that look like kisses, but I can only ever find those at the grocery store off the 210th Street exit. They probably have them closer to home, but that's the only place I know of."

"Well, we happen to be pretty close to that. Let's get

Secret Santa

you gas and then we'll head out to get her some treats."

They drove a few miles and exited the freeway, stopping at the first gas station they came to. Drake bought two five-gallon containers and filled them up with gas. He set them both in the bed of his truck, secured them with a half-frozen bungee, and climbed back into the cab of his truck. With some verbal guidance—and a lot of patience—they finally found the grocery store with the treats.

"I'm sorry about that," Lucas said as they parked. "I'm used to being the one behind the wheel."

"Don't worry," Bell said. "We aren't doing anything more important tonight than helping you out."

"It was really disheartening, you know? To see all those cars just driving by and not one stopping to help. I grew up in a different time. Your dad must have raised you right, Dirk."

Drake smiled. "That he did, sir."

They all climbed out of the car and walked into the grocery store.

"My wife and I met just before I was deployed. She was the nurse that gave me all my shots. When I got injured, she was there. She'd just been stationed."

"Which war?" Bell asked.

"World War Two. I got shot in the side and then a grenade went off that left me deaf in my left ear." Lucas pointed to his ear, showing the deformity. "But you know romances don't last between nurses and marines in the field. I was sent back out, since I healed so fast, and I didn't think I'd ever see her again. But that time I was smart." He grinned. "I got her name and address and we started writing each other the whole rest of the time I was deployed. When I got home, I stopped by my parents and said hi, and told them I was going to marry this girl. They thought I was nuts, but I left right away and drove all the way to Kansas for her." Lucas beamed.

Drake grinned. "How did you know after only a short time?"

He shook his head. "There was just something about her that made me want to be better. She was kind, always soft spoken, even to our kids growing up when they came into her nicely mopped kitchen covered in mud with a turtle in their hands," he chuckled.

"But you didn't date…or court long."

He shook his head. "We talked through our letters. That was good enough for me."

They'd finally made it to the candy aisle, and Lucas grabbed the clear box of signature candy. He glanced at one more container, then turned to go.

Bell gently put her hand on his arm. "What treat do you like?"

"We came for my wife. And I don't got that much to repay you anyway for your gas and mine."

Drake laughed. "I'm not making you pay me back for the gas, Lucas. And I'm not letting you pay for your treats either. Choose a box for you."

Lucas looked between Drake and Bell, tears coming to his eyes. "Heaven sent, you were," he said softly. "Mary asked about the treats, I was supposed to get them this morning, and then I misplaced our cash envelope that we use for food and didn't know how I was gonna pay for it. Thank you."

"Your treat?" Bell asked, gesturing.

"I love chocolate covered raisins," he chuckled.

Bell grabbed a box and walked by Lucas's side toward the cash registers. "Tell me more about you and your kids."

Drake watched them. He'd always loved watching people, but Lucas had said something that stirred Drake's heart. Bell made him want to be better, he'd realized that already. Bell was sweet. And while they hadn't written letters back and forth, he'd seen her actions throughout the community for the past two years and had mingled with her enough to know what type of person she was. Whether he could definitively say he was going to marry her or not, Drake didn't know, but he did know one thing: he sure wanted this relationship to last.

Drake paid for the treats and took as much cash out as the cashier would allow—$100—and handed it to Lucas. "This should at least help get you some groceries until you can find your money envelope. And if you need more, tell me before we drop you off."

Lucas had to pull a hanky from his pocket and blow his nose. "I don't know what makes you two so kind. You don't even know me."

"I don't have to," Drake grinned. "It's the right thing to do. And honestly, I'm glad we had the chance to meet you."

They arrived back at Lucas's car, and Drake made him sit in the truck until he put one entire gas can, and almost all of the next into the car. When that was done, he started Lucas's car and made sure it was running before he let Lucas get in.

Lucas set the bag of treats on the seat beside him. "Thank you, young man."

Drake leaned down to look through the window. "You just be safe out there, Lucas. And really, if you need anything you call." He tapped Lucas's pocket. He'd written down his number on a scrap piece of paper and put it in Lucas's breast pocket with the $100 bill.

Lucas gave a shaky salute. "Yes, sir."

"Do you want me to drive you home? Or Bell? I hate you trying to pull back onto this busy highway."

"I got it. I'm old, but I'm not too old yet."

Drake laughed. "Alright. Well, you have a very Merry Christmas."

"And you too!"

With that, Drake left Lucas's side and returned to his truck. He glanced in his rearview mirror before pulling out enough, so cars could see him, and then Lucas pulled in front, slowly gaining speed until he was safely on the freeway.

Bell reached out and took Drake's hand.

"I'm really happy we had the chance to meet him," Drake reiterated. "I know we're both starving, but that was worth it. Wasn't it?"

Secret Santa

"Do you really need to ask?" She leaned back in the chair, smiling big. "I love hearing stories of how people meet their significant other. Isn't it romantic?"

"Do you remember how we met?" he asked.

"The first time?"

He nodded.

She smiled. "Yes, it wasn't really the best way to meet someone."

"I remember you walking into the tavern," he said, keeping his eyes on the road. "Dad had just died a couple of days earlier, and I was standing in the tavern just looking around. You walked in wearing a red coat, a knitted elf hat, and you looked…well, you looked ridiculous in such a gloomy place." He smiled and glanced at her. "But I vividly remember thinking how beautiful you were and wondering why you'd come into my dad's tavern of all places. And then you asked me about the empty store on the corner and if I knew who owned the building and how you could buy it, and you told me your silly plan to open a gourmet bakery, and I thought, 'There's no way this chick is going to make it.' I figured you had big, preposterous plans. And look at you now."

Bell smiled. "And you were still gracious even after the loss of your father."

"I haven't always been kind to you. And for that, I'm really sorry."

"It's hard to imagine other people can be happy when your world is falling apart."

He nodded. "But Lucas was right. I think there's

something very special about you, Bell."

Her cheeks turned the adorable shade of red he loved, and he smiled.

Secret Santa

Chapter Twelve

Bell sat on her couch Sunday afternoon, her book open on the coffee table in front of her. It was amazing how much easier this year was than the previous. People in the community wanted to get involved in serving their neighbors and had come up with ideas all on their own of how to help their neighbors. Bell hadn't even been the one to help Dorothy Erickson. She knew Dorothy worked at the post office, and things at work had been slammed and workers had quit, but it was stuff going on at home with her kids that made things difficult.

Bell had driven by one evening to see if perhaps she could help, but when she pulled up, she noticed someone left three large garbage bags stuffed with gifts on Dorothy's doorstep. Bell had arrived just as Dorothy opened her door and pulled them in, tears in her eyes. Dorothy had looked around, hoping to catch a glance of who could have done such a generous thing, but there was no sign of people around. Even Bell had missed them.

This Sunday morning, only one name was left in the book: Nancy. And no matter how hard Bell tried to imagine ways to help her, she kept getting distracted by

Secret Santa

thoughts of Drake.

Perhaps all it would take to get her out of the Spirit List would be to invite her and her family to the town's Christmas party. Time was running out, as the Christmas party was Thursday evening.

Bell's alarm buzzed, and she quickly closed her book and grabbed her keys so she could head to church. What she hadn't expected was to arrive and walk into the foyer to see Drake standing there in his suit, talking to various people. Bell stopped and stared at him.

He must have felt her gaze because he looked over his shoulder and smiled at her. He had trimmed his beard, so it was a lot smaller, much cleaner, and his hair was nicely combed. "Hey, you're staring."

"I just...didn't expect to see you here," she fumbled.

"You and everyone else," he laughed. He walked over and kissed her on the cheek. "I figured today of all days might be worth coming. It's the Christmas program, right?"

She nodded. He took her hand and Bell felt the familiar butterflies take flight. "I'm really glad you're here. I'm just warning you, I may cry. I love Christmas music."

"I know. I hope you brought some extra tissues," he winked.

Bell held up her purse, and they both chuckled as they entered the chapel.

Indeed, the Christmas program proved to be special. Drake and Bell sat, holding hands, and singing together. Bell had never felt more complete than she did that day.

This was what she'd wanted for years: to not be alone, to have someone to share the magic of Christmas with, to have someone just spend time with.

"What are you doing for the rest of the day?" Drake asked as the congregation left the chapel.

"I was going to stop by home to grab some treats, and then I was going to head over to Nancy and her family to see if they would be interested in attending the Christmas party."

He nodded. "And what are they struggling with this year?"

Bell grinned. He hadn't even hesitated, and he wasn't looking at her like she was nuts. "That, I actually don't know."

"Wait, you don't have anything written down in your book?"

She shook her head. "Not on them. I just know something feels off. I haven't seen them at church in a few weeks, and Nancy has been picking up as many shifts at work as she can."

"Cool. Want me to drive?"

Bell stared at him. "You really want to come?"

"Of course. Like you said, any amount of time I can spend with you, I love."

She smiled and nodded. "I'll meet you at my place, then!"

"Sounds good to me." He kissed her on the cheek and walked to his truck.

Bell sat on the front seat of her car, smiling at the

ceiling. "He makes my heart so happy." She ran her thumb absently across the spine of the book in her pocket, then started her car and drove home.

She arrived first and had gone in to grab the treats from the counter but had a feeling in her gut that she needed more than just treats. But what else could she take? What else did they need? Bell sighed, silently berating herself for getting carried away with Drake when she should have been trying to learn the best way to help Nancy. Nancy was the last name on her list, and then she could finally return home.

Bell looked around her small kitchen. Maybe Nancy and her family needed a full meal, not just a treat. That's what people did when their neighbors were going through tough times, she'd seen it across multiple families. But without having prepared that ahead of time and Drake on his way over, she'd have to work fast.

She quickly pulled a deep bowl from her cupboard, another smaller bowl, and a large plate, and rested them all across the counter before her.

Drake knocked on her door.

"Just a minute!" she called.

She looked at each empty container and rubbed her hands together. "Alright, Bell. Magic." She moved her hands in a circle and gold glittery magic swept in circles around the bowls and across the plate. A steaming pile of potatoes appeared in the large bowl, while the smaller one filled with rich brown gravy. A honey-glazed, hot ham materialized on the plate, filling the kitchen with a delicious aroma. "Okay, you can come in!" she called, rushing to the pantry to grab the tinfoil.

"Wow…" Drake said as he walked into the kitchen. "That's a lot of food. I thought you said treats?"

"I meant meal and treats." She pressed the tinfoil around the edges of the items and tucked the potatoes in one arm, and the gravy in the other. Trying to grab the plate of treats as well, Bell had to step back when Drake snagged both the ham and plate of cookies before she could. "Thanks," she smiled.

"No problem." He waited for her to walk out the door first, then closed it and walked to his truck. "What made you want to cook her an entire meal if you didn't know she needed it?"

"I just felt like they might need it. I learned a long time ago to listen to that little voice in your head." She tapped her temple.

Drake climbed into the truck. "Well, it works for you, that's for sure. You tend to go all-out, don't you?"

She laughed. "Yeah, I do."

They drove over to Nancy's house, and Bell balanced the gravy on top of the potatoes so she could knock, then took a hold of if again it so it wouldn't fall.

Nancy's youngest, Phillip, answered. "Hi. Mom! It's for you!" he called, then took off running.

Nancy came out of a back room and stopped when she saw Bell and Drake standing with food. "Uh c-can I help you?" She came to her senses and walked over to them.

Bell held out the food. "I had a feeling you would need

this today. And we were wondering if you would like to come to the town Christmas party Thursday night."

"I didn't think it was happening this year."

"It wasn't going to," Drake said. "But I offered to let them use my barn like they used to, so it's happening."

Nancy smiled softly. "It's been a long time since we've been to that, or any community event. Please come in out of the cold." She waited for them to step inside before closing the door behind them. "Do you want to sit for a little bit?" Nancy walked to the couch and started moving piles of laundry.

"No, not at all," Bell said. "I mean, you really don't need to feel obligated to entertain us. We just came to invite you and bring you and your family some dinner. Is it enough?"

"Are you kidding? It's amazing," Nancy laughed. She motioned for them to put it on the empty table. "I really don't know how to thank you."

"Just come to the party," Bell grinned.

"We will see if Ty is up for it. Even being invited is wonderful," she smiled.

"Is he okay?" Bell prodded.

Nancy sighed and glanced at the stairs. "He's pretty sick right now with pneumonia, and he hasn't been able to go to school or anything for a while. It's really hit him hard."

"I'm sorry to hear that. Is there anything we can do?"

Nancy smiled again. "No. This was…this is wonderful. Did you want to stay and eat with us?"

Bell shook her head. "Have a wonderful Sunday with your family."

Nancy gave her a tight hug. "Really, thank you."

Bell grinned, and she and Drake left. "Well, that was easy!"

"Is it always that easy?" he asked.

"No. Sometimes people get mad and don't want your kindness." She waited while Drake opened her car door, and then climbed in. When he was back in the truck, she said, "How would you feel about going to Jamie's and playing games with her and Andrew?"

"You sure they want to be bugged?" he grinned.

She laughed. "I'm positive they'll be fine with it. Besides, what else will I do for the rest of the day?"

He shrugged. "You could hang out with me at the tavern. Wipe tables and listen to bad music. Help me come up with ideas of how else I can help with the Christmas party…" He made a face. "Yeah, none of that sounds fun. Want lunch before we go over there? Or do we arrive with the intention of picking their fridge?"

Bell pursed her lips. "Hmm. Let's raid their fridge."

Drake laughed, tilting his head back.

She loved that sound. He was laughing and smiling a lot more than he had in a few years, and Bell loved every minute of it. "Well, she *is* my best friend. Wouldn't you do that with Chris? Hey, maybe Chris and Heather would be interested in coming over to do games too!" She pulled out her phone. "Let me ask Jamie if that's okay." She stuck out her tongue and typed: *Drake and I are coming over for lunch and to play games. Mind if Chris and Heather come too?*

"How quick is she at responding?" he asked.

Bell's phone buzzed, and she held it up with a grin. "She's pretty quick with me." She looked down. "Alright, she said that sounds like fun! Go ahead and invite Chris and Heather. They're making sandwiches."

"I'm fine with that. As long as it's not turkey."

"You don't like it?"

"No way. Ham or grilled cheese."

"What about ham *and* grilled cheese?"

He tilted his head. "Nope. Just one or the other."

"You're picky."

He grinned. "Thanks."

They arrived, and Jamie and Andrew let them in. Shortly after, Chris and Heather arrived. Bell started helping Jamie make grilled cheese sandwiches and chunky tomato soup.

Chris cleared his throat. "We have a special announcement."

"Yeah? What's that?" Drake asked.

Chris looked at Heather with a huge smile. "Go on."

"I'm pregnant."

Drake's brows lifted quickly. "That's why she's been craving pasta!"

Chris chuckled at Drake's comment while everyone stepped forward to congratulate them.

Bell couldn't help but watch everyone, smiling like a fool, she was certain. This was the life she wanted. But something dawned on her in that moment. She didn't have a Christmas present for Drake. She'd been so busy thinking about so many others and just spending time with Drake, she hadn't thought about a present to give to him.

"Drake, come with me to pick a game," Andrew said, leading him away.

Bell leaned over to Jamie. "I need your help. I've got to find a painting Drake made for his dad. Apparently, it used to hang in the tavern?"

"Oh, I remember that…I think he painted it in high school, his senior year. Won some state contest with it too, if I remember correctly," Jamie said.

Heather nodded. "I remember seeing it on the street after his dad passed. I remember how sad I felt that it was out there, it was absolutely gorgeous."

"How do I discreetly ask people if they have it? And if anyone does, what are the chances they would part with it?" Bell asked.

Heather looked at Jamie. "What if Mister Toby took it?"

"Who is that?" Bell looked between them.

"Mister Toby runs the pawn shop," Jamie said. "If anyone took it, chances are it was him."

"What did I do?" Andrew asked as he sat back down, giving Jamie a peck on the lips.

"You stole my heart," she winked.

"You ladies are conspiring," he said knowingly.

Jamie raised her eyebrows at the girls. "Us? Never."

Drake sat beside Bell. "Alright, let's get this game

started. What are we playing?"

"Apples to Apples!" Heather said, pushing the piles of cards around.

Bell smiled at Drake. "I'm totally winning."

"I object to playing with Bell," he said, raising his hand. "She knows everything about everyone."

The group laughed while Bell gave him a playful nudge.

Chapter Thirteen

"Hello?" Drake answered, his phone against his ear. He had to step into the back to avoid the noise of the tavern. Dinner was actually busy.

"Drakey! It's Stephanie!"

"Steph! Wow, it's been a while!" He grinned. "How are you?"

"I'm doing okay. I know it's a little late to ask, but I can't get home for Christmas like I thought I would. I was supposed to fly out and all planes are grounded because of the storm. All of the other flights are completely booked."

"It's only the twenty-first," he said, glancing at the calendar by the office door.

"I know, but according to the airline, all other flights are booked. I plan on still pestering them, but if I have nowhere else to go, I want to at least be with some family. I guess I'm asking if you're okay if I come out and stay with you, possibly for Christmas?"

"Sure! I've still got that pull-out bed."

"Oh, don't tell me you're still living above that bar."

"It's a tavern," he corrected with a chuckle. "Hey, you can't argue with free. You okay with staying here? I'm sure there's probably a room at the hotel, if you'd prefer."

"Staying with you is definitely preferable," she laughed. "Thank you so much! I'll be out as soon as I can catch a taxi or something."

"Can't wait to see you. Bye." He hung up.

"Oooo who are you inviting to stay?" Chris grinned.

"Remember Stephanie?" he asked, changing out his bar rag.

"Oh yeah! She's the redheaded one, right?"

Drake nodded. "She can't get home for Christmas. At least, not yet, so she's going to stay here. Might be nice to have her help out a little with waiting tables. I had no idea this place could get this busy."

"Speaking of which." Chris set the last plate on a tray. "Here you go."

Drake slid it into his hands and hoisted it carefully into the air. "A part of me wants to stay this busy, another part is worried because we can't handle this with the two of us."

"So, you'll have to hire someone. Don't worry about that right now. Go!"

Drake walked out to the floor to deliver the food.

✻ ✻ ✻

Bell rushed down to Mr. Toby's antique shop. He sat behind the counter, arms folded over his large belly, and he was snoring softly. She walked over and knocked gently on the counter. "Mr. Toby?"

He snorted and lifted his head. "Huh? Oh. Hi." He stretched and straightened a little. "Whatcha needin'?"

"I'm looking for something and wonder if you could possibly have it. It's one of a kind, and handmade," she explained.

"What's that?"

"A dragon painting that used to hang in the Red Dragon Tavern."

He frowned, the wrinkles at the corners of his mouth making the frown even deeper. "Why you lookin' for it?"

"Oh, it's not for me! I'm actually trying to find it because…" She took a quick breath. "I really want to give it back to Drake for Christmas."

"Why dintcha say so in the first place?"

"So, you have it?" She grinned.

"No."

Bell's smile fell. "Any ideas where it could be? Or who could maybe remake it? I suppose his mother could have taken it…" she mumbled to herself. She patted the counter and stepped back. "Thank you anyway. Merry Christmas!"

Mr. Toby rubbed his moustache. "Hold up."

She stopped, her hand on the door. "Yeah?"

"You really wanna give him that picture?"

She nodded. "He brought it up a couple of different times, and said he wishes he'd never thrown it out."

Mr. Toby grunted as he pushed himself out of the well-worn folding chair. He pulled up his pants and walked through the door to the back room. "You comin'?" he called.

Bell hurried in after him. The room was organized chaos. To her right was a wall with shelves, and on those shelves were baskets each labeled with their contents: dishes, porcelain, toys, and more. To her left were stacks of furniture, and another row had pictures of varying sizes carefully stacked in a large rack.

Mr. Toby went to something hanging on the back wall wrapped in brown paper. "I spotted this on the street after his Pa died." He lifted it off the wall. "I wasn't gonna give it to you, because I was gonna wait and see if he ever came lookin' for it, but I guess you're as good as he is."

Bell smiled, her heart skipping. "This is going to be the best Christmas present ever."

He grinned, his moustache twitching, and held out the large painting. "Lemme know how it goes."

"If it goes well, I'm positive he will come and thank you for holding onto it for these couple of years. Merry Christmas!" She took the large picture, her excitement making her want to skip down the street and hand it to him right now.

Bell carefully wrangled it into the back seat of her car and took it home to wrap it in Christmas wrapping. After expertly wrapping two rows of paper to cover the whole thing, she wrapped ribbon around the seam, making it look like one giant piece of paper, and tied a beautiful bow on the front. She could only imagine Drake's face when he opened this gift and saw his painting.

Time to deliver it and help Drake with the decorations!

Again, her heart skipped. They were decorating the barn for the Christmas party. How could things get any better?

She reloaded it into her car, just as carefully as before, and climbed into her seat. She drove more cautiously than she ever had. She had to make sure the painting stayed balanced on the back seat. She had a pit of dread in her stomach that she would turn too sharply and it would hit the window and break the frame, or she would stop too suddenly and the picture would slip and the canvas would get punctured in a freak accident.

Finally, she arrived at Drake's tavern. She parked and hoisted the picture from the back of the car, safe and sound. Now she just needed to get it inside. Unfortunately, it was an awkward size, and she couldn't see her feet as she walked.

She gulped. "Please don't fall, Bell. Please don't fall," she chanted with careful steps. Her right foot slipped, she gasped, but the patch of ice was small, and her foot stopped against the dry cement. "Okay. Okay, Bell. Careful."

She got to the front door and stopped to open it. Looking through the window behind the wreath on the door, her heart froze. Drake was giving a beautiful woman a tight hug. She kissed him on the cheek. They were holding hands and talking, and Drake was smiling like they were…oh no. She had to be an ex. Why didn't Bell see this coming? Drake was happy again. Like Jamie had

Secret Santa

said just a couple of weeks ago, women in town liked Drake. He put his hand on her back and guided her to a seat at the bar.

Reality settled on Bell's shoulders. She'd been a fool. It would definitely be better for him to be interested in another human. Once he was out of her book, she would get to go home. That's how it was supposed to work. She never should have gotten so close.

Bell's heart sank, and a sharp pain made her nauseous. She'd grown to love everything about Owentown. Did she really have to leave after all the time she'd spent here?

She looked at the painting she still held awkwardly and bit her bottom lip. She managed to get the door opened, as slowly and silently as possible. She set the gift on the hardwood floor and slid it, so it rested against the wall, then quickly let the door close while she ran back to her car.

She tried to take deep breaths and calm down. Maybe the girl wasn't an ex. But why would he kiss her? Hold her hands?

Bell closed her eyes and rested her forehead against the steering wheel of her car. "I should call Jamie. She would know." She fumbled with her phone, finally getting it to call Jamie.

"What's up, Bell?" she asked.

"Does Drake have an ex?" she asked.

Jamie paused. "Of course he does. Everyone does. Why does it matter?"

"Does he have one with red hair?"

"I don't know. You're the one that stalks him, not me," she laughed.

But Bell didn't answer. She'd never seen that woman before.

Jamie suddenly became serious. "What's wrong? What happened?"

"Nothing. I just…" Tears stung her eyes and she tried looking up at the roof of her car to get herself to stop. She drew a breath to steady her nerves. "I'll be okay. Never mind," she said to Jamie.

"Bell—"

She hung up and stared at nothing in particular. Now wasn't the time for overreacting. Even if Rule #2 was: *Do not get personally involved in their lives for any reason other than to help them feel the magic of Christmas.* And she had broken that rule with Drake. She'd gotten very involved in his life, more than just setting him up with someone to love on Christmas. She had made him fall for her, of all people.

The alarm on her phone went off, telling her they were meeting to start decorating.

She exhaled. "You made a commitment," she said to herself. "You will go help them set up the decorations like you were supposed to. And you still have Drake's gift to give him. You can do this. Besides, you don't know who that was with Drake. She could just be an old friend. I don't know anything about him before I came here." She climbed out of the car. "Jamie said he was different in high school, and even if this girl is an ex, she could want nothing to do with him…"

For some reason, Bell hardly felt satisfied.

She walked to the barn sitting on the lot behind the tavern. She opened the door, expecting someone else to be there, but she was the first to arrive. Of course, she was also supposed to meet Drake inside the tavern, and he would probably be looking for her, but she needed more time to calm herself down. She knew better than to make assumptions.

She turned on the lights and looked around the empty space.

It was strange to think she and Drake had just been here Saturday, two days ago, and they'd had their first kiss. She held onto that moment, and the excited fluttering she still felt just thinking about it.

A moment later, she heard a car pull up, the car doors opening and closing with voices sounding in excitement. Bell walked to the door to open it and greet the decorating crew. Hopefully that was Mrs. Flowers with the decorations. Bell stopped with her hand on the door when she heard Drake's voice. "Go put your stuff upstairs, and then you can come help decorate."

"I might just take a shower and climb in bed. I was stuck at the airport all day." It was the woman's voice, and Bell peeked through the crack to confirm it was the same woman she'd seen inside the tavern just a moment ago.

"I'm fine with that," Drake said. "If you want to, you're welcome to join us."

"Maybe," she replied.

Bell hesitated to go outside, her heart pounding in her ears. He invited the woman to stay the night in his apartment? Was Bell really so blind she hadn't seen this coming at all? Had Drake been texting anyone frequently? Bell only saw him part of the day. Who was she to get so jealous so fast? She hadn't even met the woman yet!

The door suddenly opened the rest of the way and Drake jumped. "Bell! I thought you were going to meet me inside the tavern." He pointed his thumb over his shoulder.

"I, uh, just decided to come here first. Is that Mrs. Flowers?" She went to squeeze past Drake.

"Yeah it is." He slipped his arm around her. "You got a date for the Christmas party?"

She blushed, unable to resist. "I'm planning on coming, if that's what you mean. We should go help her." She tried to pull away.

"I think the first decoration we should put up is a mistletoe, right here."

Bell glanced up. "Then everyone who came into the door would have to kiss."

"That's the point." He grinned and leaned forward like he would kiss her.

"Hold on." Bell ducked under his arm. "Mrs. Flowers, let me help you with that!" She rushed to the car and hoisted a large box stuffed with garland.

"That needs to go along the entire loft on the railing," Mrs. Flowers instructed. "They light up, so make sure they all plug into each other."

Secret Santa

"I can handle that. I was thinking, we talked about the loft being used for the tables people can sit at to eat, but what if we made it an area for the kids? Set up some child-sized tables, get crayons and coloring pages, stuff to decorate cookies, those kinds of things?"

Mrs. Flowers tapped her round chin. "That's not a bad idea. I bet Shauna has some resources. I'll give her a call while you get that started."

Bell turned and almost ran into Drake. "Excuse me," she said.

He reached out to take the box.

"Grab the lights. I think those need to go around the pillars." Bell stepped around him and carried the large box up the stairs and dropped it in the middle of the floor. She wiped off the front of her shirt and leaned over the railing. "Do we have zip ties?"

"I have some," Drake called back, carrying two boxes of lights. He set them at the base of one of the pillars, then trotted up the stairs. "Are you okay?"

"I'm fine," she shrugged.

"I brought a speaker!" someone downstairs announced.

"Turn something on!" another voice laughed.

Mrs. Flowers cleared her throat. "As long as it's not too loud. Oh Henry, I'm so glad you're here! We need some ladders to get the lights wrapped around these pillars."

Bell had started to untangle the garland and started laying it out to see if there was enough to frame the loft.

Drake crouched. "Want to hold and I'll put on the zip

ties?"

"Sure." Bell plugged two strands together.

Drake reached out and waved a hand in front of her face. "You sure you're okay?"

She blinked and finally looked at him. She put on a smile. "Of course, I'm fine. It's just been a long day, and I've got a headache. I'm not feeling very well." It wasn't entirely a lie. Her head was still reeling with the prospect Drake had a woman in his apartment as they spoke. She really wanted to ask, but how could she? What would she say?

"Do you need to go home and rest? We can handle things. Besides, we're only doing part of the decorations tonight. We still have to set up the tables tomorrow, finish the decorating, and then you'll spend the next day baking and getting treats ready for the party, right? That's how you roll?" He rubbed his hand over her back.

"No, I don't think I need to leave yet."

Drake took one end of the garland. "If you don't want to, I'd love it if you stayed. Where do we start this?"

"It needs to start at the bottom of the stairs. Which end do you have?"

"The one with the plug." He held it up.

"Good." She stood. "I think there's an outlet on the wall down here." She trotted down the stairs and found the plug against the wall. The cord for the garland was just long enough they could plug it in and the end lined up with the beginning of the railing.

Drake turned his body, the zip ties in a bag at his hip.

Secret Santa

He grinned. "Go ahead and get one, I've got the garland nice and steady."

Bell took a zip tie and secured the first section, and then they moved up the stairs.

"So how was your day other than busy?" he asked.

"It was alright. I got a lot baked."

"Help anyone today?"

She felt his eyes on her. "I tried," she answered.

"Well, that was vague."

"I don't know yet if it helped." She tied the last tie at the top of the stairs and grabbed another piece of garland to plug into the previously placed one.

Drake reached out and gently grabbed her wrist. "You're not acting like yourself," he said in a low voice. "What's going on?"

She finally looked at him, really looked at him. For the past couple of days, just the mere touch of his hand made her heart skip, and the smile on his face made her forget what she wanted to say, but this time, she pulled away.

"I think you're right. I think I should go home. I'll be back tomorrow to help set up the tables and chairs. Morning or evening?" She stood and started down the stairs.

"Six tomorrow night. You need me to drive you home?"

She heard him following. "No, I'll be fine. See you tomorrow." She walked past Mayor Owens and Mrs. Flowers, and fled to her car, leaving Drake standing alone in the entrance of the barn.

Drake stared after Bell. To say he was confused only touched the iceberg. The day before they had enjoyed the day together at church, playing games, just being with each other. He'd been looking forward all day to seeing her again. Why did she all of a sudden pull away and leave?

"Did you see this, Drake?" Henry called. He turned and saw the man propping up a beautifully wrapped gift. "It was inside and has your name on it."

Drake walked over and looked at the tag. "It's from Bell…" He frowned. "I'll go put it back in the tavern so it's out of the way, thanks." He carried it in through the back door and stared at it. He had an inkling what it could be—though he had no idea how she could have found it. He let out a heavy sigh and rubbed the back of his neck. "What is going on?" he mumbled.

A part of him really wanted to chase after her and demand to know why she would leave a present and walk off looking upset, but another part of him wanted her to give her whatever space she needed so things would go back to normal.

The second thought won.

Drake returned to the barn and settled into the tasks. He finished the garland and then climbed onto a ladder to help Henry wrap the lights around the pillars, hook the extension cords to the overhead rafter, hide the cords behind more garland, and finally, after several hours of decorating, the barn was mostly finished.

Mrs. Flowers patted him on the arm. "You have no idea how grateful everyone will be to celebrate here again. Tables and chairs arrive tomorrow at six o'clock. We will set them up on this side with the long, thin tables against the wall for the food and treats. Shauna has asked the school to let us borrow some child-sized tables and chairs for the loft, and she will be bringing coloring books, a few easels, and whatever else kids need to stay entertained." She grinned and looked up at Drake. "This is going to be the best Christmas ever."

"I sure hope so," he sighed.

"How is your mother?" She seemed hesitant to ask.

He smiled softly. "She's doing alright. She's engaged to someone, and I invited them to come to the Christmas Eve party. We'll see if she shows."

"It's amazing that you can lose track of someone just because they move away," she said aloud. "We used to be good friends, your mother and I. When she moved, we used to talk on the phone, and then it became less and less, and then we just got busy..." She sighed. "Hardly an excuse. I need to go and give her a call and catch up some." She patted Drake on the back as she walked away. "Thank you again, Drake!"

Drake turned off all of the lights and locked the door before heading upstairs to his apartment.

Stephanie was sprawled on his bed sideways,

munching popcorn and watching a Christmas movie of some kind. "Hey!" she greeted. "Want to grab me a beer?" she grinned.

"No, I'm tired." He sat down in the armchair with a groan and kicked off his shoes.

"How did decorating go?"

"Awesome. It's really going to look great."

"And your girlfriend?" She grinned.

He rolled his eyes. "We've only been dating a couple of weeks, depending on how you look at it. I haven't actually asked her to be my girlfriend."

Stephanie propped herself up on her elbow. "You really like her."

He nodded. "I'm not sure how she feels about me, though. I mean, yesterday we had a great time with our friends, but tonight she barely talked to me, wouldn't hardly look at me, and then all of a sudden left saying she was sick. She never misses out on the opportunity to do anything for Christmas. And to top it off, she had a gift for me she just left without even mentioning it. Something's not right." He sighed and rubbed his hand over his face.

"You've done something to make her mad."

"What did I do?"

She shrugged. "Clearly, Bell is mad at you. Women aren't good at being subtle." She sat up. "Did she try and call you? Maybe a text and you didn't respond? Did you make a comment while playing games yesterday you didn't mean?"

Drake pinched his brows, trying to remember anything.

Secret Santa

"Nothing stands out," he finally said. He mentally went through the day again. "No, nothing. Do girls really hold onto stuff like that?"

Stephanie raised her eyebrow. "Like you should be one to talk about holding onto stuff."

"What are you talking about?" he asked, but he knew the answer. He didn't need her to answer, so he stood to get changed. "I suppose this means you've claimed my bed for the night?"

"Eww, no. Give me some extra sheets and I'll sleep on the couch." She hopped off the bed. "I really can't believe you're living above your dad's bar. I remember when this used to just be an attic stuffed full of boxes, and he had a desk set up right there."

"Remember that one time we got in trouble because we found someone's cigarettes and we wanted to see if smoking really would kill us?" he chuckled.

Stephanie laughed. "It almost killed me. Man, my dad was so mad. Those were the best summers, you know?"

"I wish Uncle Rod had let you guys just move out here."

"We said that every year we came," she laughed.

Drake handed her the sheets and a pillow. "I know you're going to miss Christmas with your family, but I'm really glad you were able to make it out here."

"Me too." She smiled and carried the bedding to the couch and started getting it ready.

Drake changed into pajamas, then looked down at his phone. He quickly sent a text message to Bell: *I hope*

you're feeling better. I can't wait to see you tomorrow! <3
He chewed his bottom lip, deleted the heart and put in a smiley face. He hit send and walked back into the bedroom.

"You know what this place needs? One of those little gas fireplaces." Stephanie had bundled up on the couch and hunkered down.

"It's not that cold." He turned the temperature up, turned out the lights, and climbed into bed.

"It would make it cozier."

Drake chuckled. "Probably. But it's not like I spend a lot of time in here anyway." He plugged in his phone, glancing at it one last time to see if Bell had texted back.

She hadn't.

"Well, in the morning I can make you breakfast," Drake grunted, finally snuggling into the warmth of his blankets. "And then I imagine you'd want to run around and say hi to people you haven't seen in a while."

She hummed. "Sounds fun."

Drake closed his eyes, his mind still on Bell. He could only hope tomorrow would be better.

Secret Santa

CHAPTER FOURTEEN

Bell shuffled into Jamie's bookstore, bundled up against the cold, and sat down with a mug of cocoa in her hands. She'd gone out of her way to the coffee shop to get a to-go cup, so she wouldn't have to see Drake or pretend to be happy when going to Betty's. Of course, she could have just made her own at home, but she had been hoping by getting out, she might feel less depressed.

Jamie was somewhere in the back when Bell pulled out the Christmas book. She aimlessly flipped through the pages, working her way backward toward the beginning when she spotted something she never could have imagined: her own name was written in the book.

"What does this mean?" she mumbled.

"It's the meaning of life."

Jamie's voice made Bell jump and she quickly slammed her book shut. "You scared me!"

Jamie laughed. "I'm so sorry, I just couldn't resist!" She walked around the counter and set a small box down. "You don't look like you're feeling well…" Jamie eyed her. "What happened after you got off the phone with me yesterday? Did Drake do something?"

Secret Santa

Bell sighed heavily and shrugged. "I think Drake has an ex staying with him. While I was inside of the barn, I overheard Drake tell her to go up into his room and leave her bags."

"You're sure this woman wasn't his mom?"

She rolled her eyes and looked at Jamie. "I'm not stupid. She's young, for starters, and just absolutely gorgeous." She sighed again. Her phone played sleigh bells, meaning she got a text.

Jamie raised her eyebrows expectantly.

Bell knew it was probably Drake, he'd texted her before she'd tried to fall asleep, and was probably texting her a good morning message, or something.

"Bell Winter, I am shocked by you."

"Excuse me?"

"Look at you! You're sitting here in my bookstore, sulking! I have never known you to sulk. You need to go talk to him. I'm positive you're reading more into this than you should be."

She shook her head. "I'll talk to him when I know what to say."

"Just ask him who the girl is that came last night. Or go see him this morning and when you run into her, ask her who she is!"

Bell glanced at the clock. "Right. Well, I actually have to get started baking the pies for the Christmas Eve party, because I have to get a dozen of those done today, plus all of the other stuff that will take me all day tomorrow."

"You're avoiding the problem."

"Bye, Jamie."

"Bell, seriously. If there's one thing I've learned being in a relationship, it's always communicate. Things end up much better if you just talk. Just...go talk to him. Now!"

Bell nodded. She walked out of the store and headed down the street. She didn't need Jamie lecturing her. She didn't need anyone to lecture her right now. She just needed to get out of whatever this slump was.

Once she walked into her bakery, got the ovens preheating and the Christmas music on, she couldn't help but flip to the "Rules of a Secret Santa," written in the same beautiful penmanship as everything else in the book.

1. Do not let the people in this book know you are helping them.
2. Do not get personally involved in their lives for any reason other than to help them feel the magic of Christmas.
3. Do not let anyone know you are a Secret Santa elf.

Bell didn't bother reading the rest. She ran her finger over #2.

If she wasn't supposed to even get involved with Drake personally, why did she feel so horrible that he liked someone other than her? Why did her heart skip whenever he was around? Why did she enjoy talking about him, dreaming about him, and becoming giddy just seeing a text? Why did she want to be with him all the time?

Secret Santa

Bell closed the book and pushed it away. She had to get started on these pies. She reached for her apron and from the corner of her eye saw the screen of her phone light up. She leaned over and saw Drake had sent her another text.

I made a big breakfast all by myself. You should be proud :) Come eat!

Bell drew a breath and made herself pick up the phone. *I just started baking the pies for the Christmas party*, she typed. Her fingers hovered over the "send" button, but after a moment she deleted the message and dropped her phone on the counter. She needed to get to work. She shouldn't be distracted. She needed to let Drake have time with the other girl. After all, she was better for Drake, Bell repeated. She was a human, beautiful, and he already knew her.

She hurried to put on her apron and started grabbing ingredients to make the cream cheese piecrust before she could respond.

❄ ❄ ❄

"So, am I going to meet the love of your life?" Stephanie asked as she parked herself in one of the booth seats and peered out the window.

"I don't think so," Drake admitted, setting down a plate of bacon amongst the rest of the food. "I figured she would want some breakfast. She always comes by in the morning to get a cup of cocoa."

"Cocoa? In a tavern?" Stephanie eyed him.

"Yup," he chuckled. "I thought the same thing at first." He took his seat and glanced at his phone. "Let me try calling her." He dialed Bell's number and took a slow breath waiting for her to answer. Whatever the reason, his heart was pounding.

"Hey, Drake," Bell answered.

He felt almost immediate relief. "Hey! I wasn't sure if you got my text, but I made a big breakfast and would love for you to come eat with me. I also wanted to introduce you to someone."

"I'm actually really busy. I've got to make twelve pies today for the party, and then have to get the gingerbread dough and sugar cookie dough ready to cool overnight so I can make those tomorrow, and then the next day I've got to spend all day baking cupcakes and everything else."

"Lunch, then?"

Bell paused, and he felt his stomach drop. "Maybe. I'll try and make it if I can."

"Sounds good. I hope I get to see you then." He hung up and set down the phone.

Stephanie studied him.

"What?" he mumbled.

"I've never known you to be one to passively sit by and just let things happen." She spread butter across her pancake and then poured strawberry jam on top.

"I'm just…giving her the benefit of the doubt. She really is busy and a little overwhelmed." He poked at his

Secret Santa

bacon, making it break.

"But?" Stephanie pressed.

"But I also can't help think she tried to get close to me for the sake of the Christmas party." He glanced at Stephanie.

"You think she could manipulate you like that? Because if so, then I wouldn't bother with her." She shrugged like it was as simple as that.

Drake stared at his breakfast, then decided he'd better eat or the rest of the morning would be miserable. Maybe he would give Bell some space today. Maybe she really was just overwhelmed with all of the baking. He would make her up something and take it to her for lunch. Maybe that would be a nice surprise.

But the day moved much slower than he thought it would. After breakfast, Stephanie left to go visit a couple of friends who still lived in Owentown, and Drake had a much busier tavern to run. A few people from the City Council stopped by to thank him for letting them use the barn this year, how their kids were excited, and so on.

Drake glanced at the clock for probably the millionth time and went to the kitchen to check on Chris. "So, I was thinking of taking some food to Bell and surprising her with lunch. Can you manage without me being here?"

Chris glanced past him, through the window to see the people congregated at the tables. "We have the new kids that aren't doing too shabby. I'll keep an eye on them, though."

Drake nodded and pursed his lips. "Well, let me grab

her food. I can at least drop it off for her and be right back."

"Have you actually talked to her about what's wrong?"

"I tried last night. I even tried inviting her to breakfast this morning. I was hoping to have time during lunch, but we won't have time for that conversation if I've got to be back." He lowered his arms and shrugged a shoulder. "No big deal."

The back door swung open and Stephanie walked in wearing jeans, a long white coat with a fluffy green and black scarf. "What?" she asked when the two men exchanged a look.

Drake walked over to her. "How would you feel about running the tavern for a few minutes? I want to run lunch to Bell."

She grinned. "Can I come meet her?"

"I was actually wondering if you could just take charge here while I'm gone."

She nodded slowly. "I think I might be able to do that. You may have to remind me how to do the till thing though."

Drake grinned and hugged her. "Thank you! Chris, can you get that lunch done for me?" He led Stephanie to the register behind the bar and quickly showed her how to take cash, then how to run a card.

"That's it?" she asked.

"Yep."

"Your lunch is ready, Drake," Chris said.

"Got it! Thanks, Steph." Drake grabbed the bag with

Secret Santa

the two lunches and the carrier with the two drinks. He hurried out to his truck and headed over to Bell's bakery. He hadn't been there since he'd made cookies with her, and he couldn't help but smile when he pulled up. There was a nice group of people sitting inside.

Drake grabbed the lunch and walked inside. "Hello Amanda," he greeted.

She looked up with a smile and then that smile froze. She glanced over her shoulder, where Bell was busy pulling out a pie to cool, then quickly leaned across the counter. "She's really unusually quiet today," Amanda whispered. "She usually likes to greet everyone, and she's been back there almost the entire morning."

Drake nodded. "Let me slip back there." He held up the food, like that would help convince Amanda to let him into the back, but Amanda had already lifted the counter to allow him past. He stepped into the back. Something felt…off. And then he realized there was no Christmas music playing. He cleared his throat.

Bell turned around and tightened her lips. "I wasn't expecting to see you today. Uh. Do you need something?" She looked around.

"Yeah. I brought food. You and me, we are going to eat." He set the food down on the counter and leaned back against it. "And we need to talk."

She sighed and finally walked over to him, grateful he had chosen the counter out of the line of sight of her customers. "I'm really busy—"

"No, something is definitely wrong," he said. "Look at

you. No Christmas music, you're back here alone, you aren't even wearing your Christmas baking apron!" He moved a step closer and gently took her hands. "Whatever I said on Sunday, I'm sorry. I don't want you to be upset. This isn't you."

"It's…it's not what you did on Sunday." She bit her bottom lip, looking at their hands. She finally drew a breath. "Drake, I saw you with that other woman on Monday night. I heard you invite her to stay in your room." She pulled away and met his confused gaze. "I don't blame you. You have every right to date people, and I know I'm not your type anyway, so—"

"Whoa, stop," he cut in. He couldn't resist a grin. "Bell, that other woman isn't anyone you should worry about."

"I'm not"

"She's my cousin."

Bell stared at him. Realization dawned on her face and her cheeks turned a bright red. "Drake…I'm such an idiot." She turned away, shoulders raised as she pressed her fingertips against her cheeks. "I'm so, so sorry! I just thought she was an ex-girlfriend. I thought you were…"

"You really thought I would two-time you?"

Bell looked at him. "Well, we aren't exactly seriously dating, and who wouldn't want to date you? Have you seen you?"

He laughed. "Every morning. But even if there was someone else I'd want to date, I would never go behind your back like that. I can also tell you there isn't anyone

Secret Santa

else I want to date." He gave her a half-smile.

Bell exhaled, this time her shoulders relaxed. "I really am sorry. I should have just talked to you."

"Well, now you have." He grinned and held out her lunch. When she reached out to take it, he refused to hand it over. "One condition. Get your Christmas music back on."

She laughed and nodded. "Yes, sir!" She walked around the counter in the middle of the room and turned on some music.

❋ ❋ ❋

Bell swirled an English chip in the ketchup, feet propped up on a tote full of cookie cutters. She watched Drake lick his thumb and felt an overwhelming sense of gratitude. She'd never been in a relationship, never been interested in one person like she was with Drake, and if he hadn't come and spoken to her, she wasn't sure what would have happened. At the same time, however, she felt dread squeezing her heart into a fast rhythm and curling around her stomach like a snake poised to strike. Rule #2 kept bouncing around in her mind, and if she really wasn't supposed to become emotionally invested in Drake, she needed to back out while she was already making space between them.

But as she watched him change the song, so they weren't listening to "Little Drummer Boy" for the third time in a row, she realized letting go of Drake wasn't going to be easy. This had to be why Santa created this rule in the first place.

"You're mighty quiet," Drake observed.

"Sorry, I was thinking. And eating your delicious English chips. These are seriously incredible, and I hate you for adding them to your menu." She popped it in her mouth.

He grinned. "Then I suppose I shouldn't inform you of the cheese-stuffed chips Chris is working on."

"Stop it!" she gasped. "Oh, I hate that you changed your menu. Everything is better than ever, and I just want to eat all the time."

"Tomorrow, do you want to come for breakfast? And you can officially meet Stephanie and all that stuff before you have to get over here to bake?"

"As long as it's an early breakfast." She wiped her hands on a napkin.

"I can make that work. Maybe Stephanie would like to be busy and could lend you another pair of hands?"

Bell licked her lip. "Hm. Three pairs of hands. I wouldn't know what to do with myself. Let's give it a shot."

Drake stood and dumped their garbage in the trash.

Bell wrung her hands, the thought she needed to be honest with him pressed against her. What would he do if he told her she was an elf? Would he hate her? Laugh? Just accept it? Telling him would break Rule #1 as well, but if she told him, maybe it could make up for breaking

Secret Santa

Rule #1. And he had been honest with her, so she felt obligated to do the same.

"Drake, there's something I need to tell you," she blurted.

"Yeah?" He rubbed his hands on his back pockets. "What's that?"

"I…" She bit her bottom lip. She couldn't tell him. She just couldn't. "Thank you for lunch. Thank you for everything. This has been the best Christmas ever." Bell smiled up at him.

He smiled. "You're welcome. And thank you too, for bringing me back around this Christmas." He leaned forward and pecked her on the lips. "I'll see you later tonight to finish up the decorations?"

She nodded, the butterflies in her stomach still fluttering from the kiss. She watched him leave and looked up. "Santa, if you have objections, you better tell me now." When nothing happened, she pulled out her flour, sugar, butter, and other ingredients to make the sugar and gingerbread cookie dough, her heart excited to spend more time with Drake.

She spent the rest of the day finishing the pies, and dough that needed to cool overnight. Once those were all put in their respective compartments, and Amanda had said her goodbye for the day, having spent an extra two hours there because Steve decided to watch the kids, Bell did one last sweep over her checklist. She was right on track.

Bell turned the lights off and locked up, eating her

homemade sandwich as she walked to Drake's to finish helping with the decorations. She couldn't deny that she had missed setting them up the day before. She'd never missed out on decorations before.

She walked into the tavern, seeing Drake step into the back carrying a container of dirty dishes.

"You must be Bell!"

She jumped a little and turned, not having seen the redheaded woman sitting at a table. "Oh, hello."

She stood and crossed over to Bell, holding out her hand. "I'm Stephanie."

"Oh! You're Drake's cousin," she smiled.

"He said you mistook me for an ex." She laughed.

Bell blushed, smile stiffening with embarrassment. "It was definitely a terrible assumption."

"I don't blame you," Stephanie laughed. "I am practically the sister Drake never wanted. We've always been really close. His dad was my dad's brother, and we used to spend all summer here every other year, they would come to us on the off year. I can see that you would have assumed the worst, looking at our behavior. And you probably overheard him invite me to stay in his room, which is definitely something no one wants to hear!" She laughed again.

Bell finally relaxed, chuckling with her. "At least you don't think I'm crazy."

"No, not at all."

"Hey, you came!" Drake said. He carried Bell's gift to him, still wrapped, in his hands. "I figured I'm supposed

Secret Santa

to open this?"

"It's a Christmas present, Drake," Stephanie scolded. "You're supposed to wait for Christmas."

Bell shrugged. "I don't see why you couldn't open it now, but it is the only thing I have for you."

"I have to open it. I can't wait. You should be proud of me for waiting this long."

"Then you should be able to wait an extra day." Stephanie put her hands on her hips.

Drake pouted. "But I don't want to."

"Just open it," Bell laughed.

Drake pulled the wrapping off, exposing the painting: a red dragon flying high in the blue sky amongst white clouds, its face turned to roar straight out at him. "Bell, how did you find this?" he asked softly. "I mean, I had hoped, but…"

"Turns out Mr. Toby held onto it for you."

He looked over at her, and a smile spread across his face like she hadn't seen before. "I don't…I don't even know how to thank you." He laughed and finished pulling off the paper.

"Well, let's hang it up!" She gestured at the empty space above the bar.

Drake carried it behind the counter and hung it in its rightful spot. He smiled, stepped back, and wrapped an arm around her. "You know, it's actually better than I remember it." He looked at Bell and grinned.

Bell smiled in return and gave him a peck on the lips. "Let's go finish that barn of yours."

The group headed to the half-festive barn, where the same people from the night before, and more, had already shown up. Mrs. Flowers was already at work ordering people where to set up the tables.

She made eye contact with Bell as they entered and nodded. "Good to see you here today. We need all hands on deck! Shauna is upstairs with Roy setting up the kid's area. Daxton will bring all of the floral arrangements for the tables tomorrow so they're nice and fresh for the dinner. I need you three to start putting the table cloths on—"

"I'll go help unload tables and chairs," Drake interrupted. "Hey, Quinton! You put that down." He left the conversation and went out through the open doors to help an elderly man with a table he was trying to pull out of the trailer.

Bell shrugged. "I can start with tablecloths."

"I'm going to go see that man about helping with the stage stuff," Stephanie grinned, looking a young man up and down, who was unpacking microphones on the makeshift stage.

The tables were set up in the wings, leaving the space in the middle open for dancing and visiting. The round tables had gold, and silver tablecloths. Stephanie helped get the cords untangled decorated, and the long tables against the walls were given red and green tablecloths. All of the last-minute setup would happen tomorrow, once people brought their potluck food, treats, and utensils.

Bell stood in the middle of the room, observing

Secret Santa

everyone around her, feeling a great sense of pride. She had grown to love the people of Owentown. Her heart slowly sank. This would most likely be her last Christmas with them. She needed to make it count. But more importantly…

She watched Drake. He didn't know what she really was. He didn't know she'd been working on him for three Christmases. What would happen when he found out?

Drake must have felt her gaze, because he walked over to her, smiling. "We're done for the night. Want to snuggle up and watch a Christmas movie?"

She laughed. "I never thought I would hear you say that." She put her hand in his, and they walked back to the tavern. "What about Stephanie?" she asked.

"She's going to dessert with Simon. I think that's his name?" He shrugged, and they walked up to his studio above the tavern. He looked around. "Sorry, it's not much."

"I think it's the perfect bachelor pad." She smiled and sat on the couch, noting the folded linens on the coffee table. She went to remove her coat, and her hand brushed her book. She bit her lip and looked back at Drake, who had hung his coat by the door and walked to a small shelf of DVDs to look for something.

"Wait, I almost forgot." He straightened and hurried back to his coat, pulling something from his pocket. He walked over and handed her a small box.

Bell looked from it to him. "What's this?"

"Your Christmas present."

"Drake, you really didn't have to," she smiled.

"Open it," he grinned.

Bell took the box and pulled off the lid. Resting inside was a beautiful, long gold necklace. A large golden elf girl hung from the bottom, wearing a silver glitter dress and silver glitter hat, holding a present. The necklace was simple—the girl had no face, and no detail on her hands—but she was beautiful. "Drake…I don't even know what to say."

"Say you like it?" he asked.

She gave a nervous laugh. "I absolutely love it." She pulled it over her head. "Why an elf?"

Drake smiled. "You remind me of Christmas elves. If they're real," he added with a quick wink. "You care about everyone, want to include everyone, help people remember Christmas is about love and magic and family."

"Thank you, Drake." She ran her finger across the beautiful little elf. "I need to be honest with you about something."

He looked at her. "You said that earlier and didn't finish whatever you were saying."

"I don't know how to tell you this. I just…I feel like you have the right to know."

His brows dipped. "Know what?" She heard the nervous edge to his voice.

"I really am an elf from the North Pole. I'm what's known as a Secret Santa elf. My job is to restore the spirit of Christmas to those assigned to me."

Drake's expression shifted, and he eyed her with

Secret Santa

evident confusion, likely trying to figure out if she was being honest, pulling his leg, or just plain crazy.

The silence between them was uncomfortable. Bell wished she knew what he was thinking.

"Uh. I don't know what to say," he finally said, trying to give a smile. "Sure. That's cool. What movie?"

"I mean it." She took the book out of her pocket and set it on the coffee table. Before his eyes, the small book enlarged to a full-size book. She watched Drake's face carefully.

His eyes widened, and he stared at it, and then at her, and then his brows pinched. "Wait, you're in charge of helping people feel the spirit of Christmas. That's why you spend all December helping other people?"

She nodded.

"So, when I asked if I was a project for you…I really have been."

Her throat tightened, and she shrugged her shoulder. "Well…"

He leaned away from her, his face expressionless and eyes cold.

"For the past two Christmases, yes," she said again. "But this year…I started seeing you differently. I started realizing how amazing of a person you are, and I wanted to spend more time with you, and so…" She stopped talking. His whole complexion had hardened. She had just confirmed something he'd been thinking of, and it wasn't pleasant.

"Was I on this list of yours this year?" He crossed his

arms.

Bell hesitated. "You were, but I swear what I feel for you is real."

"I think maybe you should go."

Bell felt her whole body begin to tremble. "I told you because I really care about you, Drake. We aren't supposed to get involved personally with people in our book, and I broke that rule when we started dating. When Stephanie showed up, I hoped that by distancing myself maybe a little bit, that when they reassign me it would be easier."

"Bell, you sound crazy!" he blurted. "You did some sort of magic trick and tell me you're an elf, that you're not supposed to love me? You don't need to make up a lie. Just tell me you don't want to date me."

"But I do. You have no idea how badly I want this, how much I want to be in a relationship with you. I just…can't." She took a breath, a tear escaping and running down her cheek. She quickly wiped it away.

He shook his head. "I just don't believe you. I really don't. You make me a project, make me care about you so you can feel better about yourself, and get the barn for the town Christmas party, and now that you've got it…" He shook his head.

"This wasn't about the barn!" she insisted. "None of this, I swear!"

"Go! Just…just leave." He grabbed her coat and pushed it into her arms.

Bell's chin trembled, but she didn't argue. She grabbed

Secret Santa

her book from the table and hurried out the door and down the stairs. She hurried past Chris—who was just finishing up cleaning—and out the back door.

This was worse than thinking he was with Stephanie.

Bell climbed into her car and finally burst into tears. Why did she have to tell him? Worse, why did she feel the need to do so? Why did she have to be honest? Why couldn't she just be with him and be happy?

She threw the book into the passenger seat and tried to start her car, but the engine wouldn't turn over. When she looked down at her phone, she found it somehow had no battery and had died.

This was the worst Christmas.

Bell found a napkin and blew her nose, then climbed back out of her car and started walking home. "Everyone is happy and out of the list. Why am I still here?" she said aloud, hoping Mr. Mistletoe was listening.

She got no reply.

She finally made it home, shivering, her feet and face numb from the cold. Stepping into her house, she closed the door behind her. Bell turned the fireplace on before she removed her coat, and then went to the kitchen to make cocoa. She hadn't turned on the Christmas tree lights. She hadn't turned on any of the Christmas lights. She stared at the cocoa maker and then looked around the small home she'd fallen in love with.

"Oh, Bell," Mr. Mistletoe said as he stepped into the kitchen.

She quickly faced him. "I didn't hear you come in."

"I was sort of waiting."

"I...I broke almost all of the rules." Her voice trembled. This time she was able to keep herself composed. "I understand if you want to fire me. But everyone's names are off the Spirit List. I understand it's time I need to be reassigned. I can have everything packed up tonight."

"Can you really?"

Bell finally looked at him.

He had on a soft smile and a slight tilt to his head. "I've known for a long time that you wouldn't be coming back to the North Pole. Yes, you can now your assignment is done. But you love this town, and the people in it. You love your bakery. More importantly, you love Drake Pine. *And* your list isn't done yet. You're still on it."

She shook her head. "It doesn't matter now. Drake doesn't return the feelings now that he thinks I'm insane." She looked down at the small leather-bound book in her hands. "I never should have told him. Why did I have to tell him the truth? I made a fool of myself, and I hurt him, and now he will never look at me the same."

"Look at the rules."

Bell turned the pages.

"Now tell me which one says you can't fall in love with someone."

Bell's eyes scanned the page. "Well, none of them specifically say that," she said. "Rule two."

"Not one of those rules say you can't fall in love with someone."

Secret Santa

Bell looked at Mr. Mistletoe. "It says we can't get involved personally."

"In their lives. Meaning, you can't force them to try and mend broken relationships or face relatives when they really don't want to. You can give them nudges, but you just can't force them. That needs to come from them and their own thoughts. You are encouraged to fall in love, Bell. You just need to decide that, if you love him, you will remain in a human life. If you choose to stay, you will no longer be an elf."

For a moment, she felt a flutter of joy and excitement. Then she thought of the look on Drake's face when she'd told him everything. She'd built up his trust this past month and broken it with one stupid conversation. "Thank you, Mr. Mistletoe, but I think I should go home."

"Unless you're already home."

She turned to face her supervisor, but he was gone.

Chapter Fifteen

Drake poured another mug of coffee and set it in front of the old couple. He hadn't bothered getting their names. He hadn't bothered really talking to them either. He set the coffee pot where it belonged and stepped into the back to grab the next tray of breakfast orders.

"What happened between you and Bell last night?" Chris asked.

Drake looked at him, pulled from his brooding thoughts. "Huh?"

"You and Bell? What happened? She took off out the back door crying. And now you're back to being the grumpy Grinch."

He rolled his eyes. "She told me she wasn't interested in dating me, more or less. She made up some story about her being a Secret Santa elf. Can you believe that? She didn't even have the guts to just say she didn't want to date me."

Chris stared at him. "She's a Secret Santa elf?"

"Yeah. Apparently, it's her job to—"

"Help people feel the spirit of Christmas," Chris finished.

Secret Santa

It was Drake's turn to stare at him. "So, you heard our conversation."

Chris smiled sheepishly. "No. It uh…well." He rubbed the back of his neck. "She actually told you she was a Secret Santa elf?"

He nodded.

"Did she tell you that breaks the rules?"

He nodded again. "And that she wasn't supposed to fall in love with someone on her list. You really can't believe this?"

"Actually…" Chris took a book out from his back pocket and set it on the counter. Like Bell's, it was leather bound, and when he set it down, it grew into a full-sized book. Unlike Bell's, the interlay was silver instead of gold.

Drake stared at it a good long while—at least, it felt like a long time. He finally looked at Chris. "What are you telling me?"

"I was a Secret Santa elf too, before I met Heather."

"You too?" he groaned. He snatched the tray of food. "You lied to me too? I can't believe you would stoop that low."

Chris crossed his arms. "I can't believe you would think I would do that to you."

Drake shook his head but paused before walking out into the front. "Are you serious?"

Chris nodded.

They had been best friends for at least five years, originally meeting in college. Actually, thinking on it now, it sort of made sense. Chris had always been busy around winter semester, helping at the homeless shelters, dragging him along to the retirement home to play games, running food drives...Drake could practically see the memories.

"Get it now?" Chris asked.

"Wait, that was you?" he asked.

"Christmas magic, man," he grinned.

Drake shook his head and stepped back out to the floor to deliver the food, but now the wheels in his head were turning.

Tom walked in, giving Drake a friendly wave. "Morning, Drake! Where is Miss Bell this fine morning?" he asked, looking around the half-filled room.

"Probably at her bakery, why?"

"Because her car is in your lot." He pointed.

Drake walked over and poked his head out the door. Indeed, it sat in his lot, but it was covered in frost and snow. Had she walked home last night? All the way home? And all the way to her bakery that morning? He instinctively grabbed his phone but let go. Jamie probably gave her a ride home and to work. No big deal.

He walked back to the bar. "What can I get for you, Tom?"

"One of your breakfast platters, please. And a big coffee."

"Where is your wife?" Drake turned to grab the coffee.

"She kicked me out. She's got the kitchen busy with food for the Christmas party tonight, and then she wants me back to help clean for the grandkids coming." He chuckled. "You should hear how excited they are to come to this party. It's the first time we're bringing the grandkids."

Drake gave a little smile. "I'm glad you'll be coming."

"Thanks for hosting it. Hey! You found your painting!"

Drake turned and looked at it, but all he could see was the pain in Bell's face when he'd sent her packing last night. "Yeah. Actually, Bell did. Mr. Toby had it stored in his place, apparently." He shrugged.

"That girl. She's special, you know? I'm glad you two got together." He smiled and blew on his coffee.

"Yeah…" Drake licked his lips. "Well, I'll go give Chris your order." He walked into the back. "If you were a Secret Santa elf, why weren't you the one making everyone here happy?" he asked.

Chris looked up. "Because I wasn't assigned here. I completed my assignment and asked if I could be temporarily put on leave so I could start a family."

"So why does Bell think she's going to lose her job?"

"Because we aren't supposed to tell people what we do. And if we fall in love with a human, we become one. No more Secret Santa assignments."

Drake frowned. "But why don't you…" A light bulb went on. "Heather is an elf too?"

Chris winked. "Bingo." He turned back to the sausage grilling on the skillet. "Does it really matter what she used to be? Even if she wasn't an elf, what if she had been something else? Like a thief? But she wasn't anymore?

Would that matter?"

"A thief? Bell?"

"Hypothetically, Drake."

He shrugged. "I don't know. I would have to have proof that she wasn't anymore. I don't want to get into something that could end in a disaster."

Chris laughed. "You just explained the purpose of relationships. They're meant to be risky, and to frighten you a little. What scares you more, though? That she actually might be an elf? That she actually might care for you? Or that you might actually care about her too?"

Drake pointed to him. "Stop with your philosophical stuff. I'm getting back to work."

"Just keep thinking on it, Drake. You guys aren't serious enough, so it's no big deal if she and you date other people." He said it with a smirk, like he knew how Drake truly felt, and just saying this one thing would make Drake feel unsettled.

Drake grabbed a tub to clean off a table, but Chris's last phrase lingered in his head.

It's no big deal if you date other people.

He carried the dishes to the sink.

It's no big deal if you date other people.

But what if he didn't want to date other people?

✸ ✸ ✸

Amanda walked through the back door, dusting off her

Secret Santa

coat and stomping her feet. "Morning, Bell! You're already hard at work getting things ready, I see."

Bell smiled. "Yes. Chocolate pecan cookies are ready to go in, and I'm mixing the dough for the thumbprint cookies. You can pull out the sugar cookie dough, cut them out, and put them in to bake."

"Are we opening the bakery today?"

"No, we've got to get these done in time for the party. I thought most places would be busy getting things ready for tonight. In fact, do you need to be with your family today?" She looked up as Amanda set the sugar cookie dough out on the counter and arranged the cookie cutters.

Amanda shook her head. "My job is to work here, and you definitely need the help."

Bell paused working. "Amanda, I really can't thank you enough for working with me this season. You've been an incredible help."

"You're welcome. I've actually really enjoyed it," she admitted with a grin.

"That's great! You're welcome to stay," Bell smiled. She shut off the mixer and scooped the dough into balls, rolled them in egg whites, then rolled them in walnuts, and stuck them on the cookie sheet.

"How are you and Drake doing?" Amanda asked.

"We…we had a little bit of a fight last night. I'm not sure we're going to keep seeing each other," she said, keeping her eyes on her task.

"That's unfortunate. I'm really sorry."

She shrugged. "That's the way it goes, right?" She

gave a quick smile and slid a second cookie sheet over.

"Sometimes. But if you really care about him…"

"I do. But, I don't know. I guess we'll see how the party goes tonight." She gave Amanda a quick smile. "Now, tell me what your favorite Christmas traditions are," she said, ending that conversation.

The day passed quickly. Amanda left at lunchtime, and Bell forgot to eat. When she finally had all of the food made, she had just enough time to deliver the treats then go home and get ready. She stacked the cookie sheets in opposite directions to not mess up the decorations, then hoisted them into her arms, walking out the back door. Her stomach immediately dropped.

"Oh yeah," she mumbled, having completely forgotten about her car not starting.

With a heavy sigh, Bell started carrying the heavy trays down the street, across the road, and around the block. When she rounded the corner, she spotted Jamie and Andrew walking toward her. She gave them a smile, and Jamie waved.

When they got close enough, Andrew held out his hands. "Mind if I help?"

"Please?" she asked.

Andrew grabbed half of the stack, and Jamie took two off Bell's stack.

"Thank you so much," Bell smiled. "You two showed up at just the right time."

"Why aren't you driving?" Jamie asked.

"Well, my car wouldn't start last night after helping

decorate. It's still sitting in Drake's parking lot."

"Speaking of Drake, how—"

"Are you so excited for the party tonight?" Bell asked. "I am. I think as soon as these are set up, I'm going to go home and get ready."

Jamie and Andrew exchanged a glance.

Andrew cleared his throat lightly. "I know a little bit about cars. I could take a look at yours."

"And I could drive you home in the meantime," Jamie said.

Bell nodded. "I would love that. It would really be nice to not have to walk home," she laughed. It died, however, when the tavern came into view. Why was she acting like this?

They made it to the barn, but the door was safely locked.

Jamie set her trays on top of Andrew's stack with an, "I'll be right back."

Andrew looked at Bell. "You and Drake have an argument?"

"I told him—"

"I don't need to know about your fight," he smiled. "Just know it's part of dating. You might not fight all the time, but every now and then. Just talk to each other. Honestly, without communication, you'll only make assumptions, and assumptions are the worst thing you could make in a relationship."

She looked at the back door. "That's what Jamie said."

Jamie skipped over to them and unlocked the door.

"There we go. Drake said to leave it unlocked so everyone else can start coming in to drop things off. Where can we set these?" she asked.

Bell nodded her head toward the wall on the right. "Those tables are for the desserts. You can just set the trays down and I'll arrange everything."

"Oh, we can help. Besides, I've hardly seen you since Andrew came home," Jamie said.

"I know. I didn't want to bug you. You were on your way somewhere when we ran into each other," Bell said. She set her trays down, her arms aching.

"We were just on a walk, and on our way to Emily's. I loved that Christmas candle you got me! I have to get more for the library, and for my home."

Bell smiled. "Then go on, you two. I've got this. Really."

After they left, Bell carefully arranged all of the desserts on the trays and stands. And then she took a moment to just look at everything. Mr. Mistletoe was right about one thing: she would miss Owentown if she left. All of it. The people, the community feeling, the city get-togethers, friends…

She stacked her now-empty cookie sheets and carried them back to her bakery. As soon as she locked the door, Jamie pulled up. "You have impeccable timing!" she called.

Jamie grinned. "I'm supposed to take you home, remember? Andrew and Drake are working on your car right now."

Secret Santa

"Drake?" She climbed into the front seat.

"Yes, does that surprise you?"

"A little," she confessed. Bell rubbed her hands and stretched her aching toes. "Since I don't have a car, would you mind picking me up?" she asked.

Jamie winced. "I'm really sorry. I actually made a commitment to pick up Aretha. We could probably pick you up after, you might just be late."

"Don't worry about it."

"Well I bet Drake would get you if you asked!"

Bell looked out the window. "I can walk."

"Okay, what happened? This isn't you. Usually, you're on the edge of your seat, talking about all the things you've done, and who you're going to see, and all that stuff. Are you feeling lonely because Andrew is home this year?"

"No! Jamie, no. It's not you, I promise. It's…It's me and Drake. I just don't think we're going to work out."

"Why not?"

"Because we're really different. Look, it's not a big deal. I'll get ready and I'm sure I'll be happy at the party."

Jamie stopped in front of Bell's house. "Are you sure?"

"Definitely."

"If you don't mind being late, I'll pick you up."

She smiled. "Thank you."

With that, she climbed out of the car and headed inside to get ready.

CHAPTER SIXTEEN

"Looks like it needs a new starter," Andrew said. He straightened and rubbed his hands together. "Want to take a trip with me down to the auto parts store?"

"Not that I'll be much help," Drake laughed. "This is sort of a one-person job."

"Come anyway, it will get you out of the tavern for a little while."

Drake glanced at the building. "I really should get back in and help clean and close up. Chris would kill me if I just left him. But you know what, you go get the part." He dug into his pocket for his wallet and handed Andrew a chunk of cash. "I'll pay for it. When you get back, I'll help you get it installed in the car."

"Sounds great to me."

Drake walked back inside just in time to see Chris frantically running around the dining room floor trying to give everyone their receipts. Drake walked to the nearest table, thanked them for eating, and went to make their food and drink orders. "I wasn't gone that long," he said.

Chris handed him three tickets. "Oh good. I can only do two at a time before I lose track of which belongs to

Secret Santa

who."

"Go start cleaning the kitchen, I've got it from here." Chris patted him on the shoulder and walked away.

Drake finished getting everyone's cards and receipts to them, then started bussing the tables just as the door opened. "We're actually closed," he called.

Andrew stepped in. "I got the part."

"Awesome! I was just cleaning up." He carried the full container to the kitchen sink. "Let me grab my coat and tools and I'll meet you outside."

"No way. I'm staying inside where it's warm as long as possible."

Drake chuckled and pulled on a coat. "You want to come watch?" Drake asked.

Chris paused, rubbing his chin as he looked around the kitchen. "Actually..." He looked at Drake. "I'm going to use a little Christmas magic to help get this place cleaned up a little faster. Then you and I can get ready for the party."

"Oh, that's tonight," he sighed. "Do whatever you need to. Come on, Andrew!"

Andrew followed him outside, and to the garage. They picked through the tools until they found what they needed, and then went back to Bell's car and started work. Sometime after getting everything apart, Andrew's phone rang.

"Hey babe!" he greeted cheerfully. "Yeah, it was the starter. Thanks for getting us the key. Yeah." His eyes moved to Drake. "I think we can make sure that happens.

Yes. He's right here." He grinned. "She wants to talk to you." He held the phone out toward Drake.

Drake sort of shook his head but took the phone. "Hey, Jamie."

"Alright, I know you and Bell had some sort of an argument. Don't roll your eyes."

He paused and looked around, half expecting her to be somewhere watching him.

"I don't know what it was about, and I don't really care. I'm just wondering if you would at least be willing to pick her up for the party tonight? Andrew and I have to stop and get Aretha, which would make Bell really late and as much as she says it's okay, you know what she's like. Being late to anything kills her."

"I...think I might be able to do it."

"Can you, or can't you?"

"I'll do it."

"Good. See you tonight!"

Drake hung up and handed the phone back to Andrew. He laughed. "She got you, didn't she?"

"Just to pick up Bell. It won't be that hard, right?" He said it mostly to himself, but once the car was fixed, he really had nothing else to do other than finish cleaning up the tavern, and he still had an hour before the party. Maybe cleaning up the tavern would take longer.

Jamie pulled up and Andrew climbed into the car. Drake gave a polite wave and Jamie pointed two fingers to her eyes, then back at him.

He nodded. "I got it, Jamie. Don't worry."

Secret Santa

"I'll know if you don't!" She grinned.

Drake shook his head with a chuckle and walked back into the tavern.

Chris wasn't joking about Christmas magic. All of the tables were cleaned off, wiped down, the chairs were stacked, the floor swept and mopped, and all of the dishes were either in the dish washer, or already washed and standing in the drying rack.

Chris walked back from the office, where the washing machine was, carrying the empty linen basket. "So, you get it fixed?"

"Yeah. Uh. How did you do all this?"

"I told you. Magic." He said it with such a straight face, Drake couldn't help but accept that as a reasonable answer.

"I'm going to go upstairs and shower and get ready. I have to pick up Bell."

Chris grinned. "Good. I'll see you there. Heather will have a heart attack if I don't get home now. She's probably all dolled up and already sitting on the couch waiting. See ya later!"

"You too." Drake looked around the clean tavern again and shook his head in disbelief before trotting upstairs to get ready.

Stephanie leaned close to the mirror, applying dark red lipstick. "Hey," she said. She stepped back and looked him up and down. "Please tell me you're going to shower before you go."

"Of course. I don't want to smell like car grease."

"Hey, what happened—"

"Don't ask," Drake said sharply. "I swear if you lecture me too…just drop it. I'm picking her up for the party, if that makes you happy. Besides, how did you even hear?" He closed the bathroom door and began pulling off his clothes.

"People in a small-town talk," she said.

"Yeah? And what are the rumors?"

"That everyone shouldn't get involved, but everyone is curious, because Bell is the sweet Christmas baker, and you are the tough bar owner."

"Anyone compare me to the Grinch?"

"That was me," she laughed.

Drake shook his head. "As soon as I'm ready, I'm getting Bell. Do you need anything? Want to come?"

"No way, bud. You're doing this on your own. I'm going to see if there are any last-minute things they need help setting up. See you in a while!"

Drake stepped into the shower. Of course, he could do this on his own. He was a grown man, not afraid of a Christmas-loving woman who believed she was an elf.

Bell finished getting ready. She curled her hair into light ringlets, put on some shimmery silver eye shadow, and wore a simple red dress with a high neck and no sleeves. She walked into the living room and sat down to put on her glittering gold heels.

She heard a knock at the door and looked up. "It's open!" she called. "I'm having a little trouble getting my

Secret Santa

heel on."

Drake walked through the door. "Hey."

Bell paused buckling her shoe to stare at him. He had on a suit, with a white shirt and red tie, and something crumpled up in the pocket. She cleared her throat softly and finished buckling the shoe. "I'm sorry, I just didn't expect to see you. I thought Jamie was picking me up."

"Their plans changed, and she asked if I could come get you." He paused. "You look amazing. You going to be comfortable in those shoes all night?"

"They aren't too high of a heel, and it's really the only time I get to wear these." She stood and looked him over. "You look rather handsome yourself." She couldn't resist a smile when Drake fiddled with the thing in his pocket. "Can I help?"

"I can't get this thing to look right," he mumbled. He finally pulled out a pocket square and flung it over his shoulder like a bar rag.

This made Bell smile, no matter how hard she tried not to. She reached for it and he handed it to her.

Drake sighed. "I don't know. I think it's a lost cause." He gave her a half-grin, the one that always made her melt.

Bell laid it on the armrest of one of her chairs, so she could fold it. "There you go." She tucked it into his pocket. Being this close again to him made her long to be held in his arms, to feel the warmth of his lips again. But she stepped back and grabbed her coat. "It was very nice of you to come get me. I'm sorry I left my car in your parking lot."

"It's not like you broke it on purpose."

Bell suddenly inclined her head, and half-scowled as she looked over her shoulder, expecting to see Mr. Mistletoe hiding around the corner.

"What are you doing?" he asked.

"Nothing." She wrapped her scarf around her neck.

She closed the door behind her and Drake held out his hand. She placed her hand in his and allowed him to "help" her down the stairs. But then he didn't let go. She looked up at him to find him looking at their hands.

"Sorry. I just…" He let go and opened the passenger side door.

Bell climbed in and chewed her bottom lip, unconsciously fiddling with the elf necklace Drake had given her. She'd argued with herself about whether or not to wear it, and if he hadn't noticed it before, she could still hide it, but if he had noticed it, she couldn't exactly take it off now.

Drake hopped into the driver seat and looked over at her. "Andrew and I got your car fixed. It was the starter."

"That means I can drive it home after the party. Finally get it home so it doesn't look like you have a junker hanging out in your parking lot. Sorry to be that car."

He chuckled. "It has to be someone. Might as well be a pretty girl who has to come back to get it, right? Hey, sort of like Cinderella and her shoe! Except I'm definitely not a prince…"

There was a tense silence between them.

Bell shifted. "Well, I'm not exactly a princess."

"Are we more like Beauty and the Beast, then?" He parked his truck and looked at her.

"Uh…"

Drake looked past her, and she looked through the window to see Jamie and Andrew waving to them. "We should go." He climbed out of the car.

Bell didn't hesitate to open her own door and climb out too. She'd expected Drake to still be mad, but for some reason, he wasn't. He was still stand off-ish, but at least he was talking to her.

Bell climbed out of the truck and walked with Drake toward the barn. People were already gathered inside.

Drake suddenly stopped in the doorway.

"What?" Bell asked.

He pointed up.

She looked up to see a mistletoe overhead but caught the last glittering sparkle of residual magic. What was Mr. Mistletoe up to?

He leaned across the short gap and gave her a small kiss on the cheek. "Let's go have some Christmas fun."

Bell put her hand on her cheek, and quickly went after him. She grabbed his arm. "What are you doing? What is this?" She gestured between them. "You were upset with me yesterday, and now you're kissing me on the cheek?"

"I figured you were the one that put the mistletoe there, since we talked about it yesterday. Isn't this what you wanted?" His dark brows furrowed.

"No. Yes. I don't know."

"Well. When you figure it out, let me know."

Bell dropped his arm and walked over to the coat rack to hang her coat.

She turned and looked at everyone and everything going on in the barn. People were arriving in a steady stream now, all talking and laughing. The DJ had started mixing Christmas music, and some people were already dancing. Others were picking through the treats, or grabbing plates of food, and children were running upstairs to investigate the kid's area. Everything in this room should have helped her feel the Christmas spirit. Should have made her happier. Drake should have been the golden snowflake to finish the perfect Christmas.

Now she could only stare at him as he talked with Chris and Heather.

Why did he confuse her so much?

"Bell!" Jamie called.

Bell walked over and gave Jamie a big hug. "Hey."

Andrew walked away from the group of people who had stopped him at the doors.

"I guess you are the one I should thank for fixing my car?" Bell asked.

"Drake must have told you. No problem-o."

"Where is Drake?" Jamie pried.

"Oh, he's...dancing." Bell motioned casually to the dance floor, having just spotted him. "I think you two should go have some fun!"

Jamie nudged Andrew. "Go on. Find some food or treats and go talk to people. I haven't had a chance to

Secret Santa

really talk to Bell since you got back."

"Got it." He smiled with a knowing look in his eyes. Bell knew that look too.

Jamie turned, a frown now on her face. "You're giving up?"

"Jamie, we've already talked about it!"

"I'm your best friend, I know how you feel about him." Jamie pulled her a little closer to the desserts, so people wouldn't pry. "Seriously, Bell. I thought you and Drake were finally hitting it off."

"And we were," she admitted. "But...I think I'm going to be moving, so there's really no point in getting close to him anyway. Look, you should just go dance with Andrew. It's Christmas Eve and we're going to have fun."

Jamie gave her a confused look. "Wait, you're moving?"

"Might be. It's sort of new news."

"But why? Why leave? I thought you loved it here..."

"I do. I just..." She sighed. "It's a good opportunity. I might get to go home." She smiled.

Jamie didn't. "Oh. Well...I guess I understand." She gave Bell a quick, fake smile and pointed toward Andrew. "I'm going to go dance. You should too. No reason to sulk on Christmas Eve. Besides, you said you only *might* be moving. That doesn't mean for certain. So, with that being the case, let's go have fun." Jamie dragged Bell with her to the dance floor.

"All I Want for Christmas is You" started playing and Bell felt her stomach sink.

Drake looked at Bell and held out his hand. "Would you be willing to dance with me?" He eyed her with a hint of apprehension.

He must have remembered as well as she what this song meant between them. They had listened to it less than a week before while cleaning out this very barn. It was their first kiss, and the most romantic kiss Bell could ever dream of having.

She took his hand, apprehensive of what could happen if they started dancing.

He pulled her into his arms, the comfortable, warm place she'd missed all day. Why was it so wrong if it felt so right?

They stopped dancing and Drake looked down at her. "I need to tell you something."

"Let me go first. Please?" she interrupted. "I never should have said anything to you. You're absolutely right, I never should have told you I was a Secret Santa elf, I never should have made you my project, I never should have put you through all of that. I'm sorry." She pulled away.

"Wait, Bell, that's not what I was going to say."

"I hope you have a Merry Christmas."

"Bell, stop!"

"Bye, Drake." Bell hurried over to the coats and managed to find hers before running out a side door and into the snow.

Secret Santa

❋ ❋ ❋

Drake stood in dumbfounded silence.

"What are you doing?" Stephanie asked, taking a sip from her drink.

Drake shook his head and looked at her. "I don't really know what just happened. I was about to tell her I wanted to seriously date her, and she took off."

"Into the snow?" Steph gasped. "Drake, it's freezing out there! Did you see what she was wearing? She'll freeze to death before she gets home!"

"I really don't think she wants me around, Stephanie." He finally faced her.

"You've been difficult ever since your dad passed, and Bell is the best thing that could have happened to you. You know that!" She snagged his arm, set down her glass, and faced him. "Now put on your coat and go get her back. I told you earlier, but I'll tell you again. I don't even think I've seen you this happy when your dad was alive. Bell has done more than just help you like Christmas again, Drake. You love her."

Drake thought about her words. Did he love Bell? He remembered all the times they laughed—she had made him laugh for the first time in years. They'd done activities he hadn't done in years, like cutting down a Christmas tree. And things he'd never done, like painting over drinks. Bell made him feel things he'd forgotten he could feel. And if that was love, then Stephanie was right.

He pulled on his coat, pushed open the door, and took off after Bell. The wind cut right through him, and he couldn't imagine how cold it was for Bell in her dress, heels, and fancy coat. Drake easily followed her footsteps, hating the cold the longer he walked.

"Might I have a word?" a man said as he walked down the sidewalk from Drake's left.

"Yeah, sure," Drake said as he pulled himself to a stop. He looked back up the sidewalk and could just make out Bell's shape. He looked back at the man. "Would you mind being a little quick?"

"Bell's dragging her feet," the man chuckled. "She doesn't really want to leave."

Drake's brows furrowed, and he looked the stranger up and down. "What do you mean leave?"

The man smiled softly. "My name is Mr. Mistletoe. I'm Bell's supervisor."

Drake rolled his eyes.

"Ah, I expected as much. You see, she's broken two of the most important rules about being a Secret Santa elf. She told you who she is, and she let you know she's been helping you feel the spirit of Christmas again."

"So, you're in on this joke too?"

From his pocket, Mr. Mistletoe produced a snow globe. "Take a look."

Drake took a deep breath, trying to prevent himself from being rude. All he wanted to do was take Bell back to the barn and get out of the cold. He reluctantly accepted the snow globe. What harm could there be? He tilted it

Secret Santa

upside down, making the fake dusts of snowflakes swirl around inside.

But something happened Drake wasn't expecting. The snow began to spin faster and faster until a mirror-like surface appeared inside of the ball. Suddenly, he could see Bell, small and with pointed ears, her ever-present smile on her face as she skipped around a cabin with a woman who looked almost like Bell did now, and a handsome man—Bell's father and mother. The scenes with them moved quickly, and Drake saw Bell reading stories with them, her mother taking her to school in a town with red houses, snow, and…reindeer?

The snow swirled again, and Drake saw Bell walking into a building that looked very much like a school, only it was a log cabin with warm fires glowing, people dressed in greens, reds, yellows, oranges, and blues—looking very much like Christmas lights as they bustled around the rooms.

And then there were no parents and Bell was alone in their home, standing on the faded green and red rug, staring at a picture of them above the fireplace, hugging her stuffed reindeer close. A man came in and took her other hand and took her to his home, where a round woman and three smaller children greeted her.

The next scene was a toyshop and Bell sat beside this same man. Behind them were rows and rows of robots, racecars, and more. He showed her how to attach the wires to the control panel. Drake couldn't hear their voices, but he understood what Bell meant when she said she'd lost both parents in an accident and had a family take her in.

Drake looked up from the snow globe back at Mr. Mistletoe. "You mean, she told the truth? Santa is actually…real?"

He nodded with a little smile. "Indeed. As is magic. But I have to admit, Bell has never used her magic to resolve any sort of problem. Meaning, she never used her magic on you. I did give you a mistletoe tonight, hoping the two of you would finally admit your feelings for each other. I caused her car to break down, and a few other things, but that was entirely me. You see, Bell is loyal and would never do anything contrary to what she feels is right. Tonight, she is torn between you and her duties as a Secret Santa elf." He looked in the direction Bell had walked. "But her feelings for you are very real. I must warn you, if you hurt her…"

Drake couldn't help a little grin. "You'll send the reindeer after me?"

"We have a couple of abominable snowmen." He nodded seriously.

He laughed. "Of course. Bell said she used to be afraid of them."

"And rightly so. They steal your candy." Mr. Mistletoe said it so seriously Drake couldn't help but believe it.

"*If* this is all true, then I owe Bell a big apology."

"Do you really not know Bell? Do you truly feel she would have it in her heart to deceive you in such a way? Maybe you just need a little Christmas faith."

Drake held the snow globe back out to Mr. Mistletoe.

Secret Santa

"Thank you."

"Give it to her." He tapped his nose three times, and to Drake's astonishment, a swirl of snow wrapped around him and he disappeared.

Drake stared dumbfounded at the empty place Mr. Mistletoe had stood just a moment before. His footsteps were still in the snow, and Drake still held the snow globe in his hands. Slowly, he finally turned, and took off running down the street after Bell. He'd been selfish and stupid, and all he wanted was to get to Bell and bring her back.

"Bell!" he yelled out when he finally caught sight of her again.

She stopped walking and turned to face him. She held her thin coat close. When she saw it was him, she looked down at her feet as she waited—her toes were probably frozen in those heels.

Drake finally caught up, breathing hard, his breath puffing out of his mouth like the smoke from a train. "I'm sorry. I should have listened and let you finish talking. I shouldn't have judged you about anything." He stepped a little closer, wanting to pull her close and keep her warm.

Bell finally met his eyes. "My intention wasn't to get your barn for the Christmas party and then just…drop you like a lump of coal. I never wanted to hurt you."

Drake cleared his throat softly. "I ran into Mr. Mistletoe. He gave me this." He held out the snow globe.

Bell gasped and accepted it. "I thought I had lost this. We get one when we become a Secret Santa and…" She looked up at him.

"Oh, don't worry, I'm completely convinced," he said.

She smiled. "Really?"

"Yeah. He sort of disappeared right in front of me. And he let me see your memories. Bell, I know we haven't really known each other very long. I'm so used to relationships ending badly, I thought…" He sighed. "I never should have assumed you would be like any girl I've dated. You are the most selfless person I've ever met."

Bell took the initiative to step closer to him this time. "Drake, I care about you. A lot."

"Are you willing to give this a shot then?" he asked softly. "At the barn, I was going to ask if you'd be willing to officially be my girlfriend."

She nodded, her eyes alight with the same familiar light he had always seen.

Bell felt her pocket—where the book had been stored—suddenly grow light. Her foot lifted from the ground and she wrapped her arms around Drake's neck. This was all she could have wished for. No longer being a Secret Santa elf, she could handle that. It was easier than leaving the town and people she had grown to love, and the man she had fallen in love with.

Drake cupped her cold cheeks in his hands and ran his thumb over her cheek. "You brought me back from the darkest place I've ever been in. You're the only one who bothered trying to break down the walls I built up over the years. Thank you for being the one to bring love back and helping me embrace my dad's passing instead of wallowing in it."

"I really didn't help that much," she tried to argue.

He chuckled and shook his head. "You just don't understand. Your love is what brought me back. And you know what?" he asked, studying her beautiful brown eyes. "The best Christmas gift I could ask for is right here in my arms," he said softly. The snow began to dance around them as Drake leaned down and pressed his lips to Bell's and held them there for a long while. He finally pulled back and looked down at her. "Will you come back to the party?"

She laughed lightly. "Absolutely."

He held his arm out to her.

She looped her arm through his and they began walking.

Peace filled the air around them, and Drake couldn't help but let out a relieved sigh. Bell suddenly stopped, and he looked at her. "Is something wrong?"

Bell quickly pulled the leather-bound book from her pocket. "It's growing lighter," she explained. She glanced at him before looking back at the book in her hands.

The snowflakes landed gently on the book cover, lighting it with a silver glow until the entire book glowed a soft white light. Slowly, the glowing book began to dissipate into snowflakes, fluttering away in the night.

"It's done," she breathed.

Drake eyed her. "What does that mean?"

With tears in her eyes, Bell looked at him. "I've finally

completed my mission to get all of the names off my Spirit List. I can now return to the North Pole."

His heart stopped a moment. "And will you?"

She shook her head quickly. "No."

"Why not?"

She smiled, her cheeks a rosy red. "Because that's no longer my home. This is my home. Here. With you."

His heart leapt, and he leaned forward for one final kiss.

Hand-in-hand, Bell and Drake walked back to the Christmas Eve party. It was the first time either of them had felt like they finally belonged where they were. For the first time in years, they weren't alone on Christmas. For the first time in years, they had someone to love.

THE END

Secret Santa

ALSO FROM LICHELLE SLATER

Coming December 2018!

ACCIDENTAL SECRET SANTA

Now Available

STEP RIGHT UP!

Crystal's life is turned topsy-turvy when someone from the spaceship, Sirkus av Magi, murders her father. No one else believes the murderer could be someone from the circus, and she is forced to seek revenge on her own.

As she searches for her father's murderer, she meets the performers, including the fire breather dragon, shape-shifting animals, and others. Then she learns their secret behind the closed curtains. When she discovers the truth, Crystal is forced to choose between getting the performers off the ship or avenging her father's death.

Will she succeed, or will she be played like a marionette?

Secret Santa

LICHELLE SLATER

About the Author

Lichelle grew up in Shelley, Idaho, but moved to and currently resides in Utah where she teaches special education preschoolers. She earned one of her bachelor's degrees in Creative Writing from Utah State University.

Her love for reading and writing stemmed from being read to as a child, and her love for dragons means you will always find a dragon in each story, no matter the genre.

Made in the USA
Columbia, SC
16 August 2023